MAGGIE SHAYNE

1

I was waiting, crouched behind his car in the parking lot. It was dark, and there were street lights but no cameras. I'd checked ahead of time. I'd planned this carefully, because I was going to kill him, no matter what. I figured I'd make it as easy as possible.

He came out of the bar, three sheets to the wind, which would make things so much easier. He listed to one side but tried real hard to stand up straight as he walked around the parking lot, awash in android-blue light, looking for his car. Then he took his key fob out and tapped it. The car beside me unlocked its doors and flashed its headlights. He saw it and smiled like he'd just won the lottery.

Only he hadn't won anything. His winning days were over.

He staggered to the car, opened the driver's door. I slipped up behind him, silent as a shadow, and jabbed him in the crease of his ass with a perfectly placed needle.

He spun around like a wobbling top, about to fall over. "What the hell!" he said and clocked me in the jaw. My head snapped sideways. I'd have gone down if I hadn't caught myself on the roof of his car. I stood ready to take another blow, thinking it would've been worse if he wasn't so drunk and wondering how long the drug would take to kick in.

He had one hand on his ass where I'd stuck him. His eyes rolled. I grabbed his shirt front, pulled him toward me as I opened the back door of his car. Then I turned him around, because I could not do this looking at him, and shoved him face-first onto the back seat. I climbed in after him, right up his back. He was out cold in seconds, not moving. I took the wood-handled garrote from my pocket. I'd made it out of picture-frame wire, several layers twisted together to make it thick, so I wouldn't accidentally decapitate him. I gagged a little as I put it over his head, and pulled it down between his face and the seat, over his chin to his neck. My inner voice, though it wasn't *really* mine, said, *Do it. Just do it. There's no other way. He won't feel anything. Just do it. You're so close.*

I pulled the right handle with my left hand, the left handle with my right, so they crossed at his nape. It was awful, what I was doing. My lips pulled back from my teeth with the effort it took–and not just physically. I had to *force* myself and my *self* was resisting. Tears filled my eyes. I tried to focus on my watch. It was an old-school watch, not a smart one. A delicate oval, with gold numbers and hands that swept way too slowly around its face. A narrow, pink leather band. After two minutes, he started to convulse, his body bucking underneath me, just like the internet said he would. I pulled tighter, to hold on, pressing my knees into his back like a cowboy at a rodeo. Terrible sounds started coming from him. Wet, growly, choky sounds. I wiped my wet face against my black, spandex-covered shoulder.

Just hold on. It's almost over. It's better this way. For everyone, even him.

I didn't know how many times the second hand had circled, but eventually it felt like it was over. The sounds stopped first, thank God. I'd never get them out of my head, though. Those sounds would haunt my dreams for the rest of my life. In silence, the twitching of his body eased, and he finally went still. I looked at my wristwatch and held the wood and wire weapon as tight as I could for three more minutes. My arm muscles were cramping up. My hands hurt despite the thick leather gloves I wore to protect them. Murder was not easy.

When I was sure he was dead, I let go of the garrote, slid it out from beneath him, and then climbed off him and backed down his body and out of the car. My legs were shaking so hard I wasn't sure I could stand up. But I did, I stood there beside the open car door, looking in at the man on the back seat.

I sniffed, backhanded my nose with my black leather glove, forced my gaze away from him to look around. A dozen vehicles, but no people. No witnesses. His keys were on the pavement, so I picked them up. His legs were still sticking out of the car. I bent them at the knees, so I could close the door.

Then I got behind the wheel and started the car, noticing for the first time that it was a Jaguar, a newish one. Blue or black, impossible to tell which in the dark.

I knew exactly where to put him. There was a burlap bag and a shovel already there, waiting.

I started the car. The radio blasted to life, scaring me so bad my head hit the ceiling before I got hold of myself and snapped the thing off. Then I sat there, gripping the wheel, white-knuckled. I took three long, deep breaths. Okay. I was okay. I put the car into gear and pulled out of the parking lot and onto the road.

I was driving through the night with a dead guy in the back seat, shaking all the way to my marrow. This was not me. This was not anything I'd ever imagined myself capable of, not in my wildest dreams.

Well, maybe in my *wildest* dreams.

A congested moan came from the back seat and sent a lightning bolt through my entire being.

THE ALARM CLOCK went off like a freaking mind bomb.

The murderous dream popped like a balloon at a birthday party, showering its deadly latex bits all around me. I sat up fast, blurting an overly loud, "Holy fuck!"

Mason sprang out of bed, landing in a ready crouch beside it. "What? What?"

My bulldog picked up her head, blinked sightlessly at me, then lowered it and resumed snoring.

I looked around our bedroom like I was searching for an explanation. But there were only the soothing green walls and rich walnut trim.

"Rachel?" Mason turned on the lamp.

I couldn't look at him. Not yet. Lingering sparks of murder were still blinking out one by one in my head. I swallowed hard. "I'm okay. Bad dream."

"Was it?"

I met his eyes. "You know me too well."

"So? What was it?"

"I don't know yet."

Yes, you do. It's not like it's the first time a killer took up residence in your head, or you took up residence in his, after all.

It's not that, Inner Bitch.
Then what is it?
Like I just told Mason, I don't know yet.
Yes, you do.

"You okay?"

I slid up out of our big bed, planted a big, morning-breathy kiss on his face, and said, "I'd be better with coffee."

He smacked my butt and said, "Then coffee you shall have." He pulled on a pair of pajama bottoms and a T-shirt that said, DEFINITELY NOT A COP. Yes, I bought it for him. I think it's hilarious. He only wears it to humor me. What can I say? I've got myself a keeper.

I turned back toward the bed. "Wanna go outside, Myrt?"

Myrtle did not so much as twitch her ears in reply. "I guess not." I pulled on my fluffiest robe because it was six a.m. and also September, and went out onto the balcony. It had pretty wrought iron railings and a view of the four-mile-long, mile-wide Whitney Point Reservoir.

God, I loved *seeing.* I could spend hours just…seeing. As would, I guessed, anyone who'd spent twenty years of their life blind. I went to the railing and looked at the water. It was a rippled mirror, reflecting rolling hills and blue sky. The air tasted good, but its flavor was shifting. It smelled like back-to-school.

When Mason returned, he not only had our coffees, but a pair of blankets over his arm. He set the steaming mugs on the railing, and spread the blankets over our bowl-shaped wicker chairs in case there was dew on the cushions. I sank into mine, pulled the blanket around me, and he handed me my mug.

"You are the perfect man," I said. "I don't know if you know it or not, but–"

"I do know it." He dropped the second blanket on his chair, but didn't sit. He stood by the railing like I'd been doing. Only he wasn't looking, like I had been. He was thinking.

My man was a bit of a thinker. It was his greatest flaw.

"You miss Jeremy." It wasn't a question.

He glanced back at me. "I just don't *get* living on campus when campus is only thirty minutes away."

Three weeks ago, we'd moved Jeremy into his Binghamton University dorm. Mason seemed to think we'd moved him to the moon. "It's Labor Day weekend, Mace. He'll probably be back before breakfast and not leave again until Tuesday morning."

"Yeah." He still sounded mopey. "Think we'll see him this time, or he'll just drop off his laundry and go hang with his friends?"

"Wow. Clingy much?"

"Misty sees more of him than we do."

"You're an uncle. Misty is a girl, and she's better looking. Plus, she has her aunt's DNA, so I don't know how you can blame him. You know the females of the de Luca line are irresistible."

He sighed, staring out at the water. I stretched my leg to kick his backside. "That was funny. You didn't even crack a smile."

"Sorry. You're right. I know."

"Kids grow up. It happens. Get over it."

"Right. You were the one sniffling all the way home the day we moved him in."

"Freaking campus is a pollen pit. Sue me."

"You don't have allergies."

"Did that day."

I slid over in my chair, opened my blanket and patted the

spot beside me. "BU is lots closer than the police academy, you know. You'd better toughen up by the time Jere heads to Albany." I was talking a good game, but I was missing Jeremy as much as Mason was. We might only be an uncle and an honorary aunt, but we'd been raising the boys for two years, and they felt like our own kids. Even though I wasn't nearly old enough for that.

Mason started to get in with me, then stopped because there was a ping from his PJ pocket. He pulled out his phone and looked at it.

"I reiterate my opinion," I said, "that this balcony should be a device-free zone."

"No such thing for a cop." He tapped the screen and said, "What's up, Rosie?"

Rosie was his partner. I hoped he was calling to invite us over for a barbecue.

At six-something a.m?

Yeah, probably not, I thought in reply to Inner Bitch's query. *I just hope it's not about what I dreamed.*

But it is. You know that, right?

I kind of did, but I didn't want to admit it. Not even to my subconscious Chatty Cathy.

Mason put the phone back into his pocket, and I'd missed whatever else he'd said. But his face looked more serious than before. "I've gotta go. We have a body."

I closed my eyes. "A body?"

"Yeah. Joggers found him off the Rail Trial."

I could see the man from my dream in my mind's eye. A youthful fifty-something, fit, clean shaven, hair so light it was hard to spot the gray unless you were up close to it, with a yellow-orange tint like it had been red once. He had a perfectly bald spot the size of a silver dollar on the back of his head. I'd stared at that spot for an eternity last night.

A forefinger hooked under my chin. I opened my eyes to see my guy's worried ones trying to get a peek inside my head. He said, "Anything you need to tell me, Rachel?"

"Only if he drove a dark-colored Jag and was strangled. Or mostly strangled."

"Mostly strangled?"

"I woke up before he was all the way strangled. Might've had to bash his head in with a rock or something to get the job done, for all I know."

He swore softly, sinking onto the edge of my bowl chair, no easy feat. "You okay?"

"It was pretty vivid. He spun around and punched me in the jaw, and I swear it actually aches this morning." I tested my mouth-hinges experimentally, and sure as shit, the right one felt tender. "Then I was kneeling on his back, choking the life out of him with some kind of homemade garrote."

"Do you want to come along?" he asked.

"I don't want to leave Josh home alone."

"He's thirteen."

"Yeah, but I don't know what this is yet. So–"

"You saying it feels dangerous to you?"

"It feels...personal. Close." I rubbed my arms, set down my coffee and used his shoulders to pull myself up out of my comfy nest. "I need to shower. Like, now."

"So do I. Let me call in."

I went in to start without him.

The clay-tiled shower was double sized, with multiple heads. I adjusted the water, stepped in and let the hot spray blast the remnants of that dream away. There wasn't *always* a killer dragging me into mental ride-alongs, but it had been known to happen. The first time, it had been Mason's dead, serial-killer brother. Long story, but suffice it to say I got a little something extra from Eric Conroy Brown along with his donated corneal tissue. He opened some kind of door.

I knew things, felt things. I called it NFP for Not Fucking Psychic because I don't believe in psychics.

Mason stepped into the tiled shower. He moved into the spray beside me, turned around and scrubbed his hair. I watched him until he opened his eyes and looked back at me. And then he pushed my wet hair off my face, and tucked it behind my ear, and gave me that look that said everything I needed to hear. And I forgot what I'd been so upset about.

MASON WAS WORRIED ABOUT RACHEL. She'd been shaken by her dream. It had taken minutes for the fear to leave her eyes.

He parked where there was room, got out of his restored (by him) '74 Monte Carlo, and headed down Binghamton's popular walking trail. It ran alongside the Susquehanna River. Pleasant, usually. Not so much, now. Uniforms, forensics people, and his partner Rosie stood around a pile of freshly turned black earth, and a burlap shroud that wasn't quite big enough. A pale, dead arm stuck out from elbow to fingertips. Looked like the corpse was waving hello.

He walked closer. The murmur of the river drowned out the sounds of singing birds. The body was in a hole, sort of.

"Not even deep enough to cover the poor SOB," Rosie said. He had lost twenty pounds on his latest diet, which showed exactly nowhere. He was a big guy, his Rosie. They'd been partners since their rookie days. "Jogger spotted his hand, just sticking up outta the dirt. Can you imagine?"

"It'll make a great story, I guess."

"Yeah, eventually."

"Why the burlap? Why not just bury him?" Mason

walked around the shallow grave to the bag's opening, picked up an edge with a pencil, and peered inside. "Flashlight?" he asked, hand out. Someone gave him one, cold steel cylinder in his palm, and he aimed it. "Ligature marks. Looks like he was strangled." *Or mostly strangled.* Something tickled up his spine. He shrugged it away.

"Anyone find an ID on him?" he asked.

"We're not patting him down for a wallet until we get him home where we can do it right." That was spoken with authority from a redhead with an ultra-short haircut. "Bag him up, burlap and all," she ordered. "Move him as little as possible. Don't shake off trace evidence."

As the team scrambled, she grinned at Mason. It was probably disrespectful to think she looked just like a Christmas elf. She had dimples, pink cheeks, intelligent green eyes, and a hairline that made her ears look ever so slightly pointed.

And she had her hand out, he finally noticed.

"Billie Carmichael. I'm the new forensic pathologist."

Thinking she looked about fourteen probably proved that he was getting old. "Mason Brown," he said.

"I know who you are, Detective Brown. I know your wife, too. I'm a huge fan."

"She's not my–"

"Careful!" The techs had dropped the body onto the gurney a little too hard, and the burlap came open.

Mason glimpsed the guy's face, either pudgy or starting to swell. His hair was mostly a pale orangey-gray. He looked back at the redhead. "What's an FP doing at a crime scene?"

"It's my first case. I couldn't wait." She said it with a grin, then forced a more serious expression.

"Since he's already bagged, you want to give me the

rundown?" he asked. He was trying to remember ever being that happy to be at work, and failing.

"Male, mid-fifties, maybe a drinker. He was probably dumped last night," Billie Carmichael said. He liked her confident tone. "There's a car back by the trail head. Nobody else around. Might be his."

Rosie met Mason's eyes, brows raised, clearly impressed.

"What kind of car?" Mason asked.

"Jag," the new FP replied. "Nice one. Man I'd hate to die and leave a ride like that behind."

"Shit," Mason shook his head. "Shit."

His phone buzzed. It would be Rachel, asking about all this. He wished he didn't have to tell her, but knew he did. They didn't keep stuff from each other.

He walked a little bit away before looking at the text.

"Don't forget, BBQ at noon. Wayward nephew and all."

He got a good feeling from that message. He looked at Billie, and said, "You gonna be a while with the unboxing?"

"The unboxing. That's funny." Mason didn't smile, and she turned all business again. "I'm gonna work straight through the day on this guy."

"Good. I need to go home after I finish up here. Will you call me when I can come and get a look at the victim?"

"Yeah, sure."

Rosie said, "The Jag in the parking area is registered to Dwayne Clark. Got an address, phone number, and email. We're getting more info now."

"You got a phone number, you said?"

Rosie nodded, showing Mason his iPad.

"That's a cell number." Mason tapped it into the keypad of his phone, then silenced it and listened.

The guy in the burlap bag started ringing.

"Guess we've got a probable ID." He ended the call. "Let's get some background on him."

"Already under way," Rosie said.

"Okay, good." He looked at the ground around the makeshift grave. There were plenty of tracks in the dirt, thanks to the team that had dug the body out. "I hope you got a lot of shots of the ground before it was trampled," he said to the cop with the camera.

"I did." He brought his camera over and scrolled photos across its digital screen.

Mason looked at the images of the undisturbed grave. The killer had barely dug past the grass's knotted root carpet. He'd chopped it open, rolled it back, scraped out a little of the dirt underneath, and then tried to cover the unfortunate Dwayne Clark with it again.

Mason said, "Whoever put him here expected him to be found. Anything the body and this scene have to tell us could be significant. Let's not miss anything."

Billie's guys carried the dead man to an ambulance that had driven over the grass to get close. "The forensics team will finish up here," she said. "I want to stay with the body."

Mason said. "Listen, Carmichael, just so you know, we sometimes use Rachel as a consultant on cases like this."

"I know." Her elf-green eyes popped wider. "Are you bringing her in on *this one*? Wow, I didn't think I'd get to work with her so soon."

Oh, hell. "Listen, if you fangirl all over Rachel, she'll make you her slave. If you want her respect, treat her like an equal." It was a dumb request. Rachel had no equal, but still.

The change in Billie's expression was so sudden and deliberate he almost laughed. "I'll be completely professional, Detective. And I'll call you when I've finished the autopsy." Then she unlocked her phone and handed it to him.

He entered his number into her contacts, then returned the phone. "Thanks."

As he walked back to his car, Mason made a mental to-do list. He had to go home, host a family barbecue, and during a free moment break it to Rachel that her link to the darkness was back, big time.

2

Jeremy had arrived home before nine, stuffed the washer with more laundry than it could possibly clean, helped himself to 80% of what was in the fridge, and answered my, "how was your week?" while he ate it.

I stood across the counter from him, trying to interpret his food-muffled words. "Are you too short on time to chew and swallow before talking? Gonna eat the last crumb and then launch yourself out of here at the speed of teen?"

He stopped talking, finished chewing, took a big gulp of milk. "Sorry, Rache."

"*Aunt* Rache."

He grinned. "I *am* in a hurry, though."

Josh, sitting opposite his big brother, sighed with all the drama thirteen can muster–which is, I have discovered, a *lot*. He slid off the stool and headed for the door. Hugo, Myrtle's sighted, male mini-me, was on his heels. There is nothing in the entire universe cuter than an English bulldog puppy. Hugo had also become Myrtle's seeing-eye pal.

Myrt remained where she was, sitting on the floor by

Jeremy, who had dropped enough crumbs to make it worth her while.

Josh slammed the door hard enough to make me wince.

Should've made the place kid proof, Inner bitch opined.

There's no such thing, I thought in reply.

"What's with him, Rache?" Jeremy asked.

I sent him my patented glare, which I had learned from my sister, who had learned it from our mother, may she rest in peace.

"*Aunt* Rache," he corrected. "Jeeze, what's everybody so touchy about, anyway?"

"You're neglecting your brother, not to mention your dogs and your uncle. These are dire offenses, Jeremy Brown. Just because you're a big college man now doesn't mean you get to blow off your family."

"I've barely been gone three weeks!"

"Yeah, and you're already acting like a big fat douchebag. Spend the morning with your brother."

"You can't tell me what to do anymore. I'm an adult."

I shrugged. "An adult wouldn't act the way you're acting."

"And how am I acting?"

"Like a selfish little shithead."

That pissed him off. I was kind of pissed too, but since I was technically the grownup in the room, I notched myself down a few degrees. "We're having a barbecue here at noon. My sister and Jim and the twins will be here. You and Misty can take off after, and you've got the rest of the long weekend to be together. I'm gonna come crash in your dorm room if you don't spend some time with the fam. Mason's moping like Myrtle when her dish is empty. Josh is heartbroken, and don't even get me started on the dogs."

Myrtle chose that moment to whap him in the shin with her paw. He'd stopped dropping crumbs and she didn't like it.

He looked down at the dog, then out the window at Josh. His kid bro was walking slow with his head down. Hugo was trotting beside him with a frisbee in his mouth, but Josh didn't even notice.

Jeremy said, "I'm sorry. I had a hard week."

"You wanna talk about it?"

"I've got this one professor who's a Class-A asshat."

"Language. You want me to come down there and kick him in the balls?"

The trouble in his eyes evaporated. He even smiled a little. "Yes, Aunt Rachel, I want you to come down there and kick him in the balls."

He slid off the stool, smacked his thighs and said, "Wanna go hunt some froggies, Myrtle? Froggies? Hmm?"

Myrt sprang upright and started wiggling her butt.

"I'd like to hear more about the asshat professor, though," I said.

"Later. And…I'll do better. With the family."

His mea culpa look was so much like Mason's that my heart melted.

"I know you will. We miss the hell out of you, you know."

"You, too?"

"Me especially," I admitted. "I love you, kid."

"I love you, too."

"Well, duh."

MASON GRILLED STEAKS, looking like the most content man on the planet for the first time in three weeks. My sister

Sandra had brought mac salad and coleslaw. I heated up a can of baked beans in the microwave, poured chips into giant bowls and scooped dip into small ones.

Yeah, I don't cook. It's not what I was put on the planet to do.

"Let's eat down by the water," Sandra said. We had just exited the house, our arms full of plates and silverware. "Pretty soon it'll be too cold."

"I concur." And then I whistled to get the kids' attention. "Will you guys move the picnic tables down by the water for us?"

Jeremy and my niece Misty, who'd been sitting side by side on the dock holding hands, got up and came running. Josh, too, dogs flanking him. Christie stayed put and returned her attention to her phone. Misty and Christie were twins, blue-eyed blondes like their mother, although you'd never know it today, as Christie wore a crocheted hat, with bright colored concentric circles, and it covered every lock. Jim, world's greatest brother-in-law, left his position as official grilling commentator to help them lug the old-fashioned wooden picnic table.

"Jeremy got over being mad at you?" Sandra asked.

"He couldn't deny his own assholery."

"Is that a real word?"

"It is now. As an author, I get to add new words to the language."

"I don't think that's true."

"I'm pretty sure it is. Sprounce is one of mine. You know, what Myrt does when she finds a froggie. Sprounce." I made claw hands under the plates and bounced a little.

"I love you," she said.

"Me, too."

We walked across the dirt drive that wasn't really a road,

because we were the only ones who used it, to the picnic table on the grassy patch of shoreline. The kids had already taken off, but Jere was still within earshot. I said, "I appreciate you hanging out with us today. I won't be upset if you two want to go do your own thing after we eat." I was careful not to sound like I was giving permission in front of everyone. I knew how I would react to that–instantly and with great fury– and presumed he'd be the same.

"We'll probably hang out for a while," he said. "Maybe take off later, though."

Sandra and I put the plates on the table, and I glanced over at Christie. Her full attention was on her device. I pulled out my phone and texted her, "Get off your fucking phone."

She looked up from the screen, grinning at me. "You are so ridiculous, Aunt Rache," she said, getting up, pocketing it, and walking in that way only super tall, super lean teenage girls can do. Then she pulled off her hat to release a cascade of dead-straight, jet-black hair.

I bit back the sound of horror that jumped into my mouth. Well, mostly bit it back. Half a squeak escaped. Sandra elbowed me in the small of my back, where her kid couldn't see. When I could speak, I said, "Wow, what an…extreme change."

The guys were carrying the steaks to the table, and everyone was finding a spot to sit.

"I got sick of people not being able to tell us apart."

"So you decided to become the evil twin?"

"*Rachel*!" Sandra scolded.

"She knows I'm teasing. You know I'm teasing, right?" I took a plate and a seat on the bench. Mason slid in beside me.

"I know you're teasing," Christie said. "Besides, I already *was* the evil twin. At least now I look the part."

"I've seen evil, kid," Mason said. "You ain't it."

"But it's nice to have goals," I added in my best Sandra tones.

That made her smile. Christie wasn't such a puzzle to me. She kind of *was* me. Ninety-nine percent attitude and convinced of her rightness on all subjects, regardless of evidence to the contrary.

She wasn't evil. If she were suddenly orphaned and I left the planet, she could probably go either way, but as things stood, she was going to be okay.

I looked her over thoroughly, nodding slow. "You should darken your brows a little bit."

"I hate makeup."

"Not makeup. Dye. I'll have Amy text you her brand. You now, she's naturally a redhead, right?"

"No way!"

"Way. Not since she's been my goth-Friday, but I was at her mother's place once, and there are pictures. Total ginger." A platter of food came my way before we could discuss my assistant any further. Amy does a million jobs. Most importantly, she posts as me on social media because I have zero tolerance for idiots. If I were Tweeting every day, my career would go up in smoke, you know, unless I were president.

I stabbed a big juicy steak, dropped it onto my plate, and enjoyed the friendly chaos of conversation going on around me. We talked so much when were together I didn't know how anyone ate. But we managed to decimate the meal, and get through dessert–apple pie with ice cream. It grew eerily silent once we had *that* in front of us.

We really were a family. Not officially or anything, but I was starting to wonder if Mason was ever going to ask.

Right. And it's what year, now?

I know, Inner Bitch, I know…but if I ask, he might say no.

He won't.

He could.
He won't.

Myrtle growled, which Myrtle almost never did. Hugo immediately jumped in front of her and started snarfing. (Snarf: Snuffly barking, which is what bulldogs do. Yes, it's another of my words, and also the only perfect word to describe this sound.) We looked where Hugo was looking, at a tall, young man with terrible posture, walking up our seldom used dirt road toward us.

I got to my feet, still nervous from last night's murder dream. Mason got up, too, stepped over the picnic bench and headed toward the guy. The stranger lifted a hand. He was looking right at me and smiling. "Rachel? Wow, it's really you!"

Oh my God, a fan, Inner Bitch said.
Fans put these steaks on the table, IB.
Yeah, but they don't get to show up at our house.

I kind of agreed with her on that one. The thing about writing airy-fairy self-help books like mine was that you occasionally attracted a batshit fan. Apparently, straight to your front door.

I went to stand beside Mason. Jeremy was on his feet, too, and so was the dark twin, with a distinctive touch-my-aunt-and-you-die glint shining from within her eyeliner. *She hates makeup, my ass,* Inner Bitch noted.

"It's really me," I said, polite, calm, not inviting or friendly. He had brown leaning-toward-gold eyes and thick lashes. His long brown hair hadn't seen shampoo in a while. He slouched like his backbone was tired. "What can I do for you?"

He was smiling really hard. "I just...there's so much. There's so much. I'm Gary. Conklin. I read everything of yours–" As he spoke, he came toward me, and Mason stepped right into his path.

He looked up at Mason. He was a head shorter. Had kind of a baby face. Round, with big eyes set deep that turned downward at the corners. "Whoa, man," he said, "You don't need to be worried about me." He leaned sideways, to see me around Mason. "I just...your books, it's like you're talking right to me."

"It feels like that to lots of readers," I said. "It means I'm doing something right."

"I have to talk to you, though. I walked all the way here."

I looked down at his feet. He was wearing sneakers that were more holes than canvas. "From where?"

"The shelter, um, St. Mary's."

"In Binghamton?" It was twenty miles south on 81.

He nodded.

"You want something to eat, Gary?"

"Rachel–" Mason turned fully, hands on my shoulders, leaning close, speaking soft. "This guy looks unstable," he said, for my ears only.

"Yeah, trust me I know. His head's a fucking cyclone. But his belly's empty."

"He could be dangerous."

"He reminds me of my brother."

The brother card got to him, but that's not why I played it. It was nothing but the truth.

"Gary, see the dock right there?" I asked, pointing at the square wooden dock that extended out from the shore. It was redwood stained with a railing all the way around and fish-pole holders mounted in four places. We had two Adirondack chairs out there, and a new one on the way, a double-wide one, for proper snuggling. "You go wait for me there. I'll bring you a plate of food and we'll talk a little, okay?"

"You don't have to feed me."

"We'll talk. Go, sit. Look at that peaceful lake. It's so calm. It always makes me feel better."

He looked at the water for a moment and I did, too. It was particularly placid today, its surface a smooth mirror reflecting the bright September sky. Finally, he gave a nod and went to the dock. He stood at the railing, despite the big chairs.

"I don't think this is a good idea, Rachel," Jim said. Jim, the quiet guy, who never rocked a single boat.

"I agree, but he's here and he's hungry. Besides, he's scrawny. Look at him, Jim. I could take him even if I was still blind. And you're right here, and Mason is coming over there with me, and I've got two strong kids here who'll kick his ass if he gets out of line. Not to mention Jeremy and Josh."

Misty smiled. Christie did not. She had the guy in her laser sites and wasn't even hearing me. My goodness, my niece was growing up kinda kick-ass. I liked it.

"Give me a few minutes." I was filling a plate as I spoke. We always cooked an extra steak to split up between the bulldogs, but they were going to have to muddle through with scraps this time.

"Keep the dogs here," I told Josh, who was my resident canine whisperer. Mason put an arm around my shoulders. We hadn't had a chance to talk about the body that had been found this morning, because everyone had already arrived by the time he'd got back. And now certainly wasn't the time.

I said, "Hang back a little. I want him to feel safe."

"I want you to *be* safe."

"Perfect. Pick a distance that does both." I kissed his nose. "I love you." I said, in case the stranger was going to pull out a weapon and off me within the next few minutes. And I think Mason knew it.

The timing wasn't lost on me. This guy showing up the morning after a murder dream that might've been a...I don't want to say vision. It sounds so hokey. But yeah. That. Coincidence?

No such thing.

Sandra handed me silverware and a napkin, and I carried the food over to the dock. "Sit right here, Gary," I said, standing beside the chair. He came away from the railing, sat in the chair, and I handed him the food.

"Thank you. I haven't had anything today."

"I'll box you up some leftovers to take with you when you go. Go ahead, dig in. Get your belly full first, I can wait." And I wanted to wait. I wanted to feel him first, you know, with my NFP. I went to the railing myself, leaned my forearms on it, gazing out at the water while he ate. It was always easier to feel someone with my eyes closed, probably because I'd done it blind for so long, without even realizing I was doing it. It only became a full-blown thing though, after I got my new corneas. Mason thought, in hindsight, his brother must've had a touch of...what I had. But in Eric's case, it had made him crazy.

I closed my eyes and opened my radar. What I got felt like sparks from a live wire. I tried to focus harder, but it was just chaos.

Eventually the sounds of fork hitting plate went silent, and I turned to see that Gary had cleaned it. He leaned forward to set his empty dish on the decking.

"So first, you should know, I don't usually do this. Meet one-on-one with readers like this."

"Yeah, I–I know."

"What did you want to talk to me about?"

"Your books, they say things happen to you because you think about them."

I nodded slowly. "That's a very simplified explanation. You attract the *essence* of what you think about, believe in, and expect."

"Isn't that what I said?"

"Not exactly. Say you think about dogs all the time. That doesn't mean a dog's gonna show up. It all depends on how you feel about dogs when you're thinking about them. If you're afraid of dogs, and you think about dogs all the time, other things you're afraid of will start showing up. Could be a dog, could be a stalker."

Did you just say stalker? To a fan who walked here from Binghamton to meet you? Freudian slip much?

"You understand?" I asked, to drown out the rightness of Inner Bitch's comment.

"I don't have a problem with dogs. I like dogs."

A swing and a miss!

"What *do* you have a problem with, Gary?"

"Bad stuff." Storm clouds darkened his eyes.

"Bad stuff," I repeated, and I sent Mason a yellow alert sort of look. He was standing under a river birch six feet away. He could make it to me in two long strides. But the kid could probably stab me faster.

We should've searched him, Inner Bitch said.

Now you think of it. "What kind of bad stuff?"

Honest to God, I didn't feel any threat coming from him. Hatred and anger wafted off him, but it wasn't directed at me. I usually felt that sort of thing like prickles on my skin, only not on my skin, exactly.

Gary looked away, tipping his chin down just the way my brother Tommy used to do. There was something about him. I wanted to bring him inside and clean him up and fix his life.

Like you tried to do with Tommy.

Yeah, IB. Just like that.

"What kinds of bad things, Gary?"

And he flipped just like that, jumped out of the chair and glared at me, and then Mason was in between us, hands on the kid's shoulders, saying, "Okay, now. Everything's cool here, right? We're okay here, aren't we, Gary?"

I stayed behind Mason's body like the Cowardly Lion, thinking yep, he *could* get to me fast enough, after all. Gary's eyes had turned fiery, and he thrust out an arm, pointing at me. "You're wrong, Rachel de Luca! I *don't* think bad thoughts, but they come anyway. They come anyway and I can't make them stop!"

Mason's voice was much harsher when he said, "All right, Gary, it's time for you to go now. You crossed a line coming here, and it better not happen again. You understand me? It's not okay, coming here like this."

And just like that, the fire was doused. Puppy dog eyes blinked at me through the lingering smoke. "It's not okay I came here?"

"It would be better if you asked first. That's all," I said.

Are you out of your fucking mind?

Mason's eyes asked me the very same question.

"I'd rather be blind than to feel the way you do right now," I told Gary. "I'm really sorry you're going through this." I meant it.

He relaxed, like a full-body sigh. "Do you know what it is, Rachel? What's making the bad thoughts come?"

"I know people who would. People who fix this kind of thing for a living."

He got my meaning. First time today. "I don't like doctors."

"That's okay, don't get all knotted up over it. Look, Gary, if your car's out of gas, you go to a gas station. It doesn't matter if you like gas stations or not, you go. You go because it's where the gas is."

"I don't even have a car."

Note to self. No metaphors with Gary.

"Come on. I'm gonna have Mason give you a ride to someplace you can stay tonight. Okay?"

He lowered his head, like he'd lost the battle. "Okay."

"His car's over there. The black one."

"That's a cool car," Gary said, and he walked across the dirt road, and the lawn to the driveway and Mason's car, which we all called The Beast.

When he was out of earshot, I said, "Mason–"

"No."

"You don't get to tell me no."

"This time I do."

"He reminds me of my brother."

"He reminds *me* of *my* brother."

His brother had killed my brother, if you're keeping track.

"Mason, come on." I put my hands on his chest and looked up at him. "He's sick, not dangerous."

"Those two things are not mutually exclusive."

"Put him in the motel in town. Leave him some cash. I'll get him in with a shrink tomorrow. He needs help. This is how I want to handle it, Mason."

He looked at me hard and there were so many arguments he could've made. Like what about the boys, and my sister, and her kids, and so on. But he didn't. He blew air through clenched teeth, and said, "Fine. I'll put him in the motel. One night, Rache. We get him hooked up with social services and mental health, and leave his ass back in the city. You can put him up at the Hilton if you want, but there. Not here. Okay?"

"Okay. And thank you."

He looked like he wanted to say more, but he didn't. He

went and got in the car, started it up. It had this deep, loud rumble to it that testified to my man's manliness as he drove the homeless, helpless, slightly scary Gary to a motel about a mile from our front door.

Yeah, Mason was probably right. I might've made a bad call just then. I hoped not.

"Gary Conklin, right? You have a middle name?" Mason asked.

"Robert."

"Gary Robert Conklin. Nice. And you're what, twenty-four, twenty-five?"

"I turned twenty-three my last birthday."

"And when was that?"

"July."

Close enough for a background check. "Where were you staying before the shelter, Gary?"

He broke eye contact, stared out the window.

Mason gave him several seconds, but when he didn't answer, had to move on. It was a short drive to the motel. Too short, if you asked him. "You told Rachel you don't like doctors. So you've seen doctors before, then?"

"Everybody's seen doctors before."

"Who was the last doctor you saw, Gary? Do you remember his name?"

"Her name," Gary said.

Mason thought Rachel would have kicked him for exhibiting subconscious remnants of sexism. He was woke, he swore he was.

"Dr. Guthrie. But she was wrong."

"Do you take medicine, Gary?"

Girl Blue

"I shouldn't have gone to your house," he said.

They pulled into the motel lot, and Mason headed into the office to get the kid a room. When he came back out, Gary was standing next to the car, arms full of leftovers in Tupperware.

Mason held up the key. "Got you a room for the night," he said, walking while he talked. It was only across the parking lot. He unlocked the door to room twelve and opened it wide, stepping inside with Gary right behind him.

The fan unloaded his leftovers onto a small table, and Mason said, "There's a little fridge over there to put the food in for the night, and here's your key."

"Why do I have to stay?"

"Because Rachel wants to help you make your life better."

"She thinks I'm crazy, doesn't she? I'm not, you know. I just have bad thoughts."

"They make a pill for that."

Gary frowned hard, like he was working a jigsaw puzzle in his scrambled-up head. The poor guy. Mason sighed and tried to be kinder. "Nobody thinks you're crazy. Sometimes you get sick, you take medicine, you get better. There's nothing crazy about that, kid. That's life, is what that is. That's all. It happens to everybody from time to time."

"It does?"

"It does. I'll see you in the morning, okay Gary?"

"Okay."

WE RELAXED on our balcony that night, Mason and me, in our comfy robes, with drinks in hand. There was a lopsided, almost full moon rising over the reservoir, and the little bit of vodka in my Coke was smoothing out all my rough edges.

Jeremy and Misty had invited Josh and Christie to go to the newest Marvel movie with them. Christie had laughed and rolled her eyes. Josh lit up like Times Square on New Year's Eve. So we had the place to ourselves–you know, aside from the two bulldogs snoring like bull*dozers* on our bed.

"Alone at last," I said, taking a nice big sip while regretting that it was two thirds of the way gone. "I hate to bring it up while we're in such a beautiful moment–"

"Then don't."

I looked at him and smirked. "We *have* met, right?" He closed his eyes, resolved himself to the inevitable. "Tell me about the body today."

He sighed, but he talked. "White male, mid-fifties, once-red hair going gray. You know how that looks?"

"I know exactly how that looks." Having seen it up close while I strangled him. "Cause of death?"

"Don't know yet. But there were ligature marks."

"What about the car?"

"Yeah, you nailed that, too. Jaguar in the parking area at the trailhead. Car's registered to a Dwayne Clark of Dilmun, a small lake town just past Ithaca."

"Shit."

He understood the thousand-and-one emotions conveyed by the single word. He was the only one who possibly could.

"Any forensics?"

"Wrapped in burlap."

"Burlap. Burlap. Burlap…" I snapped my fingers at him. "The Craig's List Ripper!"

"Hasn't been active since the nineties."

"How can anyone say that for sure?"

"No bodies found since twenty-eleven."

"He's hiding them better."

"They were all women."

"All but one."

"Right, but that one was in drag," Mason pointed out.

"You think the burlap's coincidence, then?" I bounded out of my chair.

My drink sloshed dangerously, so I downed it and headed inside for my phone. Unlike Mason, I respected my no-devices-on-the-balcony rule. I grabbed it off the nightstand, started tapping, and found what looked like a decent report on the Craig's List Ripper.

I scrolled with my thumb, speed reading while Mason looked over my shoulder. "Look at this crime scene." I tapped on a photo where one of the serial killer's victims had been found.

"It's very similar," Mason said, spreading the image larger, really studying it. "This might be better on the desktop."

"Way ahead of you." We hurried through the house. My office was the 30' by 30' third floor in the peak of the house, with its own mini balcony. Its front was entirely glass and faced the reservoir. My desk was on the back wall, facing the front and all that glass, with a desktop and a laptop ready to roll.

I sat, and he stood behind me, looking over my shoulder as I read aloud.

"The Craig's list Ripper, also known as the Long Island Killer, the Gilbo Beach Killer, blah blah blah. Yes. They were all strangled. Several bodies found near water."

"Not all in burlap, though. Not all in one piece, either."

"There's no such thing as coincidence, Mason."

"We're five hours away from his dumping ground."

"We're five hours away from *one* of his dumping grounds. The only one we know of." I looked up at him, daring him to argue.

"What are you doing, babe?" He tucked my hair behind my ear. "Internet research? That's not your forte. What does your NFP tell you?"

I shrugged. "Nothing about *this* guy."

"I didn't think so."

I pushed away from the computer, got up from my chair and paced across the room, closing my eyes and trying to recall the dream or vision or whatever the hell it had been. "It felt like a woman. And there was…there was a needle," I said snapping my fingers, because I'd just remembered it. "She drugged him first. We need to get to that body and check for a track mark in the crease under the left butt cheek."

"I'm meeting the new forensic pathologist in the morning. Come with me."

"To an autopsy?"

"Autopsy's already done. She texted me an hour ago."

"Okay, Mason. I'll go with you. Right after we get Gary squared away."

"I left him fifty bucks," he said. "He's not gonna be there in the morning. He's gonna go spend it to get high."

"If you felt the shit storm inside his head, you'd want to self-medicate, too."

"Not judging. Just saying."

"He came here because he wanted me to help him. He's gotta stick around long enough to let me."

He hugged me close. He'd shucked his robe, and mine was open, so I got that warm, silky rub of skin against skin. I wrapped my arms around his waist and laid my cheek on his chest.

•

3

"Happy Labor Day weekend, right?" asked the twelve-year-old pixie, standing over the open chest of a dead guy in the basement of Our Lady of Lourdes Memorial Hospital.

Mason had told me she looked like a Christmas elf, and he had nailed it.

"Rachel, meet Billie Carmichael, forensic pathologist."

She beamed at me. "It's a pleasure, Ms. de Luca. I'm excited to work with you." Her eyes slid to Mason, who stood on my left, then quickly back to me. I got, *did I do okay?*

I got it. She was a fan and he'd advised her not to gush, but it was oozing from her pores. She was doing a good job trying to hide it, though.

"Have you run toxicology?" I needed to get a look at the crease under his left butt cheek without her noticing, or she'd want to know how I knew. My NFP was a closely-guarded secret. Oh, there was gossip. I hated that there was, but there was. I'd been too close to too many gruesome murder investigations for there not to be. And you know, as far as the general public is concerned, woo-woo is woo-woo. If you're a self-help author you must also be a fortune teller, brandishing crystals and reading palms.

"Toxicology is in process," she said. "Everything else is done. Just gotta sew him up and release him to the funeral home. Widow's called three times already."

Note to self, widow's in a hurry. That probably wasn't so unusual, though.

"The cause of death was asphyxia by strangulation. Killer used twisted wire. Twice. From behind him, and from in front of him. We got a few shards of metal off the skin. You can see the pattern there in his neck." She poked the skin on the dead guy's neck with a gloved-forefinger.

I grimaced like that bothered me, and I didn't have to fake too hard. The memory of choking the life out of this human being was vivid and sickening. Here he was, dead. A life extinguished. And it felt like I'd been the one to extinguish it. "I have to step out," I said, holding one palm up. I hurried out of the room, and when Mason tried to follow, I said, "No, stay. I'll be back, I just need a breath of death-free air."

I tried to tell him I was up to something with my eyes, and he probably read it, along with my disgust and remorse for something I hadn't even done. He was way better at reading me than I was at reading him, which is ironic when you think about it.

I went out of the room into the hallway, and up one level to get a signal. Then I called the main desk. Someone answered, and I said, "Page Dr. Carmichael. It's urgent." They put me on hold.

I ran back down the stairs. By the time I was at the cutting room doors, I was distracted from my guilt trip and also aware I needed to exercise once in a while. Billie Carmichael was hurrying out the double doors to answer the fake call on the nearest in-house phone. She breezed past me, saying, "Be right back." Then she hit the stairs with effortless speed. The nearest landline was right at the top.

I rushed back into the room and over to Dwayne Clark on the table, and I slammed the door on my sickening feelings by focusing on the immediate need. "Get over here and help me roll him."

Mason grabbed a pair of gloves, struggled his big hands into them, and rolled the guy up onto his side. I grabbed a glove too, snapped it on and reached for his butt cheek. Mason looked horrified.

I lifted the guy's cheek, adjusting the overhead light with my free hand. "Look. Right there. That's where I injected him in the dream or whatever."

Elf steps pitter-pattered just outside the door.

"Put him back, put him back," I whisper-shouted.

Mason dropped the guy, yanked off his gloves, and stuffed them into a red bin. I remembered I was still wearing one and put that hand behind my back as Billie Carmichael came into the room.

"No one on the phone," she said. "Probably the widow again. Anyway, back to the victim. There are bruises on his back." She tapped the tablet that was on a nearby stand, bringing up some photos of the corpse–a far more efficient method than rolling him over like we'd done. "You can clearly see the two round bruises on his back. Made before he died, but I'm damned if I know how."

"Looks like someone was kneeling on him," Mason said.

Her brows rose, and she looked at him like she'd just realized he was the one true Santa.

I sent him a death-glare for taking credit for my shit while still trying to peel off the glove behind my back. I was not having any luck.

"Let us know when you get the tox screen back," Mason said.

"I'll text you," she promised, looking at the body, then frowning, and looking at us again. He hadn't landed in precisely the same position, and the light wasn't pointing where it had been, either.

The glove I'd been tugging on for a full minute came off my hand suddenly, and made a loud snap.

"We have to run," Mason said. "Thanks, Billie." He grabbed me by the hand, and tugged me behind him out of the room.

At the top of the stairs, he said, "The garotte. Kneeling on his back. The injection site. You got a lot of detail in that dream, Rache." We stepped out into the late morning sunshine and fresh air.

"Too much. It's creepy."

We got into his car. He reached across the space between us, smoothed back my hair, then cradled my head in his big hand. "I wish it wasn't this hard on you. But it's gonna be okay. You know that, right?"

The tension in me dissolved just because he'd touched me and told me it was going to be okay. Did I have it bad, or what?

So when was the idiot going to pop the big question?

My God, you are gagging me.

I'm gagging myself, Inner Bitch. Can't be helped.

"I know it'll be okay," I said. "I'm good. I mean, it's what I do, right? It's my gift."

"And your curse."

"Thanks, Mr. Monk." He got the reference, which made us both smile. "Can we look around for Gary now?"

"The kids–"

"Josh was picked up shortly after we left. Today was the Hershey Park thing."

"Chuckie's birthday trip. Right."

"And Jeremy's spending his Sunday reconnecting with his high school friends. I told him it was okay. Because we have to share him whether we like it or not. Like grownups."

He made a face at me.

"The dogs will be okay for a couple more hours," I said. "Let's check the shelters for Gary."

"While I drive," he said, "Find a psychiatrist named Dr. Guthrie. Maybe she'll talk to me."

"To us," I corrected.

"To me," he said. "You don't have the equipment."

"A dick?" I asked, widening my eyes at him.

"A *badge*." All fake-shocked at my gutter brain. God, I loved him.

MASON SAT in Dr. Melissa Guthrie's waiting room. The receptionist was behind glass. There was a fish tank and a patient in the waiting room with him. The patient was a brunette about forty with worry lines around her eyes. They'd exchanged a nod. He'd thrown in a smile. She hadn't reciprocated.

Once she'd found Guthrie's office address, Rachel had dropped him off and headed out to check the shelters. Mason didn't like it, but you couldn't really argue with her once she'd made up her mind. And she'd made up her mind.

A closed door opened, a woman leaned out and said, "You can come in Detective Brown. Gloria, I'll only be ten minutes. Okay?"

The worried brunette nodded.

Mason wished Rachel was there to tell him how pissed off she was. "It won't even take ten minutes," he told her as he got up, even though it might.

Dr. Guthrie reminded Mason of his mother. She had the same lean frame, dignified manner, and chic white-silver hair. His mom's was shorter and not as curly. Mason flashed his badge and said, "I need to talk to you about Gary Conklin."

"You can talk to me about anyone you want. I can't talk back." She tipped her head to one side. "So? Talk."

"My um…significant other is Rachel de Luca."

"Oooh." The sound she made spoke volumes. Mason had no doubt what the psychiatrist thought of self-help gurus like Rachel. "I've read her."

Non-committal as hell. "Gary is a fan," he said.

"Several of my clients are fans."

"Well, this one showed up at our home yesterday, in Whitney Point. Said he walked there from Binghamton."

"Oh, my." She lifted her silver brows. "Well, I'm concerned too, then. But Detective, let me ease your mind. I don't think Gary's dangerous. I really don't. He's a sweet young man."

"Thank you for that."

"I'm fond of him."

"We got him a room for the night, but he was gone this morning. Do you think you could check in on him?"

"If you know where he is, of course I will."

"We're working on that right now. I got the feeling he was off his meds. Can you tell me when you last saw him?"

"I'm afraid not." She took a card off her desk and handed it to him. "Let me know when you find him."

He took the card and headed out, texting Rachel on his way to the elevator. "Any luck?"

"None. You?"

"Pick me up," he tapped. "I'll fill you in."

JEREMY AND MASON took the pontoon boat out on the lake for some Sunday afternoon fishing. After catching up with his friends all morning, Jere had come home and actually asked Mason to hang out with him. If I was sappier, I'd have teared up. I didn't mind being left out. They needed the one-on-one time, and besides, I wanted the house to myself. I wanted to delve into every detail I could remember about that dream, disturbing as it was. And everything since. I was missing something, I knew I was.

I took a long, steamy shower, put on my most comfy cuddly fleece, and brewed a cup of herbal tea. Chamomile. It had been a Christmas present from a new editor, and still hadn't been opened. I silenced all the ringers in the house, and put a big silk pillow on the floor of my office. *I* was going to meditate. Woo-woo is woo-woo, right? Might as well play the part.

Not long ago, a phony psychic had taught me her method for "opening the channels," as she called it. And even though I'd pegged her for a fraud, I'd given it a try, cause my shit was on the fritz, and she hadn't tried to kill me yet. That came later. To my utter shock, it had actually worked.

So, I assumed the position, or what I thought was the position. Sitting on a soft pillow with my legs crossed, guru-style. I took a few deep, calming breaths, followed by a blissful sip of my herbal tea, and then I spat it all over the place.

"Ohmy*gawd*, that stuff is awful!"

I was on my feet and back in the kitchen in three point five seconds. I rinsed the cup and poured it full of coffee from the pot, added abundant quantities of French Vanilla creamer that was neither fat-free nor sugar-free. I am nothing if not a rebel. Then I headed back to my office.

Tea had seemed to go with the whole Natalia DaVine open the channels thing, until I remembered–I *detest* tea.

So I sipped my coffee–nectar of the gods–and got all comfortable. Closing my eyes, I imagined a spiral staircase descending into the ground. I tried to remember which color the first step was supposed to be. Red, that was it. So I stepped onto the red step, and–

He was a malignant tumor that had to be excised from the world.

The words echoed up at me from the bottom of my imaginary staircase, and my eyes popped open. I said it again, out loud, so I'd remember, word for word. "He was a malignant tumor that had to be excised from the world." Aiming my gaze ceilingward, I said, "Damn, Natalia. That shit really works. I guess even a murderous bitch like you isn't an entire waste of oxygen. Or wasn't. May you rest in peace. Sorry I shot you, by the way."

Meditation, complete.

I pulled my laptop over and typed the phrase into the search bar.

It was a line from an old movie starring Reginald D'Voe, arguably the greatest horror movie actor of all time. That voice. Those eyes. He'd died just a couple weeks ago, too. Was that coincidence?

There's no such thing as coincidence.
You're right, IB, there's not.

I Googled Reginald D'Voe and found about a dozen obituaries, all of which agreed that he had lived and died in the place he loved most, his gothic mansion in the small Finger Lakes town of Dilmun, NY.

The same town the late Dwayne Clark, recently strangled in the back of his Jag while I knelt on his back, was from.

Inner bitch and I had an identical reaction. *What the actual fuck?*

∼

I COULD BARELY WAIT to tell Mason my news. But Josh returned from his fun-park trip, juggling carnival prizes and a three-foot-tall alien with a straw in its head. I estimated it had a soda capacity of approximately three gallons.

Okay, one.

"You are sunburned," I said. "You didn't even take that sunblock I packed out of your backpack, did you?"

He grinned at me, white rings around his eyes. "Nope."

"I didn't think so. You have fun, though?"

"We rode the Skyrush like six times! It's awesome." Then he looked around, "Did Jeremy go back?"

"He's outside with your Uncle. They caught enough fish for supper this afternoon. They're cleaning and cooking tonight."

"I'll help!" Backpack, stuffed animals, and a four-foot alien fell like autumn leaves as he raced through the house and out the back door. The dogs raced after him, and I had to lunge to catch the door before they went out.

"Uh-uh, no way. No fishy dog breath. Not today, my friends." Myrtle sighed and plodded back to her favorite sleeping spot, a plush doggy bed I had to replace every few months because no one had the brains to make one with a waterproof inside, and a removable, washable outside. Yet. The results of their froggy hunting expeditions were constantly soaking their beds.

I worked on my newest self-help book while they made

dinner, and actually got quite a bit done. Natalia, the late murderous fraud from hell, had inspired a section about every life having value, no matter how poorly it was lived. Good stuff.

By the time Josh yelled, "It's ready, Aunt Rache!" so loud I could hear him on the third floor, I had the new section hammered out, and emailed it to Amy with a "tell me what you think of this" note.

We ate together at the actual dining room table. Everyone had enjoyed their day. I got to hear Jeremy and Mason's moment-by-moment recap of their fishing trip, and Joshua's excited retelling of his day at Hershey Park. There were thirteen roller coasters, but only three worthy of Josh and his pals' time waiting in line.

Mason and the boys and I had gone there once. It had been a crushing disappointment for me. It was hot. It was crowded–mostly with idiots. And it turned out that the park was not, in fact, made of chocolate. That name is false advertising.

The fish was so good we cleaned the platter. I convinced the kids to take the dogs for a walk, waved them off, closed the door, turned to Mason and said, "I got something!"

"So did I," he replied, and he looked like he'd been waiting as impatiently as I had.

I said, "You first," as we headed into the kitchen to stack dishes in the dishwasher. Then I looked around in surprise. "There's not oil and flour everywhere. What gives?"

"The guys and I tag teamed it. I cooked, they cleaned up as I went along."

"*That* is a *good* system!"

"Hey. I'll have you know sloppy cooks are the best cooks."

"I'm going to embroider that on an apron for you someday. Coffee?"

"Yes."

I put on a cup of decaf.

"Rosie texted me the background on the victim," Mason said.

"Dwayne Clark of Dilmun, New York."

He picked up on my excitement and paused. "Yes. Why'd you say it like that?"

"You first. Tell me the rest."

His eyebrows did that bendy thing they do when he's trying to figure out some odd thing I've said. I loved that bendy thing.

"Dwayne Clark," he said at length, "Was *recently* of Dilmun, New York. He moved to an apartment in Binghamton a few weeks ago. He and his wife Juanita were in the middle of a divorce. And there was a nasty a custody battle over their six-year-old son, Juan."

"Wait, Juanita named her kid Juan?" I asked. "Isn't that a little Norma and Norman Bates-ish?"

"Aha! Sexist!" he said, pointing at me.

"You're right. It is."

Oh, he looked so smug. "We'll meet them tomorrow. We're going to the funeral."

"Tomorrow's Labor Day, babe," I moved his coffee out of the way, stuck my mug in its place on the one-cup brewer, and deftly switched out the coffee pods. Reusable ones. They were a gift from Misty, who said if we didn't use them, we hated the planet, so you know, we caved. "It's Josh's last day before starting seventh grade."

"I haven't forgotten that for a minute," he said. "Fortunately, the service isn't until seven. We'll have the whole day with the boys. And you don't have to go if you don't–"

"The hell I don't. You need me."

"That, I do." He sipped his coffee. I was jealous that mine wasn't done yet. "What did you get today?" he asked.

"I decided to do the Natalia meditation."

"With the spiral staircase?"

"Right. I barely got my big toe on the first step when I remembered what the killer was thinking. Well, not remembered exactly. It just sort of played in my head. Like an ad in the middle of a Youtube video. Unwanted, from outside. And what it said was, 'He was a malignant tumor that had to be excised from the world.' So I Googled the phrase, just in case it was something. I mean it was so precise. It felt memorized, not organic. Not to me and not to whoever was thinking it."

"And what did Detective Google say?"

My coffee was done. I took it, added my French V–though it was darn near time for Pumpkin Spice–stirred three times and took a delicious sip. Then I said, "It's a line from an old horror movie, *The Devil's Lambs,* starring Reginald D'Voe." I sipped some more, savoring the coffee as much as the telling.

Mason frowned, clearly unsure where I was going. "Didn't he die recently?"

"Two weeks ago." I tapped my phone to bring up the page I'd saved, and turned it his way. The headline read: "Small-town Dilmun, New York plans monument to its most famous resident, the late great Reginald D'Voe."

I'd already read the story, of course. Some in Dilmun wanted to memorialize the actor with a statue depicting his role as The Headless Horseman. There was a sketch of a rearing horse with a cape-wearing body, sans head.

The head was cradled in the crook of the actor's arm, but instead of the sinister sneer and sharply crooked brow the world had come to know and love, this face wore a knowing smile, and was winking. The plan's opponents said it was undignified and too dark. Supporters said Reggie would've loved it. I guessed the jury was still out.

"He was from Dilmun," Mason said softly.

"And so was Dwayne Clark," I reminded him, though he clearly got it. "And the killer was thinking one of the actor's lines during the murder."

Mason nodded slowly. "Could be coincidence. Might just be that the killer is from the same town as the victim, and has probably seen a D'Voe flick or two. Maybe that's all it is."

"Okay, sure, it *could* be coincidental," I admitted. "Statistically, most killers live near their victims."

"Usually *with* their victims," he said.

"And people from Dilmun might be more into D'Voe horror flicks than most. But then why do I keep getting it?"

"Maybe it's just–"

"'He was a malignant tumor that had to be excised from the world.' My stuff keeps hitting the Play button on that line. And I don't get random shit. You know that, Mason. If I'm getting this, then it means something. Jeeze, where have you been the last two years?"

"Okay." He held up both hands.

Yeah, I'd been sliding into pissed off. I hadn't asked for this thing, but I had it. It was real and it was a part of me. And if Mason didn't believe in it one hundred percent, then he didn't believe in me. And that hurt.

Yes, I was over-sensitive on the issue. The merest hint of him doubting my stuff sent me into an indignant, offended, wounded spiral.

"Okay," he said again. "I didn't think that far into it. You're right. If you're getting this, it's for a reason. Maybe we'll find out more at the funeral."

I lowered my bristles and sipped my coffee. "Did Jeremy mention a problem with one Professor Asshat?"

"Professor Ashton. And yes, we talked about it this afternoon, out on the water. It was a good day."

"I know it was. I'm glad." I clinked my coffee mug to his. "So he never gave me the details. What did Professor Asshat do?"

"Gave an assignment to write about a personal trauma in the form of a police report. He told the class to pick the most emotional experience of their lives, and then write it, leaving all emotion out of it."

"That's kind of cruel."

"I think it's kind of brilliant. Cops have to learn to keep their emotions out of their work."

"Writing about a trauma reactivates it in your psyche, and therefore, in your life," I said, quoting one my own tomes, though I'd be pressed to say which one. "He's had so many traumas. Which one did he pick?"

"He wrote about his mother abducting him and Josh last year."

"Oh *hell* no."

"The professor accused him of making it up. Gave him a zero."

I got off the sofa. "Are you fucking kidding me? Hand me my phone. Who does this asshole think he is? Ashton, you said?"

"Jeremy doesn't want us to do anything," Mason said. He gave my sweater a tug and I sat back down beside him. "He says he's a man now and can handle his own shit."

"But he can't, though. We both know he can't. Do you think he's…okay?"

"I think he's shaky."

I closed my eyes. "Why the hell isn't he living at home

and commuting to school? He could ride in with you if he wanted."

"Because he's trying to grow up," he said. "And I think we have to let him."

I heaved a giant sigh. "Anything else?"

"He wanted to talk about Eric."

Eric? As in your dead brother, whose sons don't know he was a serial killer? I asked with my eyes.

"I changed the subject and he let it go, but…I think it'll come up again."

I tipped my head back. Our big fat sofa was there to cradle it. "Kids are *hard*."

"Yeah they are. That's all I got."

"I'm spent." I reached for the remote and hit the search button. "I think after the boys hit the sack, we should make some popcorn and queue up a classic old horror flick," I said, as I keyed *The Devil's Lambs* into the search bar.

4

The setting sun made the surface of Cayuga into a lake of fire. We had an excellent and stunning view of the spectacle from the Dilmun Hills Cemetery, where we'd sidled in behind the mourners without too much interaction. I wore a black tank dress with a sheer black, long-sleeved wrap. I hated wearing black. I made a mental note to put it in my will that no one's allowed to wear black at my funeral. I want colors. Bright, vivid colors.

I held my clutch, also black, in both hands, front and center, head bowed, eyes closed, feeling things out. It was kind of cool that at a funeral, this pose was not odd in the least. Usually, I had to face away from everyone or wear sunglasses or something. Oddly, standing around in public with your eyes closed is considered weird.

A cold tingle tiptoed up my spine, making me lift my eyes and look around.

Mason stood beside me in a blue-black suit. He wasn't going to go unnoticed for long. My man was hot in that suit. I liked the way it fit across his chest and shoulders.

His eyes met mine. I wiggled my brows. He flashed the

dimple of doom, then turned somber again and returned his attention to the main event. Yeah, I lost focus, there, didn't I? He tended to have that effect on me.

I looked at those gathered around the casket of Dwayne Clark, the guy I vividly remembered strangling. I used my five *regular* senses this time.

The first person I noticed was a sunshine blonde no bigger than a whisper. Late thirties, maybe forty, and pretty and somehow as soft as bunny fur. She stood between two other women, a redhead and a brunette. The brunette was Juanita Clark, Dwayne's ex. I'd scoped the widow out on social. She was even sexier in person than in her profile picture. Her black dress clung to every curve, her cleavage was capable of hiding Jimmy Hoffa, and her face was flawless. Her little boy Juan stood in front of her, dark brown hair, big brown eyes, baby cheeks that would probably be gone by the end of first grade. The blonde was stroking the child's hair. Juanita had her hand on his shoulder.

I closed my eyes behind my Jackie O sunglasses.

The blonde loved the kid almost as much as his mom did. She just sort of radiated love. I'd never come across anyone who felt like that before. She was gentle and fragile and cool, and had love oozing out of her pores.

I opened my eyes, skeptical. Maybe my stuff needed a tune-up. Nobody was *that* good.

"See the widow?" I whispered to Mason, beside me.

"I am *not* looking at the widow," Mason said. "I swear."

I looked up at him. He *was* looking at the widow, so I elbowed him in the ribcage.

"Ow! Sorry. I just keep wondering what was *she* doing with *him*?"

I shrugged. "Maybe he was handsomer alive."

He lowered his head to hide his quick smile. "Or maybe she's not as shallow as she looks."

"Nobody's as shallow as she looks." I know. I'm a shit.

"The redhead is Holly O'Mally."

"Oh, the chief's wife," I said. Mason and I had done a little research before our movie, and it turned out he'd met Dilmun Police Chief Vince O'Mally more than decade ago. The chief had been a decorated detective for the Syracuse PD when Mason had been a rookie cop in Binghamton. They'd worked a case together or something. "I think the blonde is Holly O'Mally's sister," I said. "That's the vibe I'm getting."

"Bullseye," Mason replied. "Ivy Newman. She was little Juan's Kindergarten teacher last year."

Of course the angelic blonde was a kindergarten teacher. Made perfect sense. Miss Honey.

Ivy Newman bent to the little guy and said something. He nodded sadly.

She looked our way then, sort of casually, spotted us, and then lowered her big black sunglasses over her eyes.

"You okay here for a bit?" Mason asked.

"I'm great here. The dead love me. They don't even care that it's not mutual. Why, where you heading?"

"Back down by the entrance. Gonna chat up the chief."

When we'd arrived, there'd been a Dilmun Police SUV parked in the road outside the cemetery, probably in case any press showed up. The funeral was for the victim of an unsolved murder, after all.

"I'll meet up with you on your way out, okay?"

"Got it."

He moved away from me. I edged in a little closer to the cluster of people standing around with their heads bowed, closed my eyes, and felt for anything unusual.

That tingle went up my spine again. It felt like a warning, like you might feel if there were a serial killer or, I don't know, a bear standing behind you. I'd experienced the former. Not the latter.

I scanned the cemetery and caught a glimpse of motion way off in the distance where the tombstones gave way to woods. I focused there for a long moment.

Nothing.

Back to the matter at hand, the people surrounding Dwayne Clark's open grave. I opened my senses to them. But it was what I *didn't* pick up that was most interesting. None of the mourners seemed to be mourning. There was more relief than grief at the graveside.

As the minister finished up, people filed past the widow to pay their respects. I got in line amongst them, exchanged banalities with folks I didn't know in respect-for-the-dead murmurs, as one does at these things.

"It was a beautiful service."

"The weather couldn't have been nicer."

"What a perfect spot this is."

When it was my turn, I clasped the widow's hand as the others had done and said, "I'm sorry for your loss."

I'm not.

That was it, two words, loud and clear and angry, but entirely silent. She'd felt them strongly. And so had I.

I relaxed my grip. Hers tightened, and she looked up at me. "I'm sorry, do I know you?"

Ivy stepped up behind her and placed a delicate hand on the widow's shoulder. She had the prettiest French manicure, all pink and shiny.

"I'm here with Detective Brown," I said softly.

The chief's wife, Holly, said, "Juanita, remember? Vince told you Detective Brown would be coming tonight?"

"Right," Ivy said, as if she'd just remembered that herself.

Girl Blue

I met Ivy's eyes. They were light blue like aquamarines. No, I am totally serious.

Juanita said, "Oh, the detective investigating Dwayne's… yes. Yes. Is there anything new?"

"I don't think so," I said. "But Mason–Detective Brown–will fill you in, in a little while. We just wanted to pay our respects."

"Oh. Thank you." Then she looked past me at the next in line, so I moved on. Holly and Ivy–oh my God, I just got that–came with me.

Ivy said, "It seems above and beyond the call of duty for a homicide detective and his wife to attend the funeral of a victim." Her tone was soft, her energy, curious, and she was trying not to be offensive or rude. She was a self-conscious little thing. And yet everything in me was drawn to her.

"Oh, we're not married," I said, deftly swerving around an answer. "I'm Rachel, by the way. Rachel de Luca."

"Ivy Newman." She extended a hand. I took it and made a long, slow blink a part of my smile. She felt warm, and kind, and gentle. She was also deeply, deeply wounded. It was a heart wound.

"And this is my sister, Holly."

"*Mrs.* Chief O'Mally," I said, with a friendly smile. "Nice to meet you, Holly."

She took my hand, too. And I heard her panicked thoughts, *Murdered. Dead. Strangled.* And then out of nowhere, *1, 2, 3, 4, 5, 6, 7, 8…*

Our hands separated, and I pulled myself out of her head like pulling my shoe off a piece of gum on the floor.

An older couple gathered around Juan and Juanita, sort of herding them toward the parking area. The crowd was dispersing, I realized. It was time to go. Juan looked back at

Ivy, waved at her. She waved back, and a tear rolled down her cheek.

The three of us walked together back toward the cemetery's entrance. Mason had intercepted Juanita and was talking to her, a little bit away from everyone else.

"It's a shame what happened to that family," Holly said. "First the divorce, and now this. It's just so hard to believe." The sisters were flanking me as we walked down the path toward the cemetery gate. Holly had calmed herself. I guessed the internal counting was her stress mechanism. I could sense her better now that she'd stopped. She was friendly and funny and kind, and madly in love with her husband. And she was worried about her little sister.

"I hope it was amicable. The divorce, I mean." I knew it wasn't.

Holly shook her head. "Not by a long shot. The custody fight has been vicious."

"Holly, maybe this is stuff that should stay private," Ivy said softly. I felt her not wanting to make her sister mad, but protective of Juan and his mom.

"I consult with our department on an official level," I said, like that would make it okay to talk to me.

"Really?" Ivy asked, looking at me quickly. "In what way?"

"Well, it's…" *Not fucking psychic, that's for sure.* "It's kind of my own thing."

She looked right into my eyes, smiled just a little, and I understood why kindergarteners hugged her.

Holly said, "You should come by the house before you head back. I'll make dinner. Ivy, you too. It would be good for you to get out."

Ivy dipped her head. "I don't know. Aside from school, this is the most I've been out since–"

"I know, hon." Holly touched her sister's shoulder. "Still, I think you should come. No pressure, though. You decide."

We'd exited the cemetery's open gate onto the winding country road, where Mason had finished with Juanita and was now leaning on the hood of a police department Bronco chatting with Chief O'Mally, whose photo I'd seen online. O'Mally was bigger than Mason only because he had several more years' worth of insulation. Their builds were similar, though, and I decided that my hunky honey could rock another twenty pounds and still make my girl parts tingle.

I moved up beside him. He put an arm around me, just like I wanted him to. Ivy said goodbye, hugged her sister, then walked away. She picked up a bicycle she'd left on the side of the road, an old-fashioned one with a basket on the front, and she pedaled away.

"Does Ivy live close?" I asked.

"Just up the hill." Holly pointed. "The D'Voe mansion."

"As in *Reggie* D'Voe?" I could see the top parts of the house in the distance, peaks and turrets and a widow's walk, just as creepy as you'd expect.

"They were very close," Holly said. "It's been rough on her."

I met Mason's eyes. We were both wondering the same thing; what was the relationship between Ivy Newman and the old horror film star?

While the others were discussing dinner plans, those tiny, icy shivers tiptoed up my spine again. I looked back toward the cemetery and caught a glimpse of someone walking among the tombstones, way off in the distance where I'd glimpsed him before. He was heading away from us, tall and lanky, and slouched like his backbone was tired. There wasn't a doubt in my mind that it was Gary Conklin.

"Mason?"

He looked at me, then at where I was looking, but Gary had vanished among the trees.

AN HOUR LATER, we were sipping rum-punch from an actual punch bowl at Vince and Holly O'Mally's modest white clapboard house. The place had a picket fence and flower boxes in the windows, all a'bloom with orange, yellow, gold and purple blossoms. I guessed Holly was one of those women who could actually *grow* flowers. I only seemed to be able to kill them.

"So has Mason told you how we know each other, Rachel?" The chief asked. He wasn't drinking punch, but a cold beer.

Mason dropped his chin to his chest. "You gonna ruin my image, now, Vince?"

The chief laughed softly. "He was a raw rookie on the Binghamton PD."

"And you were a decorated detective with Syracuse," Mason filled in.

I tried to pay attention, but kept glancing toward the front door every time a vehicle passed, wondering if it was Ivy.

"There was a body in a park," Vince said. "Mason was the one who spotted it. He was off duty, just happened to be there, but still, first cop on the scene."

Mason picked up the story. "I called it in. Detective O'Mally asked me to keep people off the crime scene until SPD arrived. But I, uh–got distracted talking to a bystander, and a bunch of kids on bikes blew right past me."

"Right through the crime scene," O'Mally said. "A couple of 'em rolled right over the victim. Contaminated the hell out of my evidence."

"And probably traumatized those poor kids for life," Holly said, a hand on her husband's shoulder. They were always touching, those two.

I looked at Mason. "Was the bystander a hot female jogger?"

"No." He said it with the sincerity of an innocent man.

I kept looking at him, waiting, because I knew there was more.

He shrugged one shoulder. "She was doing yoga ten feet from my face. I really had no choice in the matter."

"*Male*," I said, but I said it with love.

We were still laughing softly when Ivy came in. She entered so quietly I didn't even hear her. But I felt her. She felt like sunshine.

"Hello, again," she said. "Holly, what smells so good?"

"A frozen lasagna. Best I could do on short notice. And as a matter of fact, it should be just about ready."

Ivy dipped out a cup of punch and sat down on a pretty chair. She didn't sit back, but perched on the edge, like she wanted to be ready to launch.

Thinking I could help out, and maybe she'd drop a tidbit more about this town and the Clarks, I followed Holly into the kitchen. It was pale yellow with white cabinets and trim. The countertop was the beigest of beige with slightly beiger flecks.

"I get the feeling Dwayne Clark wasn't exactly a beloved member of the community," I said, setting my cup of punch on the counter.

"Did you? What gave it away?"

I shrugged, not answering as she took some pot holder mitts from a hook near the range.

"He was a drinker with a temper. Got into a lot of bar

fights. Didn't get along with his neighbors. Just kind of an all-around a-hole."

I loved that she said a-hole. "Do you think that might be the motive? That maybe he pushed someone too far?"

"I can't believe anyone local could've done this," she said. "It's just not that kind of town." *Anymore.*

The *anymore* part came so clearly I thought she'd said it out loud. It took me a beat to realize her lips hadn't moved. If I hadn't been looking at her, I might never have even known.

Which made me wonder how many things I'd heard people say that they hadn't actually said. I usually had my eyes closed. Wow. A flaw in my gift-curse management methodology. She opened the oven, took out steaming hot rolls, and popped them into a waiting basket, lined with a spotless, red-and-white checkerboard dish towel.

My jaw dropped a little in awe of her hostessness.

"You can take these out, if you want," she said. "Oh, and there's a salad in the fridge."

I accepted the basket of rolls, located the big salad bowl, and took both into the dining room.

Holly came behind me with the pan of lasagna, and everyone gathered around the dining room table.

The dining room and living room were both done in lake colors. Sky blue walls and crisp white trim. There were lots of framed photos on the walls, including several of Holly and Ivy as little girls, with and without their parents. But none as older girls, none as teens. The photos came to a halt when Ivy must've been around five, Holly a couple of years older. Was that odd?

Seems odd to me, IB offered.

I dug in. Holly had fancied up the frozen lasagna with extra sauce and cheese and seasonings. She reminded me of my sister.

•

Girl Blue 59

We ate, and we talked. Vince and Mason talked about police work, and the chief shared some of his war stories from when he'd served on the Syracuse PD. Holly told us that her father had passed, but that her mom was retired and living nearby, married to the former police chief, who'd passed the torch to Vince. Ivy talked about funny things her kindergarteners had said and done, and every one of them was a heartstring-tugger. But not about Reggie D'Voe, I noted. I talked about the boys and the bulldogs. I probably talked too much about Myrtle as a rule, but no one had ever complained.

After a while, we all helped clear up and then retired to the living room to sit and chat some more. Mason and I quit the rum-spiked punch after two, but Ivy was on her fourth or fifth, and as soon as she got into a big comfy chair, she started to nod off.

"Poor thing," Holly said, pushing her sister's hair off her forehead. "Honey, why don't you go lie down in the guest room?"

"I can't spend the night here. I need to be home."

"In that big empty house all alone?"

"I have to," she said. "But…maybe just a nap. If you promise to wake me in a couple of hours."

"I promise."

Ivy smiled. "You lie, though. It's okay, I'll set my phone to wake me." She got up, and I swear, I could feel the grief in her. It was bone deep, and had been lurking there the whole time. The rum had weakened her defenses and let it spill out. But she smiled brightly all the same and said, "It was so nice meeting you, Rachel. I hope we see each other again." She reached out to take my hand in both of hers.

I looked down and noticed she was wearing a watch with a delicate oval face, gold hands and numbers, and a pink leather band.

Holy shit.

I clasped Mason's forearm so hard it must've hurt. He glanced my way curiously, and I said, "We should get going, too."

"Yeah, the kids and the dogs are waiting," Mason said. No questions asked. We shook hands, Ivy hugged me. I am not a hugger. I hugged her back and I felt nothing but goodness coming from her. There was no way she was a killer.

"Thanks for dinner," Mason went on. "It was fantastic."

"We should keep in touch," Vince said.

"Absolutely."

We got into the car, and Mason looked at me. "What?"

My brain said, *Ivy's watch is the same one I saw on the wrist of the person who murdered Dwayne Clark.* But my lips only said, "Let's get over to Ivy's house so we can take a look around before she finishes her nap."

"You're going to get me fired."

"I'd do time before I'd let that happen. Trust me, we need a look inside that house. I feel it right to my bones."

He swore a blue streak under his breath. But he drove, so you know, all good.

5

My man has many talents. He popped the lock so smoothly no one would ever know it had been touched, twisted the knob with his shirt sleeve pulled over his hand, and pushed the tall wooden door open real slow. It groaned like a dying soul.

I shivered.

"You can wait in the car, Rache," Mason said.

"No way. You go in there alone, you might get eaten."

Yet another level of darkness yawned as he pushed the door wider. Mason went inside, and I put one hand on his shoulder and went with him. When I closed the door behind us, it felt like I was closing our coffin lid, and I thought, *at least we went down together.*

Way to stay with the happy thoughts, Rache.

You're as scared as I am, Inner Bitch.

Cause Ivy was wearing the killer's watch, Inner Bitch said.

Or one just like it.

Why haven't you told Mason that?

I don't know.

I smelled lemon furniture polish and old books, and it was so good I sniffed more of it as my eyes adjusted. There was a fire in a gargantuan stone fireplace that spilled orange light and made leaping shadows all around the room.

The place was just what you'd expect an old horror movie star's house to look like. Brocade wallpaper with velvet textures, and tall narrow windows dressed in deep burgundy drapes with gold cords. Above the fireplace, there was a huge painting of Reggie D'Voe in a Waistcoat and cravat, his sharp eyebrows uneven as he peered judgmentally down at us.

"That's from *The Madman on the Hill*. He played a tortured nobleman serial killer," I told Mason in my softest voice. "He'd have his servants block the road with a boulder or felled tree, and when wayward travelers came to ask if there was another way around, or for help moving the obstacle…" I drew a finger across my neck and made the appropriate accompanying sound.

"Sounds like a fun date movie."

"We should check the basement," I said.

IB said, *Are you out of your fucking mind?*

Something's upstairs.

That second voice wasn't Inner Bitch. And it wasn't a voice, exactly. It was a powerful feeling that came from somewhere else. My stuff.

I took Mason's arm. "Come on. We have to go upstairs."

We tiptoed across a parquet floor to a wide, curving staircase, and I remembered reading about how at his annual Halloween party, Reggie would wait for all the local kids to arrive, and then make a big entrance, coming down this very staircase dressed as a vampire or monster or demon he'd once played.

Tonight, the staircase seemed lonely. I put my palm on the bannister, and instantly saw him above, swooping and swirling a big black cloak with red satin lining, laughing that delicious, iconic laugh that had terrified generations of movie-goers.

I took my hand away quick and shot Mason a look.

"What was that, just now?" he whispered.

I sighed. "I'm getting stuff by touch." I lifted my hand, looked at it.

"You sure you don't want to leave?"

"You'll get eaten, remember?"

"I remember."

A deep growl echoed from somewhere above. I clutched Mason's arm so tight my nails would've broken his skin if I'd had any. I didn't. I kept them short and neat for ease of tapping the keyboard at the speed of me.

"You heard that, too, right?" My whisper was gruff because my throat was so dry.

"Uh-huh."

We moved slowly upstairs in the damn pitch dark. I pulled out my phone and flipped into flashlight mode.

"You're announcing our presence," he said.

"Yeah, but I don't want to die in the dark."

He stopped moving, looked at me. "Damn." And he touched my cheek, like he was feeling sorry for the poor little blind girl.

I shrugged. "Don't pity me. Just buy me stuff." Then, "So are we doing this, or what?"

He kissed me slow. I stood there and let him. It was kind of tingly, kissing like that in the middle of a scene right out of *Buffy*. I sighed because it was so delicious.

Then the growl came again.

"All right that's it, this thing is either eating me or I'm eating it. I'm done fucking around." I walked up the stairs, holding my phone out ahead of me like Garth Algar's backstage pass.

Mason caught up before I reached the top. There was a T, with hallways going left or right. We stopped there.

"It was coming from this way," he said. So we went left. The first door was closed. Mason turned the knob slow and pushed it open.

In the pitch dark, there were shadowy people standing all around the room. I aimed my light. Not people! *Creatures.* A werewolf and a vampire–

Music from the *Psycho* shower scene played in my head. *Ree-ree-ree!*

Mason flipped a light switch.

Mannequins, all of them dressed as characters from Reggie's films. His roles, and those of his leading ladies. A Gypsy, a sorceress, a witch.

I went almost weak with relief. "Jeeze, that scared the hell out of me."

"Me, too," he said, sliding his gun back into his jacket. "Come on, no one's in here."

"I don't know," I said, looking at each of the characters in turn. The bling dangling from the Gypsy's ears seemed to be moving and reflecting in her crystal ball.

Could've been the draft when we opened the door, I guessed.

I swore the vampire's eyes followed me.

I backed into Mason, then kept backing until we were both in the hall, with that door once again closed. Then I gave a full body shudder.

"I know." He rubbed my outer arms. "Come on, next room."

I took a deep breath, stiffened my spine, and went to the

next door. I put my hand on the doorknob, since I was in front, turned it slow.

Grrrrrrr…

My wide eyes shot to Mason's on my way to get behind him.

He frowned at the door. "That's not a growl, that's…" And then he opened it.

The room wasn't pitch dark. There was a little plug-in nightlight down low, beside the bed. The bed had a rail on the side, like a hospital bed. There was a nice homestyle comforter on it.

Someone was underneath that comforter.

I stayed plastered to Mason's back as he moved slowly closer to the bed. And then we stood there looking down at the dead actor, Reggie D'Voe. He lay there perfectly still, his skin pale. I stared at him, stunned that Ivy had somehow kept his body after he'd–

The *body* growled. I yelped and grabbed Mason with both hands just as Reggie opened his eyes.

6

I pivoted to run, and I did, right into Ivy Newman.

"What the hell are you doing in my house?" she demanded.

"What the hell are you doing in my *room*?" Reggie shouted, sitting up in his bed.

"What the hell are you doing *alive*?" Mason asked.

Alive, right, yeah. I knew that.

I knew it too, Inner Bitch lied. *And the growls were snores.*

Reggie lifted that one brow to glare at us. "It seems these strangers have discovered our secret, Ivy, my girl."

She pushed past me to hurry to the bedside. Mason came to me, slid an arm around my shoulders, and gave me a look that said he had this.

"Look, I'm gonna need an explanation," Mason said.

Oh, he was good. *He* wanted an explanation. He had more nerve than me on my best day.

"Isn't it obvious?" Reggie asked softly. "I'm...*immortal*." That brow arched up again, and he gave us his patented glare. I couldn't even turn around and run screaming like any sane person would do. I *couldn't*. It was Reggie D'Voe in full-on villain mode. It was terrifying and wonderful. I was mesmerized.

He met my eyes. And then he smiled. And then he started to laugh, and then he started to cough.

Ivy held his shoulders as his head fell forward. "Did you–" *Hack, cough.* "–see their faces?"

"You haven't lost your touch, Reggie. There, easy. Slow breaths, not too deep." She made circles on his back with her palm.

I was still catching up. I looked from the two of them to my one and only, and he closed his eyes and shook his head slow.

"Wait, so you're not dead, and you're not immortal," I said.

"Not dead yet, my dear." He'd sipped some water and got his coughing under control. "As for immortal, time will tell. But I'm afraid my final act won't be pretty, and for the first time in my life, I prefer not to have an audience."

"So you faked your death." I finally got it.

"We didn't fake it, we just…announced it early," Ivy said, running a hand over his head. "Lie back down, Reg. You've had a scare."

"Nonsense. I don't have scares, I deliver them. We're going to have tea downstairs like civilized people and confess our secrets to each other. Aren't we, Detective Brown?"

Mason lifted his head and looked surprised that Reggie knew who he was. "Take them to the parlor, and put the kettle on, won't you Ivy? I'll join you presently."

"I'll take them down and put the kettle on," she said. "Go ahead and get into your robe and slippers, but don't you attempt those stairs without me."

Her voice was full of love. But her eyes were angry when she turned to look at us. "Downstairs, then?"

We bumbled into the hallway, exchanging, what-the-hell-have-we-got-ourselves-into looks. Ivy went around us and walked briskly down the elegant staircase, across the foyer into the room with the big fireplace. She turned on the lights, revealing soft brown furniture arranged so every seat had a view of a large, empty wall. And then I saw the projector opposite it, and I understood.

"Have a seat. Don't touch anything, or I swear to God–"

I held up my hands. "We won't. I'm sorry about this, Ivy."

"You're sorry? You broke into my home when you knew I wasn't here–"

"I know. I know, I'm sorry. I wanted to see it, and then I heard something in here."

"Oh, you *heard* something." She was skeptical. She should have been, as I was lying through my teeth.

"Reggie, snoring as it turned out," I said, "but I didn't know that at the time."

"There's no way you heard Reggie snoring from outside."

"Actually, she might very well have," Reggie said. He'd donned a satiny maroon robe with ivory lining over his pajamas. His slippers were soft brown leather and monogrammed. He had a walking stick that had probably come from one of his films. Its head was a wolf. "I opened my window earlier. Wanted to smell the season. Nothing pleases my senses the way autumn does."

"No wonder you're coughing, then. And I told you to wait for me."

"I asked you to put the kettle on."

Ivy sent me a parting glare before she left the room in three long, angry strides. It felt awful, her anger. I was overcome with the most uncharacteristic urge to apologize and win back her favor. How odd.

Reggie nodded at us. "Sit, please. I'm dying to hear the true explanation. Well, I'm dying anyway." He laughed softly and sank into a giant easy chair.

We sat too, close to each other on a little love seat so soft I sank up to my waist. Mason said, "We're investigating a murder, Mr. D'Voe. All I can tell you is that evidence led me here."

He seemed to ponder that for a moment. And then he looked at me. His piercing gaze seemed capable of seeing everything going on behind my eyes. "And what about you, dear? What can you tell me?"

I wasn't going to tell him anything.

Yeah, but it kinda feels like he already knows everything, doesn't it?

It kinda does, Inner Bitch.

I had to say something, though. "I thought I was hearing growls. Like, not even dog growls, but monster growls, you know? I don't know what I was thinking, rushing inside like I did. Usually, I'd run away from monsters not toward them."

Reggie closed his eyes and leaned forward, listening with his whole body. It reminded me keenly of what I do when I'm trying to read someone. And that made me nervous. So I kept talking.

"The front door wasn't even locked," I lied. "I just ran inside, and Mason came in, you know, to make me come back out."

His brows knit a little bit, and I stopped talking, slammed my eyes closed, and tried to feel him. And I did. I felt him…feeling me.

My eyes popped open, and his did too, and we stared at each other.

He got up onto his feet. "I'm feeling unwell," he said. "Please, tell Ivy I've changed my mind. Have your tea, of course."

I got up, too. "I'm very sorry, Mr. D'Voe. I'm a huge fan."

"We both are," Mason said, and he was up, too, right beside me, as always. "And I'm sorry for the intrusion."

"It's fine, it's fine." Ivy came back into the room, and Reggie said, "Help me back to my room, won't you dear?"

She looked at him, then at us.

"We're just gonna, um, go." I was heading for the exit as I said it.

Ivy came after me, grabbed my arm, and her love for Reggie came flooding from her into me. Her heart was breaking because he was dying. He was the most important person in her entire life and she had no idea how she was going to go on without him. I felt it all so intensely that tears sprang into my eyes.

"He doesn't have much time," she whispered. "Please keep our secret. He deserves to die with dignity."

"I promise, we won't tell a soul. I hope you'll do the same about this…lapse in judgement."

"Again, I'm really sorry," Mason said. "Coming here was a mistake. I apologize." And by then we were pulling the front door closed behind us.

We crossed the porch, headed back up the driveway. Mason said, "Why would you promise her that?"

"Because if we talk, she'll talk. Did you not get that?"

He closed his eyes. "Yeah. Okay, you're right."

"But also because her heart is broken, Mason, and she's *good.* She can't have had anything to do with the murder."

Except for that watch.

Shut up, Inner Bitch.

We squeezed through the gap in the gate, and I don't think

my heart stopped racing until we were back in the car, driving away.

"So, what *was* that back there?" Mace asked. "That look between you and Reggie, just before he decided to go back to bed."

I knew exactly what he meant, but I didn't want to talk about it yet.

So this is yet another thing you're keeping from the man you love?

Not keeping it from him. Just getting my own head around it before I share.

"I'm starstruck," I said. "I'm going to dump you and run away with him. Probably before morning. That's all."

He made a face.

I stuck out my tongue. Then I widened my eyes. "Do you realize Reggie D'Voe just gave us a private performance? That whole bit with the eyebrow? 'I'm immortal. *Bwa-ha-ha-ha-ha.*'"

He looked at me like I'd lost my mind. "We broke and entered."

"I know we did. I'm sorry. But she won't tell our secret as long as we don't tell hers. And I was right, wasn't I? I knew somebody was in there."

"I think you said some*thing* was in there."

I snuggled into my seat. It was late. The soft hum of tires rolling over pavement was hypnotic. I closed my eyes. But the minute I did, I flashed on Reggie's eyes, looking into mine. Reggie's eyes, seeing all the way to my soul. And I knew in that place where I know things I shouldn't that Reggie D'Voe was Not Fucking Psychic, just like me.

7

We got up early Tuesday morning. The holiday weekend was over. Summer was over, too, and life was about to resume. Josh had school, Jeremy had classes, Mason had work, and I had a book to finish.

I took my shower while Myrt slept in and Mason cooked a whiz banger end-of-summer breakfast. I didn't know who'd fallen asleep first last night, but we'd both been exhausted. I mean, a funeral, a home invasion, stalking a monster and meeting a dead movie star were a lot for one day. On the ride home from Dilmun, I'd told Mason about Dwayne Clark not being the most popular guy in Dilmun. I'd told him, too, about Gary Conklin being at the cemetery. He said he'd get someone on Gary, get him off the streets, get him some help.

Gary might not be too easy to find, though. He seemed pretty good at getting around, for a homeless guy without wheels.

Wrapped in a towel, I burrowed for clothes. I had no intention of doing a damn thing other than writing for the rest of the day. It made me antsy to be away from it for very long.

More than a few days, and I'd be twitching like a junkie without a fix.

The uniform for the day's writing, I decided, would be lightweight gray fleece with pink trim, and a sports bra. Once the kids were out the door, the bra would be history. I piled my towel-dried hair up and stuck a Japanese hair pin through it to keep it there.

The ability to use the hair pin was a point of pride. There was definitely a knack to it, but I'd aced the technique with a lot of coaching from Misty. Christy's only use for such a device would be as a weapon.

I headed down to the kitchen where the boys were already seated at the breakfast bar, digging in. Mason was squeezing frosting onto hot cinnamon buns, so I slipped up behind him, slid my arms around his waist, and nuzzled the back of his neck.

He turned around in my arms and kissed me, minty fresh, with a touch of coffee. Even better, he then pressed a warm cuppa Joe into my hands.

"There are children present," Josh said. His voice cracked.

I sent Mason a wide-eyed look. It couldn't be!

He nodded and rumpled the kid's hair as he leaned over him to set the warm, gooey buns on the counter.

I sat down with my cup, just holding it between my palms for a second, leaning back in my chair and looking at the boys and Mason passing food around, loading their plates, teasing each other with love in their eyes. Damn, we were lucky.

Mason caught me looking, acknowledged what I was feeling, told me he felt the same, all with his eyes. His gorgeous, sexy eyes.

We dug in.

Halfway through my second bun, my phone pinged. I

pulled it out to look, a no-no at mealtime. Hey, I just *make* the rules. I don't necessarily follow them.

The message on my phone was this; "We never got to have our tea, did we? Ivy's out for the day. I think it's time we talked. Just you and I."

Holy shit, Reggie D'Voe wants a one-on-one!

I swiped the app off and slid the phone back into my sweatshirt's kangaroo pouch. Mason was looking my way, so I said, "Great news. Five-dollar footlongs are back at Subway."

He smiled at me like he didn't know I'd just lied. Well, I hadn't really *lied*. For all I knew, five-dollar footlongs really *were* back. I didn't exactly say that's what the text had been.

Are you really gonna fuck this up? Inner Bitch asked. *He's the best thing that ever happened to you, and that includes getting your eyesight back.*

I know, I thought. But I had to go. And I have to do it alone.

THE WROUGHT IRON gate with the wide-winged bat at the center was open when I arrived. I hesitated, sitting in my T-bird in the road with my blinker light on. There was enough of a nip in the air that we'd had to ride with the top up. Pretty soon it would be time to put the hardtop back on.

Myrtle tapped my thigh, and her eyes reminded me that when the car stops, we either get out, or I pet her until the light changes. I stroked her head. "Okay, we'll pull in. What's he gonna do, close the gate and trap us? We could drive right through that magnificent-yet-rickety old thing. It'd do a number on the T-bird, though."

I turned the wheel and we drove over the long, unpaved

driveway, up to the house. It stood there like an aging queen; once regal and proud, now sagging and in need of shoring up. I shut the engine off and bent to kiss Myrt on the nose. "You're going to wait here for me, okay? If anything happens, Amy knows where to find you." And she was the *only* person who knew where I was today. She was working at the house, scheduling all "my" social media posts for the coming week and handling fan mail. And, you know, keeping Hugo company. The car was running, the AC on, the gas tank full. Myrtle would be fine.

A *tap-tap-tap* on my window made me jump out of my skin. Myrtle gave a snuffly "Snarf!"

Reggie was standing there smiling in at us. He wore a red satin smoking jacket with matching pajama pants and an ivory neck scarf. He carried a different walking stick this time. It had a shiny black raven on top that might've been made of onyx. It had red jewel eyes. I'd lay odds they were rubies.

I put my window down, and he said, "Welcome, Rachel. I see you've brought a companion."

"Myrtle's my best friend and sidekick. But she's fine waiting in the car."

"Nonsense! I wouldn't hear of it. Bring her inside. I'm sure I can find a healthy treat for her."

At the word treat, Myrtle perked her ears, tilted her head, and thrust out her lower jaw, so her bottom teeth stuck up over her lip. The infamous bulldog smile. Reggie laughed, not the evil laugh for which he was famous, but a warm belly laugh that became a cough toward the end.

I watched Myrt carefully. She was completely relaxed and a very good judge of character. Reggie opened my door and held it for us. So I shut off the engine and got out. Myrtle waited patiently until I went around the car to open her door

Girl Blue

and help her down. Then she assumed the position, her body pressed to my left leg. Reggie looked at this behavior curiously, and his eyebrow rose.

God, I loved that eyebrow.

"She's blind, isn't she?"

"Just like I was for twenty years of my life. We understand each other."

"Remarkable. Will she do all right with the stairs?"

"She'll do fine." The three of us walked up the wide steps side by side, and then Reggie held the tall door for us, and we entered first. Myrtle sniffed the air as Reggie came in, closed the doors, then led the way past the sitting room with the fireplace, deeper into the house.

"I hope you don't mind having our tea in the kitchen. It's a bit easier than moving things around."

"I wish you hadn't fussed."

"No fuss to put a kettle on a burner, now, is it? The cookies are pre-existing." He looked down at Myrtle. "Peanut butter. Freshly baked."

She seemed to hang on his every word.

"Please, have a seat."

We'd arrived in a surprisingly ordinary kitchen, yellow walls, Corian countertops, light oak cabinets. Sunlight poured through a number of windows, including three tall ones, side by side. A small wooden table and two chairs were directly in front of them.

I sat down, and Myrtle promptly sat on top of my feet.

Reggie poured steaming water from a metal teapot into a glass one that held a tea-ball full of loose tea and herbs. "My favorite blend," he said, bringing the glass pot to the table. "But I do detest those flimsy paper teabags."

I was not going to tell Reginald D'Voe that I couldn't

stand tea. I would drink it and I would like it. Even if it was chamomile.

"Turn your cup, my dear."

"Oh! Sorry." I flipped over the delicate china cup that had been upside down on its matching saucer. White china with pink roses and gold trim around the edges.

He swirled the water in the pot, and it grew darker as he did. Then he filled both our cups and left the glass teapot in the middle of the table beside a platter of cookies. "May Myrtle have a cookie?"

"Half of one," I said, hating myself for saying it. Poor Myrt. "She's at her goal weight and we'd like to keep it that way."

"One of my greatest regrets is not eating what I wanted when I wanted it. But Hollywood prefers its actors thin, and its actresses skeletal. I wish I'd challenged that more."

"You're right. Give her a whole one."

He smiled, took a cookie, broke it in half, and finally sat down. Then he leaned so he could hold the cookie near enough for Myrt to smell it. "Here's that treat I promised, Myrtle."

He spoke to her the same way I did, as if he was talking to another human. And Myrt responded, got right up and moved closer. She snatched the cookie and stood while she munched it, and Reggie watched, smiling warmly. "That's a good girl," he said. He petted her head and gave her the other half. She took it with glee, then she curled up right on top of his feet.

My eyebrows arched. She *liked* him. Well, of course she'd be fond of anyone who gave her a cookie, but she wouldn't take a nap on their bedroom slippers. Only mine.

I looked at Reggie in a whole new light.

"I appreciate your husband and you keeping my secret," he said, nodding at the cookies.

I took one. "Oh, we're not married."

"Well, not *yet*." He smiled at me when he said it, like he knew something I didn't know.

"How are you doing?" I asked. "Are you feeling all right?"

"It's a good day."

I nodded. He sat there a moment, just looking at me, and then he said, "You want to ask how long I have left. It's all right. You're curious, it's natural." He sipped his tea. "According to the doctors, I ought to be gone by now."

What an awful thing to know. "And yet, you're not."

"There's a reason, as there is for all things. But you already know that."

I got a little chill.

"I looked you up after you left. Read snippets and reviews of your work. Your official biography did not mention that you were an amateur sleuth."

"Not even so amateur. I'm an official police consultant." I lifted the cup to my nose and sniffed. It didn't smell bad. It was minty. Warily, I sipped. Then I sipped some more. It was good!

"You help the police by using your gift?" Reggie asked, as casually as if he was asking for the time.

I spit tea out my nose, then started coughing, my eyes watering so hard I couldn't see. Tea sloshed from my cup, so I set it down and grabbed a cloth napkin to hold over my mouth.

"I'm so sorry, Rachel. Are you all right?"

"Yes." It came out all hoarse and I cleared my throat. "Yes, fine." I settled back in my seat, took a few deep breaths, tried again with the tea. It really was good when one didn't inhale it.

"You knew I recognized it in you. I felt you recognize it in me, when you were last here."

I just sat there, blinking at him, not knowing what to say. I did not discuss my "gift" with anyone besides Mason. Others knew about it, but they also knew the rules. We kept it to ourselves and we didn't talk about it unless there was a damn good reason.

"I understand, you see."

"You…you're…psychic?" I asked.

"Oh, heavens no. I'd never refer to it that way. It's more like a…a heightened sense of empathy. I think many actors have it. They speak of reading a crowd, or even absorbing its energy. No, I'd never call it psychic." He gave a gentle shudder. "What a pretentious word."

"I call mine, NFP," I said. "For *not* fucking psychic."

He tipped his head back and laughed, took a breath, and laughed again, dabbing tears from his eyes with his napkin. He did not break out in a coughing fit that time.

I laughed, too. It was impossible not to. He was…he was wonderful. I liked him.

You don't like anyone.

I know, Inner Bitch, and this is two in twenty-four hours. What's up with me?

"I believe we all have this extra sense," Reggie said. "But only a few notice it and spend time exercising it, and usually then, only by accident. I assume you learned to rely on your abilities while you were blind."

"Yes. And then they got a big boost when I received corneal tissue from a man I suspect also had it. Although, his, I think, drove him nuts."

"Yours won't. You've a core of solid steel, my girl."

"Wow. Thank you for saying that."

"Have you...picked up on anything about the death of Dwayne Clark?"

"Nothing that's made any sense."

"Ah." He didn't ask more.

We talked about other things for a while, sipping our tea. We talked about my books and his films, and the love of his life, an actress who'd died tragically and mysteriously in the 1960s. It was ruled a suicide but conspiracy theories were still out there. Some had even suspected him, he told me.

He never ate his cookie, and only sipped a small amount of the tea. Eventually, I felt a hot pain radiating outward from his belly. Not belly, pancreas. That's what was killing him.

"You should rest," I said.

He pulled his feet out from under Myrtle, got up and went to the fridge, then took out a tiny brown bottle, and used its dropper cap to squeeze some liquid medication into his mouth. "There. I'll now have fifteen minutes or so to get to my bed."

"Just time enough for me to clean up."

"Aren't you the sweetest thing? Juan did that, too. Helped Ivy clean up after she served him cookies and milk here last week."

He was telling me something. I was concentrating so hard I was frowning. "Juan comes over for cookies and milk?"

"Only that one time," he said. "It's been so good having you, Rachel. You can talk to me about your...NFP–" he laughed softly. "–anytime at all. At least, until I go."

"Maybe even after," I said. "I sometimes hear from people on the other side."

"*Do* you?"

"I do. That's how I know we don't end. I know it for sure."

"What a beautiful thing to say to a dying man." He hadn't sat back down, just tapped his walking stick back to the table, and stood with his hands on its onyx raven. Myrtle got up and went to press her head against his shin, a very gentle version of the head-butt she gives everyone else when she wants affection.

Smiling, he bent with much effort and rubbed her head. "It was lovely sharing a cookie with you, dear Myrtle." Then straightening, he said, "I'd better go to my room. But I won't object if you want to rinse our cups before you leave."

I got up, too. "Of course I will. This visit meant a lot to me."

"And to me." He took my hand in one of his and held it warmly for an extended moment. "Safe drive home. And if you don't mind, could you close and lock the gate on your way out?"

"Of course."

"But…finish your tea first."

He turned to leave the kitchen. Myrtle started to follow him, which was a stunner. I got in front of her and guided her back to the table. "Lie down, girl."

She did, but sighed in disappointment.

Reggie tapped up the stairs. I listened carefully in case he seemed to stumble or get stuck. But he didn't. Eventually his steps moved overhead, and I heard the creaking of his bedroom door.

I sank back into my chair with a heavy sigh and wondered what this had all been about. After I finished my tea and my cookie, I poured the remaining cookies into the cow-shaped cookie jar on the counter, so they wouldn't get stale. Then I took the teapot, cups and saucers over to the double porcelain sink to rinse them. As soon as I put my hands on the faucet, I felt something as jolting as an electric shock, but different. I jerked my hands away reflexively and stood there blinking.

What the hell was that?

I don't know, Inner Bitch said. *But I'm pretty sure it's why you're here.*

I took a deep breath and put my hands back on the faucet knobs.

And suddenly, I was doing another ride-along. Looking out through someone else's eyes, hearing through their ears. I was still there, though, in Reggie D'Voe's kitchen, at his sink. But the hands on the faucet were not my own. They were smaller than my hands, with longer nails in a pale pink French manicure. They were soaking a cloth in ice cold water. I glimpsed a pink watchband on a slender wrist.

I think this is Ivy.

We turned around, so I could see a crying child. Six-year-old Juan Clark was sitting in the chair Reggie had been in only moments ago. He was sobbing so hard his lungs were spasming. His face was red and wet and his eyes were scarlet and puffy.

We moved closer. Ivy's hands pressed the wet cloth to his face, held it to his forehead, and then to each cheek to soothe the sting of his tears. Then she refolded it and pressed it to the back of his neck, where she held it gently. "Just breathe," she told him. "Nice, deep breaths, that's it. That's it."

She got him a glass of water, and he sipped it. The sobs stopped wracking his tiny frame after a moment. He blinked up at her, up at me, big brown eyes still puffy, still wet and pleading. "I can't spend the weekend with him, Miss Ivy. I *can't*. He'll do it again. He'll hurt me again."

Ivy knew what her favorite former kindergartener was talking about. And I knew what Ivy knew, because I was inside her head.

Dwayne Clark had been abusing his little boy.

In that moment, as she held the shuddering, frightened

child in her arms, Ivy made up her mind to stop him from being hurt again, no matter what it took.

And I made up *my* mind that any way she did it was all right with me.

The flash ended, and I was just me, standing by the sink, realizing that she probably *had* stopped it.

And it was still all right with me.

I wiped my hands on a dishtowel, called my dog to my side, and went straight to my car. I didn't know what I was going to tell Mason, if I was going to tell him anything at all. And no part of me was okay with that. I felt like a fissure was opening in my heart.

If I told him, he'd have to arrest her. And if I told him why she'd done it, it would kill him to arrest her. He'd been in that position before, when doing what was right meant breaking the law he was sworn to uphold. His brother's suicide note was a confession to a string of murders. And Mason did the wrong thing for the right reasons. He destroyed evidence. He did it to protect Jeremy and Joshua from the truth about their father. And it haunted him to this day.

I couldn't put him through that again.

On autopilot, I helped Myrtle up onto her seat, buckled her custom harness, and put her leopard print sun goggles on, because her eyes were sensitive to bright light. Then I got behind the wheel and drove back down the driveway and out through the gate.

I put the T-bird in Park, but left it running, got out, and went back to pull those giant gates closed. Then I snapped the hasp on the biggest padlock I'd ever seen. I turned to get back into my car, and almost bumped right into Gary Conklin's concave chest.

•

MASON STOOD beside Rosie at the edge of the Susquehanna River, in a wild patch of tangle and scrub. Teams had excavated six shallow graves so far, all of them in different locations along the riverbank. Each body was wrapped in burlap. Three were intact. The other three, including this latest one, not so much.

Someone yelled, "I've got an arm. God, Jesus. Both of 'em."

"Oh fuck, I have the head."

"These can't all be the same killer," Rosie said. "Two were buried intact, same as Clark. Almost respectfully."

"You gotta love a respectful killer," Mason said.

"And the other three are brutal. Chopped the ef *up.*"

Mason said, "Same dumping ground, same killer. Burlap shrouds again, near the river again, shallow grave again." He nodded at the cop with the head in a bag, held at arm's length. "Any ligature marks on his neck?"

"Why don't *you* come and take a look? Sir."

"I got this!" A car door slammed, and the perkiest ME in the east came running, pulling on gloves, inappropriately eager. "Give it, give it here." And she took the bag. "Where's the torso?"

Mason nodded toward where some guys were zipping the headless, limbless torso into a body bag.

"Hang on, hang on," Billie Carmichael said, running over there.

The ground was still being photographed as the corpse-dogs widened their search. There'd been teams dispatched up and down the banks of the Susquehanna since the second body had been discovered in the wee hours of the morning. They were now up to six.

Mason followed Billie.

The male body was on a gurney beside a pile of freshly turned dirt. They'd unzipped its black bag, and Billie was already bending over it. Mason didn't need to get that close to see that the arms were gone at the shoulders, legs gone at the thighs, head gone about mid-neck. He was basically a chest, a belly, and a penis. But there were marks all over him. He frowned, leaning very slightly closer. "What do you think, Billie?"

"He's been here way longer than Dwayne Clark," she said. "There are similar ligature marks. However, this man was tortured before he was killed. There are punctures, cuts, burns… I think this mark here might've been electrocution." She poked two small round, dark red craters. "These are Taser marks." She gave the guys a nod, turning away and peeling off her gloves. "I'll know more when I get him on my table. All of them." She gave Mason a cheerful nod. "Looks like it's gonna be an all-nighter."

Standing in front of my T-bird, two feet from me, Gary Conklin said, "I know you said this wasn't okay, but I was worried about you."

My heart was beating so fast it seemed a little hard to catch my breath. It was a pretty spot. Big maple trees along the roadsides, just starting to turn a little pink and gold. I hoped I'd still be around when they achieved flaming red and neon yellow. "Gary, have you been following me?"

"Yeah."

"Why?"

"Cause you're messing around with murderers. I saw, about the bodies."

"Bodies?"

"They found bodies this morning. By the river."

"I hadn't heard about that." Part of me was relieved. If there were multiple bodies in the same place, then it wasn't Ivy. She was no serial killer. I could see her maybe offing a kindergartner's dad to keep him from raping his child. Barely. But multiple killings? No. That took a special kind of crazy. One I knew a little too well.

"I was sleeping down there, near the river. I saw. There are a bunch of 'em. Someone said Mason Brown was on the case. That's your husband."

"He's not my–"

"You were at the funeral, for that first one."

"You followed us to the funeral?" And where else, I wondered. Had he been to the house again? Had he been near Joshua? Just how close had this disturbed young man been to my family while I'd had no clue?

My spine stiffened and my chin angled up. My heart rate steadied. If I'd had fur, it would've been bristling along my backbone.

"You could get hurt," Gary went on. "Killed. And I need you." He hit himself in the head with a cupped palm. "I need you to make it go away."

"You need me to make what go away, Gary?"

"The bad thoughts. The awfulness. Evil's what it is, I think. It's *in* me and I can't get it out. And the doctor can't get it out and the pills can't get it out."

"You aren't evil," I said. When what I wanted to do was kick him in the balls, and tell him if he got near my family again, I'd secure him a life sentence in a locked psych unit.

But I could feel his pain. He was in so much pain I didn't know how he was even functioning. Then again, he wasn't really, was he?

"You are inherently good, Gary. You're a child of God." It was, I figured, the terminology he might relate to most easily. "But there's some medicine you need, that's all."

He hit his head again, then again, and again. I almost reached for his hand, but hesitated. I didn't want to initiate physical contact, here.

Finally, he just cupped his forehead, pressing the heel of his hand into his eye, tears streaming, nose running. "I saw Dr. Guthrie again. But I can't do it her way. She says I'm strong, but I'm weak. I'm worthless and weak and I can't make it go away."

"Did she give you any meds? Did you take them, Gary?"

His head came up, eyes wide and red. "WHAT DO YOU THINK THIS IS?" He lunged, grabbed my shoulders, shook me so hard I thought my neck would snap. A PILL CAN'T FIX THIS!" Spittle hit me in the face.

I honestly thought I might be about to die, and I wasn't going to go down easy. I had too much to live for. So I brought my knee up hard, and he doubled over and staggered backwards. I was in my car with the doors locked before he even lifted his head. I shifted, laid rubber, and took off.

Myrtle was panting, trying to wriggle out of her harness, so she could get to me. No doubt I was emitting the invisible scent of fight-or-flight.

Did a little bit of both, back there, Inner Bitch said. *Nice job.*

I hurt a sick young man who was already in agony, and left him outside the home of a helpless old man with no one around to protect him.

I petted Myrtle calm while driving, glancing in the rearview mirror. Gary was standing back there staring after me, getting smaller as I drove away.

I grabbed my phone and told Siri to connect me to the Dilmun New York Chief of Police. She did.

"Chief O'Mally," he said when he picked up.

"It's Rachel de Luca. Um, I was leaving a message for Ivy, in her mailbox, when I was interrupted by a very disturbed young man who's been sort of stalking me–"

"*Stalking* you?"

"Occupational hazard," I said. "I had to hurt him a little bit."

"Are you all right, Rachel?"

"Fine. I'm fine. Just shaken. And so is he. He's in the road in front of the D'Voe mansion. I need you to pick him up so he doesn't get any wild ideas about breaking in. The gate's locked, but still."

"Sure I will. Sure."

"And I need you take care with him, Chief. He's not bad, he's just sick. Very sick, I'm afraid."

"I'll take care of it, Rachel. We'll get him some help."

"Thanks." I almost asked him not to tell Mason, but I hesitated, because that was so unnatural, so downright wrong, that my mouth refused to speak it. And by the time I unlocked my jaw, he'd hung up.

8

Two Days Later...

Rachel was sitting on the dock in the dark when Mason came out of the house with a drink in each hand and crossed the front lawn. He didn't go right over to join her. He stood there for a second, watching her. She was in the new two-person Adirondack chair with her feet up. He closed his eyes for a second to tune in. Rachel was always tuned in, but for him, it took a minute. Shut the mind down. Let go of the day. The job. The kids. The case.

His worries about the things she was keeping from him.

Vince O'Mally had called Wednesday morning to let him know that Gary Conklin was all right. He said to tell Rachel that he'd locked him up overnight, fed him, even had the local doctor check on him, and then he'd put him on a bus back to Binghamton. A social worker was supposed to meet him at the bus station. Gary had asked the chief to tell Rachel he was sorry for scaring her outside the D'Voe place.

So Rachel had gone back out there, to Dilmun, to Ivy Newman's house for some reason. He still didn't know any details, and was almost out of patience waiting for her to tell him. But he *had* to wait. He had to know whether she would. It was killing him, though.

To top all that off, he was dealing with another serial killer, way too close to home on way too many levels. The press was all over it. And why wouldn't they be? Six bodies. All strangled to death, three of them intact, including Dwayne Clark. Three had been tortured for what Billie Carmichael said might have been a couple of days, *then* strangled to death, then mutilated. They had not one single clue or suspect, and the pressure was on. Most of it was directly on him.

It was damn strange that Rachel had only connected to the killer that one time, with the most recent victim.

But he was supposed to be letting go of all that and being in the moment.

So he tried to be in the moment. Shut off the flow of thoughts and just be.

A low bullfrog baritone kept the rhythm for a cricket symphony. A fish jumped; he heard the splash. In the distance an owl hooted twice.

He knew Rachel was listening to all that. He opened his eyes again. The sky was full of stars. No moon yet. She'd be admiring that, too. She loved being able to see. Her sheer enthusiasm for all things bright and beautiful made him appreciate them more himself. He'd never known anyone who used their senses the way Rachel did.

He had the ring in his pocket. He was waiting for the right time to pop the big question. He had to be ready when that time came. But this was not that time, because she was lying to him, and he didn't know why.

"You coming over here or what?" she asked.

"Ears like a bat," he said, and joined her on the dock. He

handed her a drink. Vodka diet, her fave. Ice chinked in the glass. Water lapped against the moorings.

"How's the new chair?" he asked.

"Needs cushions. Thank you for the drink."

"Didn't we order cushions?"

"We did. They shipped separately. They'll be here next week."

"That's logical," he said.

"Isn't it?"

He sat down beside her in the Adirondak-chair-for-two. "It's roomy." There were four inches to spare on either side of him.

"Yeah, too roomy. Get over here." Rachel tugged his shirt, and he slid closer, put his arm around her shoulders. "Yeah, that's better," she said, snuggling close. "Is Josh in bed?"

"Out cold. School's messing with him. We should've made him get up early all summer."

"Fuck that! Let the kid sleep in as often as possible. What they ought to do is start the school day at a decent hour. Nine, nine-thirty. Ten would be better."

"It's kicking his butt, though."

"He'll adjust in a few days. Better a week or two of being tired, than a whole summer of bed times and alarm clocks."

"You're a whole new kind of parent, you know that?"

She stopped talking, sipped her drink in silence. He thought the word "parent" was probably why. That's what she was, though. She was parenting his guys. She was good for them. Potty mouth and all. Josh was making a killing off his swear jar. Sometimes she only pretended to slip, just so she could drop a few bucks in there.

"They love you," he said.

"Well, duh." She sipped again. "I love them, too, in copious amounts."

She did, he knew that. And she loved *him*. This wasn't about the two of them, it was something else.

She settled into her seat and seemed to fall into the night. So he tried to fall into it with her, putting his feet up, leaning back. Out beyond his toes was nothing but water. You could fool yourself into thinking you were floating on it, surrounded by it, if you tried. Baby waves lapped and splashed. Somewhere a deep, croak-like sound came. He wondered what it was.

"Blue heron," Rachel said, like he'd asked out loud. She said she couldn't read him. The truth was she read him so well she didn't know she was doing it. He read her the same way. Sometimes it was like hive mind, just for two.

He didn't know when he'd put his hand into his jacket pocket. He was holding the little box, turning it around and around, willing her to open up and tell him the truth.

Rachel took a deep breath, and without looking at him, said, "I went to Dilmun Tuesday. Reggie invited me for tea. I know I should've mentioned it before now." She still wasn't looking him in the eye.

"You went out there alone. To the home of a horror star who's supposed to be dead. You put yourself at risk, you know."

"He has it."

His words tripped over hers. And they didn't compute. "Has what?"

"It." She finally looked at him, right into his eyes. "The same thing I have."

"The *stuff*?"

She nodded slowly. "I thought I felt something when we were there together."

"Something like…?"

"It felt like he was poking around inside my mind. I

looked at him, and I saw him react. Like he felt me feeling him. Like he knew that I knew. You know?"

"I think I get what you mean."

"So when he texted and invited me, he kind of let me know that's what he wanted to talk about. And that it would be just the two of us."

He opened his mouth, clamped it closed again, took a deep breath, reminded himself this was the woman he loved. The woman he wanted to marry. "The boys and I would be devastated if anything happened to you, Rache. I don't know if you realize how much....and I know we're not supposed to hang our well-being on your shoulders, but we love you a lot."

"I wasn't in danger. At least, not from Reggie."

"You can't be sure of that. It's not always reliable, your stuff. Not a hundred percent."

"Seventy-five, anyway."

"I'm asking you to weigh all that next time you're deciding whether to do something risky."

"I weigh all that when deciding what to *eat*, Mason. And how fast to take a curve in my T-bird, and how far out to swim when there's no one else nearby. I wouldn't put the boys through another loss. You know that."

He held her gaze for a long beat before he answered. "I do know that."

"I wouldn't have gone if I thought it was dangerous. I took Myrtle with me, for heaven's sake. I wouldn't put my dog in danger."

"All right." He sighed, because she wasn't hearing him. And there was still that part about Gary. So he leaned back in his seat again. "All right. Just…all right."

"All right." She sighed, too. "You don't get to tell me what to do, you know."

"I know." She was all prickly now. Defensive.

"You have one of the riskiest professions in the known universe."

"I know."

"The boys would be devastated if anything happened to you, too."

"You're right."

"And so would I." Her throat was tight, her voice thicker than before.

He turned sideways in his chair, pushed her hair up off her forehead.

She said, "It's beyond stupid how much I love you. You know that, don't you?"

"I do," he said. She had tears. "I'm sorry. I didn't mean to make you feel attacked."

"Scolded," she corrected. She snuggled up closer again, and they relaxed into their former position, his arm around her, her head pillowed on his chest and shoulder. She gazed out at the water.

"So what happened, during your high tea with the dead man?"

"Well, he told me he knew I had it and that he did, too. He calls his a heightened sense of empathy."

"Do you think it fits?"

"When I feel people's emotions, it fits. But it doesn't fit when dead guys are talking to me, or when I take a ride-along inside some crazed killer's mind."

She was breathing slow. He didn't ask. Just waited. And eventually, she said, "Ivy's everywhere in that house. I sat in the chair where she sits to have her breakfast every morning. I rinsed tea cups at her sink. I tapped into her, and I didn't feel anything dark or evil."

Her words felt absolutely genuine and true. Maybe he'd been wrong, before, when he'd–

"So, even though my stuff led me to her door, literally, I don't think she had anything to do with the murder."

There it was. There it was, that tightness underlying her words. That quiver just beyond the range of human hearing. He felt it. He was a cop. He knew what a lie sounded like, and he knew her. And that was a lie.

He could hardly wrap his head around the fact that his Rachel was lying to him. He couldn't even move on yet, to what that meant. But he left it there, lying on the floor of his mind, waiting to be picked up. If she was lying when she said she didn't believe Ivy had anything to do with Dwayne Clark's murder, then that meant she believed the opposite. That Ivy *had* something to do with it.

"Anyway," she went on, "when I got out of my car to close the gate Gary came up behind me. He'd followed me. He kind of grabbed hold of me. Yelled in my face. Shook me. And I *did* feel I was in danger, then. But that wasn't my fault. I mean he came to me here, at home, so that could've happened anywhere."

"I know," he said.

"I had to knee him in the balls. And I hated to. He's already in so much pain."

He nodded slow, seeing her anguish in her face. "Did he hurt you?"

"Just scared me. My neck's been a little stiff, and he left some finger-bruises on my shoulders. Nothing too serious. I got back in my car and just left him there. But I called Chief O'Mally to go pick him up."

He nodded slow. "I know you did."

She blinked twice, then looked at him intently. "What do you mean, you know I did?"

"Vince called the next day. Said he wanted to let you know he did what you asked. Fed the kid, had the local MD check him out. He kept him overnight and put him on a bus to Binghamton the next morning. Someone from Social Services was supposed to meet him at the bus. I wanted to let you know he was okay, but…."

"But?"

He shrugged one shoulder. "I was waiting for you to tell me."

"To see if I would?"

He sensed he might've unwittingly walked into a mine field. "I…*guess*?"

"Don't you think that's just a little bit sneaky?"

He'd been sneaky? She's suddenly keeping secrets and *he's* the one who's sneaky? How did she *do* that? Turn this whole thing around like that?

His phone vibrated. Probably work. It was past midnight. Nobody called about anything good after midnight. He pulled out the phone and looked at the screen.

Jeremy.

His heart jumped into jackhammer mode as he answered on speaker. "Jeremy, what's wrong?"

"What's going on?" Rachel leaned over the phone. "Jere? You okay?"

"I'm fine, don't panic. I've just um…one of my professors is missing."

Mason looked at Rachel. She looked as confused as he felt. "You're calling us at midnight-thirty to tell us your professor is missing?" she asked. "Wait, do you mean Professor–"

"Ashton," Mason cut in, before she could say asshat.

"Yeah. There were signs of a struggle near his car, which

is still in the campus parking lot. He didn't go home last night, and he's nowhere on campus."

Rachel said, "And that's a problem because...?"

"I punched him in the face yesterday."

"You punched him in the face?" Mason asked. "You want to be a cop, and you punched a guy in the face?"

"I know. It was stupid. He flat out called me a liar. Someone saw, I guess, and told the police when they came around asking about him."

"So the police are involved," Mason said.

"Yeah, that's why I'm calling. I'm…at your work, Uncle Mace."

"At my *work*?"

"At the *police department*?" Rachel went bug-eyed. "Jeremy, are they *questioning you* about the professor's disappearance?"

"Not yet, but yeah, I guess that's the plan. And I was alone last night, so…."

"No alibi," Rachel whispered.

"Don't answer a single question, Jeremy," Mason said. "You hear me? Not a word. If they question you without a lawyer, I'll–"

"Chief Cantone says no one can question me until you get here."

"We'll be there soon, Jere," Rachel said. She was already out of the chair. "You're gonna be okay. Just…be okay. Be smart. And don't worry. We've got this."

"We'll call a lawyer on the way," Mason told him. "Put the chief on the phone."

"Just a sec. She went out of the room to give me privacy."

"There's no such thing as privacy in a police department," Mason said.

"Well, she let me use her office, so…." The door creaked

when it opened. "Chief?" Jeremy called, very softly, so she must've been close.

A second later, Vanessa Cantone's voice came over the line. "Mason–"

"Not one question, you hear me? This is my *kid*, Chief."

"That's why he's in my office and not an interrogation room. And yeah, you're welcome."

"Thank you," Rachel said quickly.

"Get here," the chief said. "Bring a lawyer. It looks bad."

9

He's losing it, Rache.

I can see that, Inner Bitch.

Mason had been up and down the stairs five times in about a minute and a half; first for clothes, then keys, then wallet, then phone, then shoes, all at a dead run. I'd already called his mother, woke the poor thing up and asked her to come over and stay with Josh, who was sleeping upstairs. Josh had no clue about any of this. Yet.

I was rapid scrolling the search results for "criminal defense attorney, Binghamton NY" on my phone when Mason headed out the front door, keys in hand.

I caught up fast, snatched his keys, and said, "I'm driving. You're too distracted. And we're waiting for your mother to get here." He looked at me and blinked. I figured my words were bouncing off his skull into space. "Here." I handed him my phone. "Pick a lawyer."

He took the phone, looked at it, looked at me. The poor guy's head was spinning.

"I'll help," I said. "Imagine you've arrested the most

detestable criminal in the universe, and you know he's guilty. Who's the lawyer you really hope he doesn't hire?"

"Celia Moon." He said it without hesitation. "I hate her guts."

"There you go. Find her number and call her. There's your mom."

Angela's headlights bounded up the driveway and stopped. I was at the door of her Mercedes before she even got out. "Thanks so much for coming."

"Of course," she said. She hadn't put on makeup, and I was super touched by that, because Angela never so much as checked her mailbox without full hair and makeup. I'd told her everyone was fine, but it was urgent. Her grandsons were everything to her.

"Is Jeremy all right?" she asked. "What's going on?"

"We don't really know."

"Bullshit," she said, and she held my eyes.

"You never say bullshit."

"I learned it from you. Now tell me the truth."

Mason's mother was growing on me. We'd had a moment, a while back. It had changed things. We were bonding. I decided to give it to her straight, because in her place, that's how I'd want it. And I respected her. I respected even fewer people than I liked, so that was saying a lot. "He had a fight with a professor who has since gone missing. They've brought him in for questioning. That's honest to goodness all we know. No bullshit."

Angela nodded. "Thank you. I hate being protected from harsh truths. It's ageism, you know. Is Josh in bed?"

"Sound asleep. Doesn't know any of this."

"What should I tell him if he wakes up?"

"See how much easier this would've been if you hadn't called bullshit on me?"

"I know nothing," she said. "I'll get him off to school if you're not back in time."

"Thanks. You're a life-saver."

"No, Rachel. You are." She clasped my shoulders and kissed my *actual* cheek, instead of the air near my cheek. "Go, before my son's head explodes."

Mason was outside, pacing and talking on his cell. Apparently, the defense attorney he hated most was on the other end of the call. I went to him and touched his arm. He was already pocketing the phone and getting into the passenger side of my T-bird without even arguing in favor of taking his own ride.

"You get ahold of Celia Moon?" I asked, backing out and around, then heading up our beaten path toward civilization.

"She said she'd be with Jeremy in fifteen minutes."

I lifted my brows. "Why do you hate her again?"

"Because she's good."

When we walked through the beehive a half hour later, Mason was greeted with sympathetic looks and shoulder pats all around. Chief Cantone came out of her office. Sleek dark hair pulled behind her head with an abalone shell clasp to hold it there. She wore a blue suit that hugged every curve, and an attitude that dared anyone to say shit about it.

She didn't meet Mason's eyes, but marched ahead of us to an interrogation room, tapped twice, and opened the door.

Jeremy was sitting at a table with a woman beside him. She was leaning close, one hand on his shoulder. He looked as if he'd been in lockup for a month on bread and water. He was pale, shaky, puffy. We'd just seen him off Tuesday morning. It was Thursday. Technically, Friday. There was only one thing I could think of that could make him look that bad, that fast.

The woman beside him got up and faced us. She was a tall black woman with piercing green eyes and cropped brown hair with blond tips. I was sure I'd never seen her before, because I'd remember if I had. She was impressive.

"Detective Brown," she said, giving Mason a quick nod. Then she extended a hand to me. "I'm Celia Moon."

"Rachel de Luca," I said, and I shook. Her grip was cool, dry and firm. Her energy was *fierce*. "Thanks for coming."

"Can you fill us in?" Mason asked.

"Absolutely not," Celia replied, almost before he'd finished the question. "Jeremy is of age and our communications are privileged. But I'll give you some privacy so he can fill you in as much as he wants to." She looked back at Jeremy. "Ten minutes? Then I'll be back with Chief Cantone to get your statement."

Jeremy nodded. "Thanks, Celia."

She gave him a nod and left the room, pulling the door closed behind her. He looked like he was facing a firing squad. I looked up at the camera in the corner. Jere said, "It's fine, Celia made sure they were off. And nothing I'm going to say is incriminating, anyway."

"Are you under arrest?" Mason asked.

"No. Celia said I can leave any time I want, but I thought I should cooperate as much as possible." He closed his eyes. "I can't believe this is happening."

"You look like hell, Jeremy," I told him. I knew why. I wasn't sure if he would admit it or not, or whether Mason had picked up on it, in the state he was in. But it was obvious to me Jeremy had been drinking hard.

It had happened before. He'd been drinking and hiding it until hiding it was no longer possible. He had a problem. It would have been pretty naive of us to think it was going to be once and done. Especially with his history. This damned missing professor had triggered him with his asinine assignment. I wished I'd have punched him myself.

He had no way of knowing, though, Inner Bitch tried to reason.

He called my kid a liar. Fuck him.

Mason said, "Tell me everything." It was a clear contradiction of Celia's parting shot. Not that it had been a shot. It had been a message. Mason was the one who'd called her, but she worked for Jeremy. He was calling the shots, not his uncle the cop.

Jeremy didn't have any reason to keep secrets from Mason, though. Mason would die for the kid–had done worse than die for him.

"I told you about the assignment. Last week Professor Ashton assigned us to write about our most traumatic experiences in the form of a police report. He said it would count for half our grade. I wrote about Mom. He gave me a zero and said I'd made it up."

Jeremy's mother Marie was in a locked psych unit for the rest of her life. That hadn't stopped her from breaking out and wreaking havoc in her kids' lives, though. Writing about that would've brought it all back. It was no wonder Jere was drinking again.

"And this is the part we already know," I said, an impatient edge to my voice.

He took a deep breath. "I went to see him again today. I mean, yesterday. I don't even know what time it is."

"It's after one."

"We argued. I punched him in the face." Jere shrugged, and lowered his head. "I stormed out of his office. That's the last time I saw him."

I was counting time in my head. Jere had gone back to campus Tuesday morning. He must've started drinking almost immediately to look as bad as he looked. He might've even been drunk when he'd hit the professor.

"God, I'm an idiot. I never should've hit him. I wanna be a cop. Maybe I've messed that up for good."

"You haven't," I said. "Not unless you choose to believe you have. You need my bullshit books right about now, Jere."

He smiled a funny little smile. "I've been reading your bullshit books since I was sixteen, Aunt Rache."

My heart turned into a thick, pink puddle of love. He laid me low with it. I swallowed so I could talk again.

"And you have no alibi for the hours between that last encounter and the time the police picked you up because…?" I asked.

He lifted his head and looked me in the eye, like he didn't know I could see right through him. He said, "I was alone in my dorm room all afternoon and night. And that's the truth." He shifted his eyes to Mason's. "Find him, Uncle Mace. That's the best way to clear me. If you can just find him, this all goes away."

"I'll find him," Mason said. "I don't want you answering questions right now. I want you to get up and walk out of here with us. Not a word to anyone."

"Celia says–"

"I don't give a shit what Celia says. Get up and walk out with me. Go straight to the car, not a word to anybody. *Now.*"

I had to pick my jaw up off the floor. Mason didn't talk to the boys that way. And then I saw the look in his eyes. He knew. He knew Jeremy had been drinking.

Jeremy knew we knew it, too. He got up onto his feet like he had an assload of lead. Mason opened the door and walked out first. The chief was out there, and so was Celia Moon. Static energy hung between them.

"Wait, what's going on?" Chief Cantone asked when she saw us.

"Not a word," Mason said. He clapped an arm firmly around Jeremy's shoulders. "I'm taking him home. You want to question him, you can do it there. But not today."

Celia looked at me like I was the one in charge.

Usually you are.

I know, right? This is a different side of Mason.

It's kind of hot.

I didn't have a clue what the hell was happening with my mild-mannered man, and I told the chief so with a shrug of my shoulders.

Mason led Jeremy straight through the beehive and out into the hallway. I was right behind them, and Celia walked with us while Chief V yelled, "Brown, come on. You know better than this shit. Let me talk to him."

Celia turned around and stood in her path while Mason and Jere kept walking. I was sort of hovering in between, not wanting to miss a trick, either way.

"Detective Brown is right," Celia told the chief. "Jeremy's exhausted and shocked. It's the middle of the night. He's barely out of high school. Upon reflection, I'd prefer my client be well-rested before answering any questions or making any statement. I'll call you and we'll set something up."

"Goddammit, Brown!" the chief shouted, ignoring the lawyer like she wasn't even there. "Mason!"

Mason looked back at her, and if I'd been on the receiving end of that glare, I'd have wilted. Then he pushed the front door open and ushered Jeremy through. I hurried up to him. "What can I do?"

"Get him home. I need to be here."

"I can give them a lift," Celia said, having come out right behind us.

Mason looked at her. I couldn't believe he disliked her. She was powerful, capable, confident, and a little bit scary. She didn't take shit from anybody. You could feel all that wafting from her pores. I could, anyway.

So I said, "I think that's a great idea. That way she can consult with Jere on his own turf and–"

"It's the middle of the night," Mason said. "She can come over tomorrow." Then, to Celia, "Afternoon."

She held up a palm. "All good. All good."

I sent Celia Moon a grateful look, then escorted Jeremy out the door and down the wide stone steps to the T-bird, parked a little bit crookedly by an expired meter in front. We both got in. Celia gave us a wave. "See you tomorrow, Jeremy."

"Thanks for coming, Celia."

He closed his door, and I pulled away from the curb. I knew damn well Mason wasn't going to leave the office until he knew everything there was to know about the disappearance of Professor Asshat.

I planned to do a little digging of my own.

But there was one thing I didn't need to dig into at all. "So you were alone in your dorm room all afternoon and all night tonight?"

Jeremy looked at me. There was a mix of guilt and accusation in his eyes. "You already know, don't you?"

"That you were drinking? Maybe ever since you went back? Yeah. And Mason knows it, too."

"How?"

"Um, have you walked past a mirror lately?" I reached up and twisted the rearview mirror his way. He looked

Girl Blue

into it, then looked away shaking his head, and I put it back.

"Even in college I can't have any privacy, can I?"

"Privacy to do what? Fuck up your life beyond repair? No, you'll never have that as long as you have people who love you, dumbass."

"One of whom is fucking psychic."

"I am *not* fucking psychic. And watch your mouth."

He rolled his eyes, turned toward the window.

"So how drunk were you when you decked him? Blackout drunk? Do you remember it?"

He exhaled so slowly for so long I thought he'd run out of air. Then, "I remember most of it. I went straight back to my dorm room."

"When?"

"After class. After I hit him."

"What time was that?"

"Ten a.m."

"So you went back to your dorm room and kept drinking. Didn't you?"

"Rachel–"

"You wanna be a cop? You wanna be a *cop*? Look at you. Still too fucked up to even give a decent alibi."

He leaned sideways against the door.

"When did you start drinking again? And don't you even *think* about lying to me. You know I'll know."

He said nothing.

I slammed the brakes so hard he almost hit the dashboard. Then I took him by his shoulders and made him face me. "Talk, dammit!"

"Fine! All right! I partied with some friends last week, and I did fine. I was handling it. You saw me over the weekend. I was fine."

"You were *not* fine. Mason and I both knew you were shaky."

"I *felt* fine." He pushed a lock of mink brown hair off his forehead. "And then…and then…I don't know."

"And then you weren't so fine." I said. "That's what happens with addicts."

"Don't say that. I'm not an addict."

"You prefer I call you a drunk? An alcoholic? A chemically dependent little shit? What? You tell me. You can't drink, Jeremy. Period. And you *know* it, that's the worst part. You know it."

"I know it." He closed his eyes, sighed. "I know, I know, I know."

"Good." He was hanging his head. I ran my hand over the back of it. "Knowing it's everything. We'll help you deal with it. You didn't give any blood or urine to those assholes at the department, did you?"

"Celia got there before they had time to ask."

"So tell me everything you remember."

He looked at me, finally. Maybe another layer of booze had evaporated from his teenage baby veins. "I will, if you'll stop swearing at me."

"I'm not making any promises, kid. Talk."

He rubbed his jaw in such a Mason-like way, my heart cracked a little. "I worked hard on that paper. It was like…"

"Opening a vein," I said, because I knew.

"Yeah. I thought it might help, getting it out, you know? It was raw and honest. Then I went back and took out all the emotion, but I still felt it, you know? And for that asshole to accuse me of making it up–I just lost it."

"But not until today."

"Liquid courage, I guess." He was quiet for a long time.

I looked across the car at him. He was scared to death.

"Hey, Jere. You know we've got this, don't you? There's not a doubt in your mind that we've got this. Is there?"

He looked at me. I reached out and pushed that lock off his forehead. "Your uncle is the best detective on the planet. Your honorary aunt has NFP and piles of money. And I will spend every bit of it, or cash it all out and fly you to Mexico myself before I'll see you do time for this. You know that, right?"

Some of the tension eased from his eyes.

"So you punched him in the face," I said, so he'd pick up the story where he'd left off.

"Knocked him right on his ass." I could tell he wanted to smile a little.

I nodded and said, "*Nice*."

Probably not the best response, there, Rachel.

I know, Inner Bitch, but you gotta admit–

Yeah. Asshat had it coming.

"The drinking, though. That had already started up again before that, yes?"

"Started the day I started writing the paper. Last week. I thought I had a handle on it. And then yesterday...I don't know, I just fell. And you're right, I don't remember much about yesterday or last night."

"When did you find out he was missing?"

My roommate, Raj, said a cop had cornered him on campus to ask about Professor Ashton, and all kinds of questions about me. Raj said he never went home last night. Hadn't been seen since. So I took a shower, drank a couple of sports drinks, and took a handful of Ibuprofen."

I nodded, listening, feeling him. He was telling the truth as far as he knew it.

"Were you worried that something might've happened to him?"

"I figured he just didn't want to show his face on campus with a black eye. I finished off the bottles I had on hand and went to sleep. Next thing I know, there's a cop at the door asking me to come in for questioning."

I nodded. "And you don't remember leaving your dorm room after you punched the professor?"

"No."

"But?" I said, because *he'd* said it, just not out loud.

"But I don't remember much else, either."

"Was your car in the same spot where you left it?" Parking spots on campus were like gold.

"I don't remember where I parked it, so…" He lifted his head, looked me right in the eye. "I couldn't have killed him, though. You'd know if I did, right?"

"Of course I would," I said, because he needed to hear it. "You didn't kill anybody Jere. You're good right to your marrow." I pulled into traffic again.

"They probably think I did it, though. Because of Mom."

"Your mom broke under pressure. I don't think it was DNA, I think it was stress."

I felt his eyes on me. I felt him wanting to say more. I tried to feel for what it was, but Jere poked the Sirius button and started singing under his breath to an acoustic version of *Marry That Girl* on Coffee House, my favorite channel. He preferred hip hop.

He didn't want me to know what he'd been about to say just then. And apparently he'd figured out a way to keep my nose out of his head.

I'll be damned, Inner Bitch whispered.

I know. Hell, I wonder if Josh has figured out how to do that yet?

10

"You know damn well you can't be involved in this case."

Vanessa Cantone was a professional. Mason knew she had to be. You couldn't look like she did and be taken seriously as a cop otherwise. But she wasn't a hard ass. Not deep down.

"I'm *already* involved in this case," Mason said.

"As a parent, yes–"

"As a cop." Mason paced the length of her office, expressing with his hands. "Middle-aged white guy. Married with kids. Missing without a trace. Sound familiar?"

She frowned so hard her eyebrows touched. "You mean the Riverside Strangler?"

"He has a name now? I missed the memo."

"Mason, there's no evidence this is related–"

"Rachel thinks it is." It was an outright lie and he blurted it anyway. Anything to get the focus off his kid. Vanessa was one of a small number of people who knew about Rachel's ability. And she believed in it. It had saved her life once.

Fair or not, the lie worked, at least enough to distract

Vanessa from throwing him out of the office. She looked at him hard and he looked right back. Then she slammed a hand on her desk and said, "I don't even know if you're telling the truth or saying that to save your kid."

Damn, she knew him better than he thought.

She let her head fall forward. Some of her hair had come loose from its clip, and fell over her intense brown eyes. "Hell, I can't say I wouldn't do the same if it was Bunny."

Tension-laden silence stretched. He decided to ease it. "Rachel says if you don't quit calling her Bunny, she's going to end up pole dancing."

"*That* sounds like something Rachel would say."

"Jeremy didn't do anything to his professor, Vanessa. He's a good kid. You know that." Maybe first names were a good idea here. Maybe it would ease her off her professional high horse and get her feeling like a fellow parent. Like a friend.

"He's been drinking hard, Mason," she said, first-naming him right back. "I could smell it across the room, even though his hair was still wet from the shower."

He'd smelled it too, and seen it in Jeremy's puffy eyes and red nose. "That's not unusual in college, is it?"

"No."

"Jeremy's been through a lot, you know. Lost both his parents."

"Both to mental illness and violent behavior."

She had him. Why had he brought it up? Mental illness on both sides, father dead of suicide, mom in a locked psych unit, probably for the rest of her life. That made it look worse for Jeremy, not better. Imagine if she knew Jere's dad had been a serial killer.

"That kind of thing can be handed down," she said, like she'd heard his last thought out loud.

It startled him so bad he snapped his head up fast, and there was probably fear written all over his face. She wasn't referring to his thoughts, of course, but to her own words about mental illness. *That* could be passed down.

But she'd planted an icy seed deep in his mind. Could that kind of thing be in someone's DNA? Was there a serial killer gene?

He'd never seen any hint of darkness in the boys. Then again, he'd never seen it in his brother, either.

No. No, the boys were fine. And he *had* seen it in Eric, he just hadn't known what he'd been seeing.

This was ridiculous. He was pissed at his boss for putting ideas like that into his mind. It was sick, was what it was. "I want everything you've got on Professor Ashton. Full file."

"It's a conflict of interest, Mason. You want me to lose my job?" She walked around her desk and said, "You need to go on leave."

"I can't–"

"It's not optional. Rosie can step into the lead on the Riverside Strangler investigation. I'm going to oversee the missing professor personally. Go home."

"How long?"

"Until I tell you. Now, I need some coffee, before I drop. No freaking lackeys around at this hour to make copies. Had to do it all myself." She took her coffee cup off her desk, moved a manila folder to the front edge. Then she walked out of the office and left him there alone.

He looked at the folder. It had Ashton, James printed on its tab. And his irritation with his boss faded a shade or two.

He picked up the file, tucked it inside his jacket, and pulled the door closed behind him when he left.

The best smell in the known universe is the combination of coffee brewing and bacon cooking. That's the scent that woke me up. I opened my eyes, inhaled deeply, and smiled. Nothing like a little motivation to get my ass out of bed. Myrtle lay beside me, horizontally across Mason's vacant pillow, her butt aimed at my face.

"Hey," I said. "You smell that, Myrt?"

Her head rose, and her nose twitched, and then she sprang up onto all fours and ran to the edge of the bed.

"Whoa! Wait!" I grabbed her before she could dive over the side. I swear to God, my geriatric, blind bully thinks she's Underdog sometimes.

I put her portable stairs right in front of her, then spotted her while she waddled down them. Going down stairs is hard on bulldogs, because they're so top heavy. As she went down, her back feet barely touched. I'd tried, once, to just scoop her off the bed onto the floor, but she'd detested it. It was the only time I'd ever heard her growl. I figured it must hurt her and never tried it again. If my bulldog wanted stairs, my bulldog would have stairs.

I pulled on my flannel robe, stepped into comfy slippers, and headed down to get in on the stuff that smelled so good, Myrtle close beside me the whole way. We stepped into the kitchen, just as my sexy man finished filling a giant coffee mug. He turned, handed it to me. I kissed his cheek, and took my usual seat, relieved. He'd been mad at me for waiting two days to tell him I'd gone to Dilmun and run into Gary. I'd been mad at him for knowing about it the whole time and not saying so. But today, it felt like we were fine. Thank God.

There was a laptop and a file folder in front of me.

"Thanks for getting up with Josh," I said.

"I didn't get up with Josh. I slept til ten," Mason said.

"He got him*self* off to school? My God, we're horrible parents."

"Thirteen is plenty old enough to get himself off to school," Mason said.

"Well, yeah, he can do it. But jeeze, somebody oughta at least say good morning, make sure his shoes match and tell him to have a great day." I closed my eyes. "I'll make it up to him."

"You'll buy him something."

"Great idea! What time did you get in?"

"Three, I think. I don't know why I came to bed, I barely slept. You were out cold, though."

"I slugged back a vodka diet to help me drift off." He gave me a look, and I said, "Right before I locked every trace of liquor in my office safe, behind my locked office door, across from which I surreptitiously taped a strand of my own hair, which will be broken in twain, should the portal be breeched. Plus, I told Jere if he touches my stash, I'll kick his skinny ass. Is this Professor Asshat?" I flipped open the folder to see a headshot.

"Yeah. I thought we'd start digging over breakfast." He was sliding eggs onto slices of warm, buttery toast.

I started reading, sipping coffee, thinking life was pretty good, even when we were facing something awful.

Mason brought two plates to the table, sat beside me and turned the laptop his way.

"He lived in a nice neighborhood," I said.

Mason craned his neck to read, then typed rapidly. "You want satellite view or street level?"

"Street." I shoved my chair closer.

We leaned together, looking at an arrogant Georgian with black accents and trim. Three-car garage, detached with a connecting covered walkway. The landscaping was sparse.

Crewcut hedges across the front. Grass mown to within an inch of its soil, not a blade out of place. Blacktop so perfect it must've been installed yesterday.

"Nice place."

He clicked off and began searching the net for mention of the professor himself, and in a few minutes, he was clicking through photos of the man, and his wife, and his little girls at various stages of childhood, in school, at sporting events.

"It's creepy how easy that is," I said.

"Everyone's gone public these days. Makes my job a lot easier."

"I bet." I returned to my file folder, flipping a page, looking for dirt, not finding any.

"Can I help?" Jeremy had come in, looking like he belonged in rehab.

"I thought you'd sleep in," I said.

"I would've–"

"Whatddaya mean sleep in? It's noon already!" Josh said. He came running from somewhere, pushed past Jeremy in the doorway, and slid onto a chair. "Where's mine?"

"We thought you were in school," Mason said. "Which begs the question, why aren't you?"

"Nobody woke me up."

With that Mason sent me a look, as if to imply this was my fault. "What? I thought you got him up. I told you that."

He closed his eyes, shook his head. Apparently, I wasn't getting it. He said, "Nobody should *have* to get him up. He's thirteen. He has a cell phone with the same alarm clock app everyone else's has."

I blinked at him. "You're right." Then I looked sternly at Josh while I slid my plate over in front of him and went to the stove to cook a couple more eggs for Jeremy and me. "Josh, from now on, it's your responsibility to get yourself up in the morning. Start setting your alarm."

"Okay," he said slow, like he wasn't so sure about it. "But I might need backup in case I forget."

"Eat quick, and I'll drive you in," Mason said.

"Really, Mace?" I asked. "Cause it's already after noon, and by the time he eats and showers and changes it'll be one-thirty. Is it really worth all that for an hour and a half of school?"

Mason rolled his eyes. "It's a mile down the road."

Jeremy said, "Don't cook me anything, Aunt Rache." He poured himself a coffee, sat down and started picking through the file while I cracked some eggs into a pan and popped in more toast.

"Toast or oatmeal, Jere? You need something in your stomach."

"To soak up the booze," Josh said, shoveling my perfect sunny-side up eggs at the speed of sound.

Everyone looked at him. He noticed, stopped shoveling, and said, "What, you guys think I'm in a coma while I'm asleep?" around a mouthful. I poured him some OJ and set it in front of him. He took a gulp, swiped his mouth with the back of his hand. "So why were you in jail, Jere?"

"I wasn't in jail. They just wanted to ask me some questions."

"'Bout what?"

"One of my teachers up and vanished. They think something might've happened to him."

"And they think you know something about it?" Josh asked. He set his fork down. "Why would they think that, Jere?"

"Because I punched him in the face, and I can't remember for sure where I was after that, because I was drinking."

"Jeremy!"

"No, Uncle Mace. Protecting us from the truth about things never did us any good. It's not doing *me* any good, that's for sure. I mean, look at the mess I'm in."

"You're stupid, that's why you're in a mess." Josh stood up so fast his chair tipped over backwards.

"Josh, hon–" I got up and put a hand on his arm, but he shrugged it off.

"He knows how much trouble drinking gets him into. Jeeze, Jere, we already went through all this. Now you're gonna start it all up again?"

"No. I'm not."

"But you are! You did! What if you go to jail? Huh?" His face was turning bright red. "What am I gonna do if you go to jail, Jere? Don't you think about anything but yourself anymore?" He whirled and stormed out of the house, slamming the back door behind him.

I stood there blinking in shock after him. Mason came right up beside me, one hand on my shoulder. We looked at each other, then turned and looked at Jeremy.

"I'll talk to him." Jeremy got up, his coffee mug in his hand. "But after that, when we're alone, I want to know the truth about my father." He met Mason's eyes and held them. "I need to know. I need to know more than you need to not tell me. So…just tell me."

Then he followed his brother out the door, taking his coffee, bitter and black, with him.

11

Jeremy came to us after breakfast. Mason and I were cleaning up the kitchen, and Josh was outside with the dogs. He said, "I'm going to meet Celia Moon and Chief Cantone at Celia's office to give my statement," he announced. No preamble, no nothing.

Mason scowled. "I thought we were doing that here."

"Josh is here. I don't want him around for that."

"I don't either," I said.

"I should be there." Mason wiped his hands on a towel, dropped it on the counter.

"No," Jeremy said. "Look, there's no reason for you to be. And frankly, I don't think your hostility toward my lawyer does me a lot of good, Uncle Mace."

"What the hell are you talking about?"

"I'm an adult. I'm going to meet my lawyer and give my statement. There is nothing for me to do but tell the truth. I don't need help for that. I was alone in my dorm room and I was drinking and I never left until the police came for me. That's it. That's all. It's simple and its honest. I'll have time to go over it all with Celia before the chief gets there."

Mason looked like he wanted to shake him. Then he looked at me.

I shrugged, and said to Jere, "It's really hard for us not to take hold of this thing for you. Do you get that?"

"Cause that's what you do. You protect us from everything. From the truth about our father to our own bad decisions. I did this, though. And I need to deal with it. Myself. Like a man. And I need you to let me."

I looked from him to Mason. Mason looked like he was in physical pain. But he said, "Okay. All right. If that's how you want to handle it."

"It's how I want to handle it. When I get back, I'm gonna take Josh out on the boat for the afternoon. This is tearing him up."

"Okay."

"Lifejackets are not optional," I reminded him, like he was ten. God, no wonder he was rebelling a little.

"They're also the law," he replied. "I'm sorry I brought all this down on us. But I'm gonna do the right thing from now on."

I hugged him hard. He was two inches taller than Mason, and my head barely reached his chest. He was still a skinny teenager. He was still a kid. I wanted to take on the world to protect him.

"I DON'T like them on the water when we're not home," Mason said for the tenth time since we'd exited I-81.

Jeremy had gone to the meeting with Celia and the chief alone, and we'd sweat bullets the whole time. It wasn't long. Two hours and he was back, with a copy of his statement for Mason. His version of a peace offering, I guessed.

"Jere wants you to stop babying him."

"Me? You gave up your breakfast for Josh this morning."

I shrugged. "Jeremy's a cop in the making, and Josh is a teenager."

"Putting them both at more risk than a pair of ten-year-olds," he replied. "No matter how grown up they think they are."

I thought about that for a second, then said, "You're right," pulled out my phone and tap tap tapped it.

"Who are you texting?"

"Amy. She'll watch them without them knowing they're being watched."

"She really is an all-purpose assistant, isn't she?"

"I'm paying her to lounge around the lake reading pages and keeping my dog company on a gorgeous autumn day. Yeah, she's a gem." Then I smiled softly. "She really is. She'll be there in ten minutes. They'll still be sorting their tackle boxes."

That's weird, isn't it? How they sort through all those shiny, hooky things and doodads before every fishing trip?

I think it's some kind of man-zen exercise, IB.

"Feel better?" I asked.

"About Jeremy? I'll feel better about *that* when we find this missing professor."

"You say that like it's not the only thing you're feeling bad about."

Instead of answering, he pulled up to the curb a block and a half away from Town Hall. Everything closer was taken by press vans and curious bystanders. Apparently, Professor Ashton was kind of a big deal.

As we got closer, I gave Mason's hand a squeeze, met his eyes for a second. We could share a lot when our eyes met. It was like a 1000G connection. He said, *be careful*, and *be smart*, and *I love you*. But there was something else underneath all that. Something worried.

My eyes replied, *keep your gorgeous boss off my back* and *I love you, too*.

I hadn't told him yet. I hadn't told him Dwayne Clark had raped his child. I hadn't told him that Juan went to Ivy begging her to save him. I hadn't told him about the pink watch band. Because if there were multiple victims, it couldn't be Ivy.

I didn't know if he would agree with me on that. But I *did* know that she couldn't have killed all those men. Tortured half of them. Chopped them into pieces. There was no earthly way Ivy Newman did any of that.

But not telling him was in between us like a poison-tipped thorn.

I sighed and tried to focus on the jobs we'd come here to do.

Mason's job was to run interference and keep people from noticing me doing my job. *My job* was to get close enough to the professor's family to *feel* them. I might even have to engage them in conversation, which would make it a little harder.

I looked at the floor where Hugo sat in an unzipped gym bag at my feet. "Okay, little buddy. You ready?"

He was still puppy-cute. I dropped a handful of tiny treats into the bag, zipped it up and slung its strap over my shoulder. I wanted the pup to go *un*-noticed for the first little bit.

Myrtle had been mightily offended that Hugo got to go with us and she had to stay home in the lap of luxury. Amy had promised to keep her company, and I knew damn well she'd spoil her with calories. But everybody needed a cheat day.

I had a book with me, too, pre-autographed. A prop, but

hey, I was a semi-famous self-help author. This was probably the sort of thing people expected me to do.

Not in front of cameras, though. That's why I had on big sunglasses and a straw visor with a sunflower embroidered on it, like something my soccer mom sister would wear.

Or Myrtle, Inner Bitch opined.

I nodded. *Yeah, Myrt would rock this visor.*

That's what I'm saying!

I wove into the crowd, trying to face the "stage" (which was really just a section of sidewalk) while side-stepping my way past it. I needed to get out past stage left, where the professor's kids were waiting with a chubby redhead who was probably their grandma but didn't look her age.

Who does, these days, am I right?

You are right, IB.

I held Hugo close to keep him safe while I got elbowed, stepped on and briefly, tangled in someone's camera bag. I managed to get to my goal. The chief had come to the podium, so all eyes were on her. She wore a brown skirt to her knees, cream blouse, buttoned up and tucked in, jacket, unbuttoned. Brown pumps, with 2.5-inch heels. I always noticed what Vanessa Cantone wore, because she wore everything so well. All business, and all woman. It was a remarkable thing she did with clothes. I admired her for it.

And still I heard some dick in the crowd saying, "Damn, I'd like to get with that–*OW*!"

"Aw, I stepped on your foot there, didn't I?"

I kept moving. Didn't know or care if he replied.

"I'm Binghamton Police Chief Vanessa Cantone and I have an update on the Professor Ashton case. We are currently analyzing evidence retrieved from his car, and we're hopeful it will bring us closer to finding the professor. In the meantime…"

I tuned her out, moving into the shaded area away from the crowd, where the family was standing. They could see the chief at the podium, but still remain a reasonable distance from the public. I might be stopped by one of the officers patrolling the space between, if they saw me. I waited until they were facing the other way before sidling into the small group of VIPs as if I was one of them. I unzipped the bag and scooped Hugo out, set him on the ground and snapped on his leash.

With the part of my brain that was still listening to the chief, I was aware the missing professor's wife was going to make a public appeal to the person who'd apparently taken her husband. There had been signs of a struggle in his car, which had left campus and then been returned to campus. Mrs. Ashton was going to beg the public for their assistance, the usual bit. Then the chief would take questions.

Hugo spotted the missing guy's daughters, and tugged me right to them, and they responded in the way all children respond to puppies, crouching low and loving on him. I leaned in closer to the grandmother and whispered, "The kids don't need to be here for this, do they?"

She looked at me. She had blue eyes the same color as those dishes people collect. "Where else would they be?"

I pointed my chin over her right shoulder. A little park, a swing set, a duck pond. She turned and looked at all of it, then crouched between the two little girls and the happiest pup on earth. "I wonder if there are ducks in that pond?"

The girls spotted the park and bounced in excitement. The older one looked up at me. "Can the puppy come?"

"If your grandma doesn't mind."

I felt her ripple of suspicion and I said, "I'm Rachel de Luca. The author." I took off my sunglasses in case that helped. "I've brought one of my books for Mrs. Ashton. People say they're quite uplifting, and I thought it might–"

"I'm familiar with your work," she said. She took the book from me, looked at it, flipped it over for a glance at the author photo on the dust jacket, then dropped it into her tote bag. "Thank you. That was kind of you." She started walking again.

The girls had run ahead to the swing set.

I fell into step. She didn't object. A few cops looked our way, but since I looked like part of the family, not an eyebrow was raised. Hugo was tugging like crazy at his leash. I opted to keep him on until we caught up to the kids. He wouldn't go anywhere they didn't go. Once attached to a child, Hugo did not allow much space between himself and said child.

We caught up, and I unhooked the leash at last. The girls and Hugo hopped, skipped and giggled their way behind us as we walked around the pond. When we found a bench, we sat, me and the grandma, whose name I didn't know. The girls started finding things to throw into the shallow water. Sticks, twigs, pebbles. Hugo waded right in to fetch the things back out again.

Why is every little kid's first act upon seeing a body of water, to throw something into it?

The girls giggled, and I was glad I'd brought the pup. Anything that could make them happy in the middle of all this drama in their lives was fine by me.

"What would you say about all this, Ms. De Luca?" their grandmother asked slowly. "You embrace the theory that we somehow create the events of our lives. Why would my son-in-law have created something like this for himself? For his family?"

"I'm sure he didn't. Not on purpose. A simpler understanding is that like attracts like. Energy matches up with similar energy."

"You're suggesting Peter's energy matches the energy of whoever took him?"

"In some way, maybe. Or maybe he was fearful. Was he a fearful man, Mrs..."

"Santiago. And no, I would not call my son-in-law fearful. But he is not a kind man."

Her eyes shot to the girls.

The two of them were floating leaves on the water, like little boats, and Hugo kept snatching them out of the water and shaking them.

"They're going to get soaked," she said, "Becka and Kate, get away from the water now, that's enough."

The girls came running, puppy right behind. I felt a little bad about that, until Mrs. Santiago leaned low and said, "I'll take you to the big park, later on, with even more water. But you're wearing your good clothes now. Why don't you go play on the swings for a while?"

"Is Mommy done talking to the TV yet, Gram?" the smaller one with the dark ringlets asked. "Will it make Daddy come back?"

"I hope he never comes back!" the honey blonde said. She had that pre-adolescent chub that would vanish by middle school. I figured her for around fifth grade, maybe ten or eleven years old.

I closed my eyes, feeling for her anger, and there was a flash, a scene in my mind. The professor holding her down on a twin bed with a purple comforter, his hand between her legs. She was twisting away, "No! Stop! I don't like it!"

"Yes, you do. You know damn well you do."

My eyes popped open, my stomach lurched, I wobbled on

my feet, pressed my hand to a tree trunk to keep myself upright.

"Are you all right, Miss. de Luca?"

Another flash, bang. My head snapped backward, and I was in the car again, strangling Dwayne Clark again, my knees in his back again. I looked at my wrists, and the familiar watch, and then at my hands. They were small, and sporting a shiny pink French manicure.

I opened my eyes.

"Miss de Luca!"

"Um, yeah." I brought my head level, opened my eyes. "Yes. I'm okay. I probably need to drink more water. It's a warm day, for September."

"You should get inside, out of the sun. Here, here." She took the leash from my hand, clipped it to Hugo's collar. "Thank you for the book. We're good now. You can go."

I got it. I was weirding her out. I was weirding *me* out.

I couldn't protect Ivy anymore. I didn't know how it could be her, but somehow it was her. She'd killed Dwayne Clark. The watch might've been a coincidence, but now the watch and the manicure.... She did it. She killed him, and she'd done it to protect Juan.

And now there was another child molester missing.

Was this the connection? Were all the men whose bodies had been buried along the banks of the Susquehanna pedophiles?

It was kind of ridiculous to think that Ivy could have done one and not the others. But God, she didn't feel like a murderer to me. She felt like an angel.

I had to come clean with Mason and hope for the best. Frankly, if what I suspected was true, and all the victims were pedophiles, I'd rather throw Ivy Newman a freaking ticker tape parade.

I TEXTED MASON THE ALL-CLEAR. He'd been with his partner Rosie and a handful of other cops, watching the presser go down. I saw them as I wended my way back out of the crowd. I walked a block and a half, then around a corner to the waiting car, got in, started it up. I did not want to believe Ivy was behind this. Not after I'd given her the benefit of the doubt.

What if all you gave her was the chance to prove you wrong?

Everything in me said it wasn't her. But the evidence was saying otherwise.

Mason joined me in the car, and I started driving as soon as he closed his door. "Well? What did you get?"

"Not what I wanted to get."

"What's that mean?"

I took a deep breath. "We have to talk."

"About Professor Ashton?"

I shook my head. "About Ivy Newman."

He exhaled so thoroughly I think he deflated a little. "It's about time." I frowned at him. "Ever since you said you didn't think she did it I've known you thought she did."

"If you knew, why didn't you say something?"

He shrugged. "You want to keep shit from me, it's your prerogative."

He was hurt, and maybe a little bit mad at me. Mason almost *never* got mad at me. This was happening too often. "I just...I was unsure. And I–"

"You like her."

I pressed my lips and didn't look at him.

"You don't like anyone. But you like her."

"You almost sound jealous." He didn't answer that. "She

doesn't feel like a killer to me. It's confusing. I'm getting mixed signals and that just…threw me. I've been struggling with it."

"When I'm struggling with something, you're the *first* person I want to talk to about it." He was looking at me and I was not looking back. "I thought we were on the same page."

"We are. I'm sorry, Mason. And I'm talking to you about it now."

He nodded. "So, talk then."

He wasn't over it yet. Shit. I had some serious kissing up to do. "Dwayne Clark was abusing his son, the gorgeous little sweetheart with the biggest, brownest eyes in the known universe."

He shot me a look of surprise and dismay. "Ivy told you that?"

"No. I saw it, there in Ivy's kitchen the day I had tea with Reggie. He got tired and went to his room, asked me to clean up after us before I left. I think he just wanted me to be alone in that kitchen. I think he knew I'd pick up on it. And I did. I saw little Juan there with Ivy. He was crying because he was going to have to spend a weekend with his father, and his dad was going to hurt him again. I felt Ivy decide that someone had to stop him."

"So you *know* she did it?"

"I saw her wristwatch when she was strangling him. It was the same one she was wearing at Vince and Holly's."

He nodded slow. "And you didn't tell me because…."

"I just…hesitated. That's all it was, hesitation. Because I keep thinking I must be wrong. And a wristwatch could be a coincidence. Same town, same jewelry store, that kind of thing. I haven't had any hint at all that she killed any of those other men you found along the river banks, Mason. Not one. But now…."

"Now?"

"The manicure was the same, too. And it turns out Professor Ashton was abusing one of his daughters. The older one, Kate. I got it just now."

He shifted into cop mode so fast I got whiplash. "We need to find out if the other victims were also sexually assaulting children. If that's the connection–"

"If that's the connection, then whoever killed them deserves a medal."

He looked at me like I'd lost my mind. "Jeremy is a suspect in what's looking more and more like a murder. Did you forget about that?"

"Of course I haven't forgotten about that. That's all I'm thinking about here. We have to catch whoever did this to clear Jeremy."

"Even if it's her?"

"Of course, even if it's her. Shit, Mason, how can you even ask me that?"

"We need to tell the chief. Ivy Newman needs to be under surveillance until we can–"

"Based on what? My gut feeling? My NFP? We don't have any real evidence. Just a connection we can't prove."

"They could question the kids."

I sent him a look that should've melted his face. "We don't have enough yet. And if we put Ivy under surveillance, we'll be blowing Reggie's cover. He wanted to spend his final days in peace."

"And that would be a shame, but Rachel, we're talking about a serial killer here."

I shook my head. "That just doesn't feel right."

"In what way?"

"In the way that I've known too fucking many serial killers." I shook my head angrily and pulled off an exit ramp and into a fast food joint. "I know it makes no sense, I know that, but I'm telling you–there's something else going on here. And if we jump on the wrong person, it's gonna look like we're just trying to scapegoat anyone we can to clear Jeremy. And that makes him look even more guilty. We need *proof*, Mason."

"Why are we at McDonald's?"

I put my window down. "Because I need to take out my frustrations on a quarter pounder with cheese, okay?"

"You want to make that a meal?" the crackly-speaker-voice asked.

"Yes, I do. With a vanilla shake."

"Anything else?"

I looked at Mason. He rolled his eyes. "Make it two," I said. "Only make the second shake strawberry." I put the window up, pulled ahead, and waited for the person in front of me, who was apparently counting out payment in nickels.

"Don't bring the chief in on this yet," I said. "We have no evidence. Let *me* surveil her, instead."

"Yeah, right."

"Yeah. Right. Me. You don't have the evidence to do it officially, and you can't do it off the books because you want to keep your job. I'm self-employed. I'll surveil her."

"It's dangerous."

"If I was going to get hurt or killed, I'd know it."

"You would not."

It was our turn to pay. I put my window down again and handed over my plastic. She rang me up with a smile that died at my return scowl and handed it back.

At the pickup window, the guy ahead of us was checking each item in each bag. Dick.

"Would you, Rachel? Would you know?"

"Seems like."

"You've got yourself into some risky situations before without knowing you were in danger. Most recently with Gary Conklin."

"And yet, I'm still here." I patted my chest, belly thighs. "All intact."

He rolled his eyes.

"Look, does it matter? I'm gonna do this, either way. We have to untangle this mess. For Jeremy's sake."

"Yeah." He nodded. "Yeah, you're right."

We finally got our food. I found a relatively empty space in the parking lot, and shut the motor off. I felt the uncomfortable and unusual tension between us and I hated it. Eventually, I said, "What are we gonna do about Jeremy, anyway?"

"The drinking," he said, like it wasn't a question.

"No. Not the drinking. The drinking is easy. We kick his ass all the way to rehab if he takes another sip. He's not gonna throw his life away on booze. That's a no-brainer. It will not be tolerated, that's all."

"I don't think it works like that," Mason muttered.

"I meant, his questions about his father. I think you have to tell him the truth about Eric, Mason."

His eyes widened so much I wondered if I'd sprouted antlers. "Rachel, if writing about his mother sent him into a binge, what do you think finding out his father was a serial killer is going to do to him?"

"I think he already knows. Or has a pretty good idea. I think it's the uncertainty bothering him. That and the fact that the person he trusts most in the world is keeping the truth from him."

He looked at his burger, then dropped it back into its box.

"You always knew it was going to have to come out someday, Mason. Secrets like this can't stay buried. He's gonna be a cop. If he doesn't ruin his life first. Sooner or later he's going to dig into this and find out on his own. And I'm betting on sooner. Don't you think it's better coming from you?"

He took a breath, sighed it out again, shook his head. "I'll talk to him." Then he looked at me sharply. "Not Josh."

"Hell, no. Josh is too young."

He nodded again. "Okay. I'll do it tonight."

"Maybe arrange an overnight for Josh with Hunter, so you can have time alone with him, since I won't be home to run interference." I unwrapped my burger, and bit in. The fries' temperature window had closed. I sucked a swig of my shake through the foldable metal straw I kept in my purse, a gift from Misty. Then I checked my watch. "We need to get moving."

"Why's that?"

"Cause I want to be at Dilmun Elementary when the teachers leave for the day."

He looked at me and his eyes said, *I don't like this one bit*, and mine replied, *I didn't say you had to like it.*

I needed to get this thing done. *We* needed it done. It was tearing our perfect little family to hell and gone.

12

"U still ok?" The text was from Mason.

I was parked in my crossover, because it was less conspicuous than the T-bird even though it was burnt orange, outside a Methodist church all the way out in Endwell. Ivy had gone inside, and so had five other women.

I was nervous as hell and watching everyone around me. I'd just had an anonymous call from someone who said she thought I should know Gary Conklin was missing. He'd been in-patient since his return to Binghamton on the social worker's recommendation, but this morning, they'd released him. He was stable on his meds, and doing everything he was supposed to. You know, make your bed, take a shower, pick up your room. The way violent psych patients can demonstrate their sanity these days is equivalent to the way an 8-year-old earns his allowance. Except the mental patient can go home and buy a gun after. Great system.

The informant said someone had found Gary's meds in the trash can near the exits. I was kind of scared shitless.

"I'm fine," I texted back. "Ivy went into a church. Looks

like an AA meeting sort of thing. Weird she comes this far, though. I'm going in."

"She'll see u."

"No. She won't." I silenced the phone and pocketed it. I was wearing that perky little visor, but that would look odd indoors, without sun. So would the sunglasses. I left the shades on anyway, and as a last resort, ditched the visor and grabbed Josh's Maroon baseball hat off the back seat, Whitney Point Eagle and all. Not even a little conspicuous, right? I stuffed my hair all up inside it. Then I went to the red double doors on the side of the beautiful stone church and walked in as the other women had done.

A hallway that only went one direction led me deeper into the building. Rooms with doors lined it. Most were closed, a few were open, one was a restroom, but all felt empty. Voices, the sounds of scraping chairs, and the smell of bad coffee wafted from the end of the hall where it formed a T. There were two entrances on the facing wall. One led into the room where the women were pulling their chairs into a circle. The other was closed, and closer to me. I ducked around the corner, and holding my breath, opened that door.

Storage closet. Score.

I ducked inside, pulled it closed, and listened. I could hear them in the meeting room. A second door in this closet led directly into the room where the women had gathered.

"So glad everyone could come," someone said. She had a good voice, strong, but soft at the same time. An approachable voice. "How's everyone's week been?"

"Mine sucked," someone said. "So much in the news triggers me. All this *Me, Too* stuff."

If *Me, Too* was a trigger, then these women were survivors of sexual assault. My brain put that together as quick as a *eureka!* finger-snap.

"I love the *Me, Too* stuff," another woman said. "Don't you feel like it's about time?"

"I feel like, why the hell didn't I have the gall to say something when it happened to me? Why didn't any of us?"

It wasn't time then, I thought. *Too few of us were woke. Now the scale's starting to tilt the other way.*

"It makes you feel ashamed for not speaking up," the first woman said. I took her to be the group leader. "But how many eight-year-olds do you see speaking out against their parents, even now?"

Eight-year-olds? Oh my God, they're survivors of childhood *sexual assault.*

So…Ivy was sexually assaulted as a child?

My stomach tied itself into a knot. I imagined her aquamarine eyes in a little girl's face. I heard giggles, glimpsed pigtails, and wanted to vomit. Suddenly her closeness to a wealthy old man took on a sinister hue.

"Children aren't strong enough to speak out." I recognized Ivy's voice, and it reminded me that she'd survived. She was okay. You know, aside from possibly being a vigilante serial killer. Serial vigilante killer. Whatever.

"That's why it's so vital that the adults in their lives protect them," she went on. "And I think for the most part, we do a crappy job of that in our society."

"You never did anything wrong," said the leader, refocusing on the woman who felt guilty for not speaking out against her childhood abuser. "Not one single thing you did was wrong. Telling isn't wrong. Not telling isn't wrong."

Another woman said, "But abusing children *is* wrong. There's no redemption for it. There's no cure for it. No surgery, no medication that can make it go away. There's no sentence long enough and no God forgiving enough. Not for that. It was *his* fault. Every single part of it was entirely his fault. It was never your fault."

She sounded angry. I wished I knew who she was.

"It wasn't your fault." Everyone repeated. They said it several times, all in unison. I heard chairs scraping, footsteps, some sniffling. I think they were hugging her.

My eyes burned, and I couldn't swallow for a minute.

There was muttering, kind of hard to distinguish as several small conversations broke out between individuals. It felt like they were taking a break.

"Where's Gloria?" I heard Ivy ask. "Why isn't she here?"

No one seemed to have an answer. I tapped my phone to light it up, typed a note to myself. *Find out who Gloria is.* Then I noticed my surroundings in that muted glow and switched to the Flashlight app to take a look around. Folding chairs. Folding tables. Brooms and mops. A big Tupperware tray with a tight-fitting cover stood on a shelf beside stacks of paper plates, napkins, a giant can of cheap coffee, foam cups, and a two-gallon jug of Hi-C, fruit punch flavor.

I could see storing everything in a closet except for the cookies. That didn't make any sense at all.

As if in response to my thoughts (that's how it works, folks, it's not coincidence), one woman said, "These cookies are fantastic."

"That reminds me," said the leader, and her chair scraped. "I have a batch of peanut butter, too." I heard her footsteps coming nearer. The footsteps stopped. I clicked the phone to douse its light, moving quickly to the door I'd come in by. But there wasn't time to duck out. That second door was opening. There was nowhere to hide. So, I just bent my knees and dropped into a crouch so deep I worried about leaving organs on the floor. I pressed my face to my knees and held my breath.

I heard rattling, breathing, then the door swung closed again.

I lifted my head. Door, closed. Cookies, gone.

Holy shit that was close.

Too close, Inner Bitch.

I ducked out of that closet so fast I was surprised I didn't knock things over, and headed back up the hallway to the exit. I heard heels tapping behind me, too close to not see me, unless they were blind like I used to be. I didn't look back, though. Just went right out the double doors, up the sidewalk and crossed the street.

I'd parked in a space on the opposite side of the road, and I headed for my car, but didn't get in. I sat on the curb beside it, instead, completely out of sight, but with a view of the stone church. It would've been stunning by itself. But instead it was wedged in between The Corner Cigar Store on one side, and a brick building currently housing an insurance agency on the first floor and a lawyer's office on the second. I watched the red doors to see if anyone came out looking for me. Seconds ticked by.

But no one emerged. Then something moved in the glass part of the door, and I swore a blue streak. She'd been looking out the window, whoever she was. One of the members? The leader? Ivy, herself? *Someone* had been looking out the window. Had I made it to my cover before she'd cupped her hand to the glass? Or had she seen me, and therefore my car. Had she jotted down the plate number?

Normal people don't go around jotting down plate numbers, Rachel, Inner Bitch pointed out. *That's more a you thing.*

That's what living with a cop will do for you.

There was no more sign of anyone looking at me, and I breathed. It felt like the first time since the closet.

It had turned gloomy while I'd been inside. The sun hadn't set, but it was hiding behind a thick bank of clouds, and a stiff breeze was whipping up dead leaves along the sides of the pavement. The entire length of the short side street had parking spaces along one side, angling outward from the curb. Anyone going into that support group would probably have parked there, just as I had. Just as Ivy had.

I got upright again, and looked at the cars parked side by side, their asses facing the church, and their noses, the little park at my back. It had a couple of benches and a fountain.

There were five cars besides mine and Ivy's. I took out my phone, and walked the edge of the park, snapping shots of all five license plates. Breech of privacy? No doubt about it, but it wasn't like I was going to out them on social.

Were they watching me?

I couldn't tell a thing by looking at the church. Its windows were black mirrors. Unless someone moved, I didn't think I'd know if anyone was on the other side, looking out. On top of that, the meeting might let out any second.

I took a pic of the final plate, then jogged around the cigar store's corner. There was a bench there and a Bus Stop sign. I sat on the bench, and I texted the photos to Mason.

"We need names, addies."

He texted back, "Why?"

"Later."

Every inch of me was yearning to check the car doors, starting with Ivy's and go through the shit inside the unlocked ones. See if anyone was carrying a homemade garotte with braided picture wire. I wasn't going to do that, though. It was broad daylight. People were walking and driving past. I pocketed my phone and went to look back around the corner.

The church door was open and the women were coming out. I pulled Josh's baseball cap down lower and leaned on the building like I belonged there. I could hear them talking, female voices, low and confidential. Not loud and laughing like when I hang out with my friends.

What friends? Inner Bitch asked.

You. And you know, Sandra and the girls, and Amy.

Sister. Nieces. Employee.

And friends. Stop being so literal.

You should snap pics of these *friends,* my alter ego suggested softly inside my head.

I leaned around the corner for another glance. Three had emerged and stood on the sidewalk talking. I had a full-face view of two of them, and I snapped a quick shot. Another came out and I snapped again. The third one turned my way and I snapped. She saw me, and I moved my phone around, like an idiot looking for a signal. By the way, holding your phone as high as your arm can reach will never give you more bars. Still, I did that, and turned and walked out of sight. I entered the cigar store, and pretended to browse until they'd all driven away. Then I went back to my Crosstrek and pointed it toward home.

My phone, face-up on the seat beside me, lit up. Sandra.

I smiled and poked the button on the dash to answer hands-free. "I was just thinking of you."

"Good. I like when you're thinking of me. What were you thinking?" Sandra asked.

"I was counting my women friends–"

"What women friends?"

"You, among others."

"I'm your sister."

Told you so.

Shut up, Inner Bitch.

"Jim wants to cook steaks for dinner Saturday. You want to come over?"

"Sure. Unless you want to do it at my place."

"He was hoping you'd offer."

"I know he was. Why wouldn't he? I have a lake."

"It's not your lake."

"It is in my head."

"I bet it is. How's Jere? And why did I have to hear about all the drama from my daughter? He punched a professor who later went missing, and was taken to the police department for questioning?"

"Misty buried the lead. He's drinking again."

"Holy fu–dgesicles."

"Yeah. He's home. I think his on-campus living days are over for a while."

"You can't make him live with you forever, sis."

"Who says?"

She sighed. "He has to learn how to deal with this on his own."

"Why? He has us."

"Arguing with you is hard work."

"That's why you shouldn't do it. How are things? How are the trouble twins?"

"Senioritis. They don't want to go to school, they don't want to stay once they get there. They don't want to do anything. Mentally, they're done. All Christie wants to do is party with her friends, and the justification for it is, 'I might never see them again after June.'"

"It's only September."

"I've pointed that out. It hasn't helped."

"And Misty?"

"Wants to hurry up and graduate so she can go to college. I'd be excited about that, except she could care less about college. To her, going to BU is something like her and Jere moving in together. She says she's not even applying to any other schools."

"And this is why men have been in charge for so long. Women are idiots until thirty-five."

"Um, AOC?"

"A rare exception," I replied. "She's gonna be president someday."

"Twenty twenty-eight," Sandra said. "If we haven't all gone extinct by then."

"Amen, sister."

"So what's up with this missing professor?"

"We're looking into it."

"Well, duh. What are you finding out?"

"Nothing yet, other than that Jeremy had nothing to do with it." I knew more than that, and she *knew* I knew more than that. But she didn't ask. I'd driven around the block, and spotted Ivy's old Subaru at a traffic light. I followed from three cars back, until I was sure she was going home. I mean, there's not much else on the way to Dilmun. Less than there is on the way to Whitney Point, even, which is why I love it.

"I'm not…comfortable with Misty being around him when he's drinking," Sandra said. "I can tell you that because you're my sister. I know you love Jeremy, but–"

"If she dumps him, he brought it on himself. I've got no sympathy for this, Sandra. Mason's all, 'but it's a disease,' and I just call bullshit on that. It's a choice. Period."

"Not everyone's as strong as you are."

"Everyone is as strong as they choose to be. Not everything I write is bullshit, you know. And hey, I'm on your side here. I don't like him seeing her when he's drinking, either. "

"Easier to put a halt to a runaway train than a pair of lovesick teenagers."

"I can guarantee you he's not drinking now. He's home

where we can keep an eye on him. And he knows how badly he fucked up."

She sighed. "I hope he can beat it."

"Me, too."

"Maybe he should consider therapy," she said.

I rolled my eyes. "Yeah, that's the agreed-upon norm in these situations, isn't it?"

"We'll talk before Saturday. Love you, Rache."

"Love you, too." I hit the end call button on my dash and pressed the accelerator harder, eager to get home. I swear I must be getting old. Were you old when home was your favorite place to be?

Not old. Just lucky. Very, very lucky.

13

The guys had already eaten and were engaged in a raucous video game battle by the time I dragged my sorry ass home. I walked in with a box of donuts I'd picked up at Dunkin to ease my guilt for missing dinner.

The fresh pot of decaf I set to brewing worked its magic. Before it finished chugging, the boys had floated into the kitchen on its steamy, wonderful smell.

"Mmm, coffee?" Mason asked, coming to slide his arms around my waist and pull me close. "You are a goddess."

He might get mad at me, but he didn't hold onto it long. Thank goodness. "And you are a very lucky god."

Jeremy was already filling his mug.

"You're welcome." I looked at Josh, the only one not waxing ecstatic over my brewing skills. He was looking around expectantly, and I said, "On the table, hon."

He spotted the box and shouted, "I knew there'd be donuts!" on his way to get one.

I poured him a glass of milk.

We had our donuts and beverages of choice in the living

room while the men folk wrapped up their game, and I watched. I wondered if I'd have got the gaming bug if I hadn't been blind growing up. It used to eat at me, when I was a kid, hearing the other kids going on and on about the latest system or game. Maybe I should learn. Make up for lost time.

Josh was the first one to turn in. The rest of us were alone, still sipping coffee around the counter in the kitchen. Jeremy said, "I should get back to school next week. I haven't been expelled. Yet."

"Yeah, about that–"

Mason put a hand on my shoulder. I broke off, and he said, "Jere, do you think you'll be able to stay sober if you go back?"

Jere lowered his head, started to say something, then closed his mouth again. "Because if you stay here, it'll be easier. We'll be here to help you."

"To watch me, you mean. I don't need a babysitter."

"The hell you don't." They both looked at me. Jeremy all defensive and insulted, and Mason kind of long suffering and pleading. I put my hands up. "Fine, you two work it out. Just know that if it were up to me, you'd be on house arrest, with the sole exception of classes, for your entire freshman year."

He pushed his chair out, got up, and stalked from the room. "I'm an adult. You can't tell me what to do."

"Oh, yeah? Watch me."

And he was up the stairs and out of my anger's reach. I didn't even realize I'd jumped up onto my feet. Mason gaped at me. I sat down and took a long sip from my mug.

"Tough love," I said. "Look it up."

"I don't think that was helpful."

"You're right. It would've been more helpful if you'd backed me up. You can't let him throw his life away, Mace."

"The operative phrase there is *his life*. It's *his* life. Not ours. And if we lock him in his room and do this for him, he's never going to develop the strength to do it for himself."

I set my jaw.

"That's almost straight from one of your books," he said.

My jaw went lax. "Damn you for being right."

He shrugged. "Let's not fight. I love you too much."

We were still okay. I didn't even know how worried I'd been until he reassured me with those five words. I managed to hold my form, even though my insides had all turned warm and melty. I hid my mush-rush behind a layer of smug. "You should be thanking me. He only hung out down here after Josh went to bed, so he could ask about his father again."

"Probably true." I got the distinct feeling he did not want to discuss that particular issue. "What did your surveillance tell you?"

"Top news is that I got an anonymous text telling me Gary Conklin was released from the psych unit, and that he trashed his meds on the way out."

"Whoa. How long ago did you get–never mind. I don't want to know. You're gonna have to be careful, Rache."

"Trust me, I plan to be. I also learned that we're barbecuing on Saturday here with Sandra and the gang. Jim's bringing the steaks. Amy's coming, too."

"So the same thing we do almost every nice weekend from May to September?" he asked.

I blinked at him. "Is it getting to be too much?"

"It's my favorite thing on planet earth. I miss it when it gets too cold and snowy. I wish Mom would come more often."

"Well, you know. Your mom has her garden club." I stroked his calf with my toe. "Also in today's news, Misty wants to go to college so she can shadow Jeremy's every step. And he thinks *booze* is his biggest problem."

He pushed out his lower lip and nodded. "Sounds about normal. Anything…about the case?"

"Maybe. Ivy attends a support group all the way in Endwell for childhood sex abuse survivors, all female including the group leader."

"Ivy was abused as a child?" He looked stunned. Then his brows rose even higher. "Reggie?"

"I don't know. Can we find out?"

"I've already tried to look into Ivy Newman's background, ran into a log jam of sealed files. If I want to see them, I need a court order. And to get one, I need at least some evidence connecting her to the crimes."

"And not to be on forced leave, probably," I said. I wanted to know what was in those sealed files.

"I still don't think she killed all those men," I said.

"So you keep telling me."

"Those were the group members' license plates I photographed. I want to put names with their faces."

"I gave them to Rosie, since I'm persona non grata at the department right now. He's gonna run 'em for us. He got a few back so far. Here." He gave me a printout.

The three vehicles on the list were registered in the women's own names. All were local within Broome and Chenango counties. Inspiration struck, and I started typing each name and city or town into the search bar on my various social sites. Facebook returned a couple of hits. I downloaded profile photos and hit the print button. My office was upstairs, its door closed, so the printer shouldn't wake Josh. I seriously doubted Jeremy was sleeping.

Thinking about Jeremy set off a red alert in my brain.

"We should've searched Jere's room! He might have booze stashed up there."

Mason rolled his eyes, and said, "Again, he's an adult who has to make his own decisions. Besides, I did that earlier today when he was outside with Josh and the dogs. I put a mini fridge in there too, stocked it with Gatorade and candy."

"Electrolytes and sugar. Good thinking."

He nodded.

I didn't want to ask, but I had to. "Did you find any alcohol?"

"No. I take that as a sign he's trying."

"He's gotta stop trying and just do it." I sighed, and got up to carry my empty mug to the sink. Mason was scrolling his phone, and came to join me there, holding it in front of me.

I was looking at a photo of an oval medallion with an image of a fiery woman engraved on its face. It was familiar.

"What is it?" I asked.

"A pendant of some sort. It was found between the seats of the professor's car. His wife said it wasn't his."

It clicked in my head where I'd seen it before, and I wished to hell I didn't have to say it out loud. "I recognize this."

"From where?" he asked.

I started swiping through the photos I'd taken of the women outside the Church, and stopped on the one of Ivy. Mason was leaning over my shoulder.

"Is that…?"

"I don't know." *Please don't be the same. Don't. Don't. Don't.* I spread the image bigger and centered the oval pendant. Mason held his phone beside mine. "It's the same," I said, with the inflection doctors use for "It's cancer."

"This is it!" Mason said with the inflection new fathers

use for "It's a boy." "This is the physical evidence I need to get those files unsealed."

"Is it…are you going to arrest her?" I asked.

His face went from eagerness, to disbelief with an edge of darkness. "Does it matter? If it clears Jeremy–"

"I know you think I'm protecting her, but I'm not." The image of little Kate Ashton, humiliated, sobbing, as her father violated her replayed in my head. So did Juan's brimming, brown eyes. Okay, maybe I *was* protecting Ivy, just a little bit. But not at Jeremy's expense. Never that. "If it's her, arrest her. But make sure, Mason. It has to stick or we make it worse for Jere. Okay?"

He said nothing.

"Let's try to identify this image on the pendant. Who is it supposed to be? What does it represent?"

"You saw her commit one murder. Your stuff is usually accurate, right? And now we have physical evidence tying her to the second–"

"No, we don't." I snapped my fingers. "We actually don't. She's *wearing* her pendant. The one in the car can't be hers."

He shot me a look that said I was treading on his thinnest layer of patience. "It's identical."

"Have my feelings ever been wrong before, Mason? How can you not believe me when I tell you Ivy did not kill anyone except possibly Dwayne Clark?"

"How can you defend her when the police are looking at Jeremy for this?"

I shot to my feet. "I'm just trying to get to the truth."

"Any truth that clears Ivy Newman, you mean."

"*Mason–*"

"No. No, I can't even talk to you about this right now." He shook his head hard, got up and walked right out the door.

Mason was sipping his first cup of Joe, still in a pair of pajama bottoms and a T-shirt, barefoot, when his phone pinged. He'd already seen Jeremy off to class and Joshua off to school. He'd stayed up late, going over and over the murders, and everything he had on the other victims. Only one of them, besides Dwayne Clark and the professor, had kids. The others included a teacher and a coach. Access to kids for sure. Two more had priors. One for sharing kiddy porn online, and the other had been arrested for molesting his seven-year-old niece. The kid had later recanted, and the charges had been dropped.

So that was four with a definite predilection for sex with children. Two with obvious access to kids, and one he still had nothing on. He was pretty sure that all the victims had been killed because they were pedophiles.

Rachel had been asleep by the time he'd gone to bed. And he'd got up before her…and yeah, it was on purpose.

He felt like a real shit for that.

She came scuffing into the kitchen wearing a silky navy nightgown with a lace inset in its v neck under an open spa robe. Her bulldog was at her side, and her hair was a fluffy bat's nest. Her eyes were puffy, too. If he said she looked like she'd been crying, she'd have clocked him in the jaw, but she looked like she'd been crying.

She stopped in the wide entryway and leaned against the side. Myrtle stopped and sat down. She never missed an opportunity to sit, and if Rachel stood there more than a minute, Myrtle would go perpendicular and probably start snoring.

He decided the best approach would be with coffee in

hand, and made her a cup, heavy on the cream and sugar. She took the cup, sniffed it and muttered, "Checking for arsenic."

"Don't be ridiculous. Nobody uses arsenic anymore."

"Hmph." She scuffed to the nook where she could look out the windows. Myrtle never let much air between her and Rachel's leg.

He went there too, but didn't sit. He was casting around in his head for something to say, but as usual, she was ten steps ahead of him.

"So, do you really think there's anything I wouldn't do to protect Josh and Jeremy?"

"No. I don't think that."

"And you really think I'd lie to you to protect a serial killer?"

"I don't think that, either."

"Do you, in fact, Mason Brown, honestly believe I would put anything or anyone, even myself, above you and those kids?"

"I know better."

She nodded hard, looked at her cup. He knew she wanted to be furious at him, maybe yell at him for a while, but he was deliberately making it hard for her to find a reason.

"I'm sorry," he said. "I'm out of my mind over Jeremy, not just the case, but the drinking, and the questions about Eric. Especially the questions." He took a sip of his coffee, but it was more than half gone and already getting cold. Then he said, "To tell you the truth, it hurt my feelings that you didn't feel like you could tell me what you saw. That you didn't trust me with it."

"I *couldn't* trust you with it."

"Rachel, you know you can–"

"Did you tell Chief V about Ivy's pendant?"

"Yes."

"See?" She sipped her still-hot coffee. And just like that, she was the one mad at him. How did she always manage to do that?

"Rachel, I don't understand this. I thought I knew you inside and out, but I have never met this side of you."

"This *side* of me? You *know* this side of me. This is the side of me who susses people out. The side that can listen to an interrogation and tell you if the guy is lying. The side that keeps telling me that Ivy Newman is good."

"And yet you're pretty sure she killed Dwayne Clark."

"She's a level of good I've never encountered before. And it's not about what she *did*, it's about what she *is*. It's beyond good, what she is. It's…." She exploded her head with her fingers.

He looked right into her eyes, listening with his whole being, because he wanted to get this. He didn't like the rift he felt forming between them.

"This isn't a *different* part of me, it's the same part of me. I know things I shouldn't know. That's the part that knows she's…good."

"Whether she killed him or not."

"She saved Juan from being raped by his father."

"And the others–"

"I don't think she killed them."

"But is that your stuff or just what you want to believe?" he asked. "Because I think she did. I think she's a vigilante, and I think she feels good to you because she *believes* she's good. But she's just a killer, Rache."

"No. She's not."

He sat across the table from her, put his cup down, reached across and put his hands over hers. "I love you. This–" He touched her heart with his fingertips, then his own. "This right here, this is a zillion times bigger than everything else. That's all static. It's not about us. We're gonna take care of Jeremy, whatever it takes, but that's about Jeremy. We can't let it affect what's between us. Okay?"

She was quiet for a minute, processing what he'd said. Probably having one of those inner monologues she sometimes spoke aloud. She had entire conversations with her books while she wrote them. He'd heard her up there in her office, talking away. She was fascinating to him. Still. Always.

Then she got up, and came around the table, sat on his lap and kissed him like there was no tomorrow.

And then the phone rang, and he snaked his hand around her waist and picked it up.

"We need you, buddy. Rachel, too."

"Rosie? What's going on?"

"Rachel's obsessed fan, Gary? He's losing it big time. Hurry it up, okay?"

I KNEW it was about Gary before Mason picked up the phone. I'd felt it buzz through me like a mild electric shock. I heard his plea inside my mind. "You've gotta help me."

It took us mere minutes, maybe three of them, to throw on clothes, and hit the road in Mason's Beast. He wasn't far, one exit down 81. We off-ramped to Castle Creek. Mason used to have an old farmhouse there. He was all about fixing it up for the boys, before some psycho hosebeast firebug torched it, we thought with the boys inside.

Just driving by the site, an uncapped basement in the middle of a weed field, brought back the same feeling I'd had when we'd come home to find it engulfed. When we'd gone out, the kids and the dogs had been inside. When we'd returned, it had been in the process of burning to the ground.

Mason covered my hand with his. "It gets to me, too," he said. "But they're okay. We all are."

I gave a sad smile, a fake firm nod.

The address Rosie had texted wasn't hard to find. There were five police cars lined up. Three of them were Binghamton black & whites, and two were the blue and yellow of our New York State Troopers with their dorky wide-brimmed hats. I'm sorry, but they are. It's New York and you're wearing cowboy hats? What's wrong with a freaking fedora?

There was a Bearcat with SWAT stenciled on its sides, but what chilled me most were the two ambulances.

All the vehicles' lights were flashing. I always thought it would be better if they'd just turn them off. Seemed to me flashing bright lights at criminals might just agitate them.

We parked at the back of the line and ran forward. Mason grabbed hold of my hand on the way. As we approached, we could see all the action was in the back yard of a little white clapboard house with sky blue shutters. There was a picket fence, a mob of cops, and a pair of T-poles connected by clothes lines. No clothes, though. Just clothespins, every few inches, leaning this way and that way like drunken soldiers on parade.

We crossed someone's lawn, kitty corner. Mason hopped over their back fence, then reached back, gave me a hand over. I'm not weak, I'm short. We made our way between the cops. I smelled the gas first. Then we finally breached the front line, and there was the whole story right there. Old man on a chair, duct tape wrapped around him every two inches from his shoulders to his ankles. All he could move was his head. His face was wrinkled and puffy and red. He had tufts of iron gray hair, pointing every which way. He was very wet.

There was a gas can lying on its side near his feet. We stood outside the picket fence, looking in.

Near the back door of the little house, a very round woman in a kaftan and a long green sweater was shivering and crying and saying, "No, Gary. No Gary, you can't. You can't."

Gary was standing a few feet away from the old man, holding a lighter that was already lit, like a true believer at an emo concert. It was one of those Bic lighters, a red one.

I looked past the lighter at Gary. I tried to tune in, but I could not close my eyes. I took a step closer to the white picket barrier between us. One of the cops said, "No closer, ma'am."

I ignored him. "Hey, Gary. What's going on?"

He slid me a sideways glance. He wasn't puppy dog Gary, he was pissed-off Gary. He said, "This is the only way to make it stop, Rachel. I've tried everything else, I swear to God I have."

I took a few more steps, and the cop started toward me, and Mason said, "Let her go." Then to me, "Careful, Rachel."

I gave a single nod. "Gary, this isn't gonna make anything stop. But it will make a lot of even worse things start."

"There isn't anything worse."

"I didn't spend enough time with you," I said, moving right up to the fence. "I'm sorry about that, Gary. Sometimes we all mess up. Will you give me another chance?"

He looked at me again. His face was wet, chin dripping. His eyes were red from the burn of all that salt.

"We'll sit down. We'll talk. We'll talk for as long as you want. Just put that lighter down, hon. Please put it down."

He sniffled, looked past me at the police, I glanced behind me, too. Every gun was raised, and trained on this brokenhearted, broken-minded kid. God, he reminded me of my brother.

Gary said, "If they lower their guns, I'll put the lighter down." He said it loud enough for the responders to hear, and Mason made downward motions with his arms. Slowly the rifles and shotguns tipped barrel-down. Sidearms slid into holsters.

Gary nodded and bent his knees to put the lighter down. I looked down as he did, and spotted the little channel he'd dug into the lawn, no more than an inch wide, but easy to see. Brown earth splitting green grass. It formed a Y, one arm leading to the old man's feet, the other, toward the picket fence between him and me.

And then I understood, all within the same nano-second, and I lurched backward and my hands went up and I yelled, "No! WAIT!"

Blue flames shot along the channel in a violent *whoosh!* The fence became a wall of fire, knocking me back even further. I slammed into a cruiser, one arm shielding my face. Gary must have soaked the fence and filled his little trench with gasoline before anyone had got there. Even with the barricade of flames between us and the back yard, I could still see the burst of fresh fire when the old man went up.

He only screamed twice. The woman, never did stop.

14

By the time they'd doused the flames enough to see past the black and crispy picket fence, Gary was long gone. His father was a charred chunk, unrecognizable as having ever been a human being. His mother was sitting on the top stair, tugging at her hair and wailing. Poor thing.

One of the EMTs gave her a shot of something, and the cops spread out to search for Gary. I closed my eyes to feel around for him, but I couldn't sense any trace of him.

So there was that.

Despite having been on the scene, Mason was still on involuntary leave until the Ashton disappearance was solved. So we went home. It was all there was to do.

\#

WE'D SHOWERED and changed clothes, and I was standing in

front of my closet, looking for a sweater and trying to get that scene to stop replaying in my head.

Mason said, "We need to walk the dogs."

"Oh, yeah, they look like they're dying to go out." I nodded in the direction of two comatose, snoring lumps, lying side by side in the pool of late morning sunlight that slanted in through the French doors.

He held up his phone. "I've got Ivy's formerly sealed file. I'm probably not supposed to be seeing it while the case is active, but a do-gooder who shall remain anonymous sent me a copy."

"Rosie?"

"Him or the chief. Like I said, anonymous."

I walked over and sat on the bed, leaned back and stretched my legs out. "Where's your laptop?"

"You...aren't furious that I got this?"

"Curious," I said, emphasizing the C. "If she did it, I want to know. Come on, come on. Let's see what it says. I need something new to think about besides watching Gary burn his father alive."

He took his laptop off the nightstand, took up position in the bed besides me, on top of the covers, legs stretched out, crossed at the ankles. He'd pulled on shorts and nothing else after his shower. I'd put on a football jersey after mine. Don't break my heart again, Giants. I sat up straighter, adjusting the pillows behind me. He clicked on the file.

The first page was a missing child poster with a little girl just exactly the way I'd seen her in my mind, right down to the pigtails and aquamarine eyes. It said:

MISSING: IVY NEWMAN

AGE: 5

"Holy shit," I whispered.

Mason flipped pages, and we performed a tandem speed-reading worthy of Olympic gold. "Ivy was fucking kidnapped off the street, walking home from school with her sister, when she was five years old. It happened in Syracuse."

He picked up there. "She was held prisoner for years with no one looking for her. Another child murderer had confessed to killing her in a plea deal that saved him from the death penalty. That son of a–"

"Wait, wait, let me skim." I took his laptop right off his lap, and moved my finger over the mousepad. "She was kept chained to a radiator. One night she managed to pull her wrist free, and got away. Claims she climbed into the back of a truck, not even knowing it was her abductor's. When it stopped again, she was in Dilmun. That's where he lived."

"What a scumbag."

"Her family spent vacations there. A couple weeks on the lake every summer. But she didn't know that's where she was. Hell, I doubt she even remembered. She wandered off when the truck was still and quiet. The first person she ran into was Reggie D'Voe. There's a statement from him in here, it says." I scrolled, then I found it.

"'When I found her, Ivy was alone and frightened. She was in torn, filthy clothes, obviously malnourished, with restraint marks on her wrists and ankles.'"

"Ah, hell," Mason said.

"She told Reggie her daddy had done all that to her. Turns out the perv was her uncle. But he always wore a mask so she didn't know that, and he made her call him daddy. She was so young, she got confused."

He took the computer back. "So Reg decided to keep her. Passed her off as his niece. Since there was a pedophile in prison, having confessed to Ivy Newman's murder, there was no reason for anyone to think it was her. And since she wasn't from Dilmun, no one there would've recognized her, even if he hadn't kept her out of sight. But he did. Home schooled her. Protected her. Raised her as if she was his own. Apparently the police chief at the time and a local doctor helped him keep the secret."

"The police chief who's now married to her mother?" I asked, wide eyed, leaning over the screen.

He nodded. "James Mallory. The doctor was Ernie Graycloud. Their statements are in here, too." He scrolled a little more. "Hell, they thought they were saving a kid from a monster. No charges were filed. Even Ivy didn't know who she really was for twenty years or so. But when her uncle started up again, and kids went missing, it all came back." He went quiet, but I could see he was reading, so I elbowed him in the ribs.

"Ungh. Sorry. "Ivy was a grown woman by the time they found out who she really was. Her mother and sister had both moved to Dilmun, had even interacted with her. But she was an adult by then, and still reclusive." He gave a sad sigh. "All in the same town and didn't even know." He closed the laptop.

"She's been through so much," I said softly. "It's a hellish history."

"Yeah. And sorry to say, a helluva motive."

I wanted to argue with him, but I knew he was right.

"She could get off on an insanity plea," he said softly. "Who would doubt it, after going through something like that?"

"I don't sense insanity from her," I said, shaking my head. "She's not crazy, Mason."

I SPENT my Saturday morning stalking Ivy Newman and the

other members of her support group on social, looking for clues about the one who hadn't shown for the last meeting, Gloria. It didn't take long to find her full name.

Ivy, apparently still worried, shared an "I miss you" kitten meme and tagged Gloria Orr.

I clicked on the tag, and found out where she lived. Vestal. From there it took no more than a few clicks of the mouse to get a home address. Hell, I could look at her house from satellite if I wanted to.

Anybody can be a PI these days, Inner Bitch opined.
You downplaying my skills, IB?

It was pushing toward noon, though, so I saved my notes, jotted the address on a scrap of paper and shoved it into my jeans' pocket. The gang was on the way, and Mason was already outside arranging picnic tables on the lawn. The kids were down by the water, laughing hysterically at the dogs' antics. The froggy hunting team of Hugo & Myrt was something to behold. They flanked unsuspecting frogs and *sprounced*, often banging into each other while the frogs hopped away unharmed. They never hurt them. Sometimes they caught one, Myrt more often than Hugo, despite that she was blind. But when they did, they never bit down, and quickly dropped it again. Myrt would shake her head to get the frog taste out of her mouth, and then go after another.

I went out to help.

When we got the tables where we wanted them, in a spot that would stay shady for the afternoon, Mason pulled out his phone and checked it.

"That's the third time you've done that," I said. "Is something up?"

"I don't know. Rosie says he's suddenly being kept in the dark, and the chief's not answering my texts. I'm worried."

A horn honked. A shiny, dark red Ford Edge pulled into

the driveway. The twins got out and headed for the water and the boys before their parents could even alight. Misty was in Jeremy's arms a split second later. Christie claimed one of the older Adirondack chairs, the single ones, on the dock. She put her feet up and pulled out her phone.

"Hey, new wheels?" Mason asked, pumping Jim's hand, which was how they always said hello.

"Picked it up yesterday. It was time," Jim said. He and Mason walked around the vehicle, manspecting it, while I hugged my sister, which was how *we* always greeted each other.

"Your idea or Jim's?" I asked.

She rolled her eyes. "I tried to tell him we didn't need all that room. The girls will be off to college a year from now. I think he's in denial, though."

"Get some dogs. They're better than kids anyway. I know, having both."

She shook her head at me, and knew I was kidding. "How's Jeremy doing? With the drinking."

"He wants to go back to campus. I flat out said no. Mason says it's up to him."

Her brows arched. She was so pretty, my sister, brown hair at the moment, with so many blond highlights she might as well be entirely blond. "You and Mason disagree on something?"

"A lot of things, lately."

"Awww, *hon*...." she said, just the same way she'd say it to a three-year-old with a sliver.

"Don't. It's fine. Couples don't have to agree on everything. God, how boring would that be?"

"Just the right amount of boring," she said with a look Jim's way.

She loved him. I mean, I *knew* she loved him, but, she really *love* loved him.

Amy arrived in her impossibly tiny Yaris. She was all about saving the planet these days. She got out alone. I always expected a herd of circus clowns to pile out behind her, but nope.

"I'm here," she announced. "You can start the party now."

"I'm so glad you made it."

"Yeah, every once in a while I'm willing to hang out with old people. Gotta give back, you know?" She pushed her short black hair off her face. She had a deep side part, and a long lock of bangs that was perpetually hiding one of her always thickly lined green eyes. Her lips were lilac today, and she wore her standard uniform of black leggings, with black boots, a black tee, and a black leather jacket.

"So what's to eat?"

"It's not ready yet," I said.

Sandra said, "You should check out Christie's hair."

Amy looked toward the edge of the water, where the kids were, then whistled long and low. "That looks sweet. Did you have a meltdown over it?"

"Only in private," Sandra said. "It's growing on me."

"Good for you. My mom screamed at me for a week when I did mine. She still complains whenever she sees me." She took a bowl of chips and a container of dip off the picnic table and wandered over to the shore to join the youngsters. She was twenty-six going on seventeen. My nieces were seventeen going on twenty-six. It worked. And she was a good influence. Strong, opinionated, independent, reliable as hell. She'd been my assistant since her junior year of college. I honestly didn't know how I could get by without her.

The guys wasted no time putting steaks on the grill. Mason

had it heated up and ready. Sandra and I unloaded the rest of the feast from her new car. Salads and desserts. In addition to the chips and dip, I'd contributed the salt potatoes, because it only involved boiling water and adding salt. Our other contributions included soft drinks, which were still inside.

"Jere!" I called. "Can you guys get the sodas for me?"

Jeremy came across from the reservoir, Misty hanging on his arm. They ignored us to go inside for said items.

"Sis, you gotta talk to your daughter. She's being way too clingy."

"Too clingy for who?" Sandra asked.

"Anyone with a gag reflex."

She rolled her eyes at me. "She misses him. And she's worried about the drinking. Said she didn't know. She couldn't believe he could hide something from her so completely, and I think realizing that shook her sense of security a little."

"I thought you didn't want her seeing him when he's drinking."

"I also said stopping teens in love would be like stopping a stampede of wild horses. But you said he's not drinking. Has that changed?"

"No. I'm sure he's still dry. I'll keep my eye on things." Misty was walking so close to him I thought their legs would get tangled. "She can't think this is a lifetime commitment they've got going, can she?"

"She's a teenage girl," Sandra said. "She's probably already got the wedding gown picked out."

I lowered my head, shook it. "They should wait until they're thirty."

"Just because you did?" She frowned at me. "Jeremy's not going to break Misty's heart, is he?"

"Not that I know of."

"He'd better not. I'll kick his ass myself."

I gaped at her, because my sister never swore. I loved her. She was a great parent. I'd love to ask her advice about Jeremy; whether we should tell him the truth about his father. But that secret was one even my sister didn't know.

The kids came back out. Jeremy was carrying the ice chest full of ice and pop.

I loved our summertime barbecues. If I had to pick any day of my life and relive it over and over forever, it would be a Saturday barbecue in my own front yard, with these very people. It felt great to know Mason felt exactly the same.

Myrt and Hugo abandoned the kids and came running as soon as the smoke from the grill reached their little smushed noses. Josh stood on the shore, feet in the water. It was already getting too cold, but you couldn't tell him that. He was gazing out kind of pensively. His hair was getting shaggy. The wind was blowing it a little. He'd grown unbelievably tall over the past year. He was almost as tall as Mason, but no bigger around than before. He had spaghetti arms and gangly legs. I reached behind me for my phone, zoomed in until it was just Josh and the sunset over the water and snapped.

Then I felt eyes on me, and shifted my gaze. Mason was looking at me, goofy smile halfway on his face. It was a perfect moment. I loved him so much it was ridiculous.

And then I saw a police car pull in, Rosie at the wheel, and right behind him, Chief V in her ride. They got out and I backed up five steps, right into Jeremy by some kind of sonar. My hands spread wide all by themselves.

Rosie was shaking his head, coming closer. The chief strode right up as Mason closed in beside me. Misty was there, too. Sandra and Jim had instinctively flanked Josh. Christy was sitting up in her chair, lowering her phone.

"I'm more sorry for this than I can say, Mason," the chief said. And I could see her eyes were troubled and maybe even damp. "There's new evidence. I have to place Jeremy under arrest."

"The hell you do."

Rosie pumped his hands for calm. "Mace, this don't mean a damn thing. He gets booked, he makes bail, he gets out. And you know we're gonna find who really did this. You know we are."

"I can't believe you're a part of this," Mason said. He was holding his long-time partner's eyes.

Rosie said, "I thought if it was me, I could make sure he's okay. Take care of him. But if you don't want me on this, I'm out." He raised his hands. "I'm out."

Mason stared at his friend for a long moment, but he didn't say either way.

Behind me, I heard a phone ringing, you know, from the other side. Jeremy was making a call–to Celia Moon, I hoped.

He took a few backward steps and I could only hear his low murmurs. I said, "How can you do this, Vanessa? I thought we were friends."

"I don't have a choice."

"No? What's this new evidence that's so compelling?"

"I can't tell you that."

"You'll have to tell his lawyer."

"And I will tell his lawyer."

"I will never forgive you for this."

Vanessa lowered her head. Her dark wavy hair fell over her face, and she just let it hang there. "I wouldn't, either."

She looked at Mason. He had an expression on his face that I had never seen before. It was one of pure disgust.

"I'm trying to keep you from destroying your career,

Brown. And I think that when all this is over, you're going to realize that."

Jeremy stepped around his uncle and me. Misty was wrapped around him like a spider monkey.

"It's okay, you guys," Jere said. "Celia says I should go with them. She'll meet us there."

Misty gave a yelp, like if someone had hauled off and kicked a puppy. He kissed her head. Said something soft in her ear, then gently unlocked her arms from around his waist.

She straightened up, lifted her chin, nodded once and gave two sniffles that crooked her nose each time. Jeremy stepped forward, held up his hands.

"Jere, no!" Josh torpedoed out of nowhere, hitting Jeremy so hard he almost took him down. "They can't do this!" And then he let go and turned to face Vanessa and Rosie. "You can't do this to us! Haven't we been through enough already? Dad killed himself and Mom went crazy–jeeziz, haven't we been through enough? You can't take my brother, too. You can't!" His face was red, his nose running, by the time he ran out of steam.

I started to go, but Jeremy beat me to it. He turned his kid brother around, and looked him in the eye. Josh was only a few inches shorter.

Jeremy said, "I didn't do anything, Josh, except drink myself stupid. I'm sorry. I can't stand seeing you like this, knowing it's my fault."

"It's not–"

"It is. But I didn't do anything to the professor. We're gonna prove that, and everything will be okay. I'm not gonna leave you, bro."

"You already did," Josh said. He pulled free of his brother's hands and ran into the house, slamming the door behind him.

"I'll go," Sandra said.

"Let me." Christy had come over from the dock. "Josh and I've been bonding lately." She headed inside.

Jeremy looked shocked by his brother's outburst. Then he looked at Mason, and then finally at me. I was the one he asked, "What the hell have I done?"

"You fucked up," I said. "We all do. You've got the best detective on the freaking force on your side, and me with my shit and Celia Moon, a badass attorney. We've got this. I promise."

He nodded, turned to Vanessa again and started to pick up his hands, even though he knew damn well you never cuff a suspect's hands in front of him. She shook her head, "No need." Then she nodded at Rosie.

Rosie looked at Mason. Mason nodded. "Take care of him."

"Like my own," Rosie said, one hand on Jeremy's shoulder. They started toward the car.

Vanessa called out, "Mirandize him, Rosie."

Rosie paused and sighed. I could see his big shoulders rise and fall from behind. He hadn't intended to do it, I realized. He was gonna skip reading Jere his rights so if worse came to worse, his lawyer could use it to have the case tossed.

And then he began the refrain we've all learned by heart from TV cop shows. "You have the right to remain silent...."

"I'm going with them," Mason said, "I'll call you to pick me up."

"Okay. Try not to punch anybody."

He looked confused.

"You look like you might want to punch somebody. I'm just saying, it won't help."

"It *might* help." He jumped into the passenger side of

Rosie's car, pretending not to notice Vanessa Cantone objecting.

When they pulled away, she met my eyes. She should've melted from the fury they beamed. "Never set foot here again, Chief Cantone."

"I'm sorry, Rachel. I really am."

I held up my hand, palm out, closed my eyes. "Go."

She turned and walked back to her car. I maintained that pose until I heard the door slam, the engine start, the tires crunching as she backed out. Then my sister put her arms around me, and I burst into noisy, messy tears. So did Misty, while Amy did her best to comfort her.

BY THE TIME I got it together, reassured Josh, and convinced him to have an overnight with Aunt Sandra and the girls, who adored him, Mason had been gone for an hour. We'd been texting the entire time. Jeremy was being questioned. He was only allowed to watch from outside the room. They hadn't booked him yet. Mason was trying to delay that for as long as possible. He was going to tell the chief everything we had on Ivy Newman, even though it wasn't much. He was going to mention the support group, the childhood abduction, the similar pendant, the whole nine. But he was afraid we'd need more to clear Jeremy.

I asked if I should come. I wanted to come. He said it wouldn't help. He said I should try that meditation of Natalia's again, see if I could get anything new, anything that would save Jeremy.

Hugo had gone to Sandra's with Josh, so it was just me and Amy and Myrt. Amy was sitting at the kitchen bar. She'd made us each a cup of decaf, cracked her knuckles, opened my laptop, and said, "Okay, what can we do?"

"What?"

I was distracted, watching my phone for texts, itching to go to Mason, to Jeremy.

"What can we do? Come on, you've been on this. Isn't your stuff telling you what we should do?"

"I can't think about anything but Jeremy under arrest. My God. He's just a kid." I was pacing the kitchen, my mug in my hands. "I should go. Mason says it wouldn't help, but at least I'd be close–"

"Or," she said, "You can use the skills God gave you and save your kid. So I repeat, what should we do? Ask your stuff, right now. Go on, I'll wait."

I rolled my eyes. "It doesn't work that way. I can't just say, 'hey stuff, what should I do?' and expect an answer to–"

Gloria Orr

I stopped talking, stopped pacing. "Gloria Orr," I said.

"Who's Gloria Orr?"

"Someone who might have some answers. And I know where she lives."

Amy slid off the stool. "Let's go, then."

"It could be dangerous. Maybe you should stay here."

"You kidding? Your crazy-ass stalker who burned his father alive is on the loose somewhere. I'm coming with you."

About forty-five minutes later, we were pulling to a stop in front of a cute little cape cod. Dried gourds, straw brooms, and a scarecrow paid homage to fall. I felt a little thrill in my veins at the reminder.

Fall was like fireworks to me. Only better. Where we lived, fall was, all by itself, sufficient reason to possess the senses of sight and smell.

"You wait here, I'll go to the door. See if she'll talk to

me." I'd filled Amy in as much as I could without revealing Ivy's secret past or Reggie D'Voe's secret still-aliveness.

"What are you going to say?"

"I don't know yet."

"Well, you ought to have something in mind, don't you think?" Amy asked. She had a nice diamond stud in her nose. Bought it for herself for Galentine's Day.

"Fine, um. 'hi, when I was stalking your support group last week, I noticed you skipped the last meeting and haven't posted online lately. Do you know anything about a bunch of murders?' And, scene."

"Just go," she said, rolling her eyes at me.

I opened the car door and got out. She said, "Wait! What's the signal? If you need help?"

"I'll text HELP."

"What if someone takes your phone?"

"Then I'll *scream* HELP."

"Okay." She nodded nervously. "Okay."

I went up and knocked on the door. There was a doorbell, but a doorbell wouldn't convey the correct–*ohmyGod, what is that smell?*

You know what it is, Inner Bitch said. *Nothing else smells like that.*

I hate when you're right, Inner Bitch.

I didn't want to put my hand on the doorknob in case there were prints. But as it turned out, I didn't have to. The door wasn't closed all the way. A nudge of my shoulder pushed it open. I edged my way inside, rethinking my stance on gun control. Sue me, in that moment, I was wishing for a big, manly *piece* in my hands, and not the good kind. I pressed my sleeve over my face because of the smell, peeked around a corner. I could see her bare feet. She was face up on the floor in front of the sofa, the rest of her was hidden from my view.

"Hello?" I asked, even though the feet were gray-blue. "Hello, are you okay?"

I'm dead. How could I be okay?

"Holy fuck fuck fuck *fuck*!" I skittered backwards all the way out the front door.

That wasn't you, was it, IB?

Nope.

Is it gone?

I don't know. You want it to be?"

A horn beeped. My horn. "You okay?" Amy called.

I held up a hand her way, like quiet or stop or something, while I looked around at nothing, listening, aiming my attention with my eyes. "Are you there?" I whispered.

Nothing.

"Sorry I freaked, okay? That never happened before. Exactly."

Nothing.

"Fine, be that way."

"Who the *hell* are you talking to?" Amy called.

"Gloria Orr is dead," I called back. "And I've gotta go back in and take a look around before the cops get here."

"Wait, she's *dead*?"

"Yeah, has been for a while, by the smell." I tapped Mason's number.

Amy puffed her cheeks out and lowered her head.

Mason finally picked up. "Hey, babe. What's up?"

"I decided to visit the missing support group member."

"How'd you…when did you get the address?"

"I tracked her down on social. Took two minutes. Thing is, I'm here, and she's dead." I dropped my phone into my front pocket on speaker, and pulled the scarf from my collar around my face. "Can you hear me?"

"Barely."

"There should be an anonymous tip, okay? I don't want them all distracted trying to figure out what I was doing over here."

"Don't poke around the scene," he said.

"How can I poke around? I was never here."

I hung up, and continued my walk-through. Nothing in the house seemed disturbed. The coffee pot had burned black, but nothing else seemed at all unusual, other than the dead woman on the living room floor.

Ahh, laptop. Maybe I should take that. And her cell phone, and yes…that little address book by the phone. Good, good.

You have to look at her.
I know I do, Inner Bitch.
Get it over with and get out of here.
Okay, okay. Stop rushing me.

I moved around the sofa, my face pulling into a grimace behind my scarf. She looked really bad. Eyes all sunken, skin all blue. Looked like she'd slid off the sofa. She lay on her back, between it and a coffee table. There was a needle on the table, a rubber hose on the floor.

So she overdosed.

The fuck I did.

I jumped damn near out of my skin that time. Then I noticed she wore a chain around her neck, with an oval medallion.

Wait a minute, wait a minute. It matched the one found in the professor's car, and the one Ivy had been wearing in the photo. I set down the laptop and pulled out my phone, scrolled back to my photos of the women coming out of the church after that meeting, enlarging each one, trying to see their necks. Of the three I could see, besides Ivy, two had chains on them, but they were tucked into their blouses.

Take the computer or leave it for the police? That was the question. Gloria Orr was connected to the murders. She was a member of the same child abuse support group, and she was wearing the same pendant. Chief V would have to see that. I snapped a pic of it on her body, just in case the police didn't. I left the computer where it was. Phone and phone book, too. The best way to clear Jeremy was to let the police find the real killer.

"I have to go now, Gloria," I said. "Unless you want to tell me who killed you."

Not just me.

I felt a whoosh. Not the sound, but the clear sensation. And she was gone. I knew it. I didn't know if she would return or not. I didn't know if she'd been hanging around waiting for her body to be found, or if she'd just popped in to provide a little commentary.

I tugged the scarf away from my face as I stepped outside and took a few grateful breaths of air. Then I headed for the sidewalk, angling across the lawn to put more distance between me and the corpse house.

Amy was waiting right where I'd left her. I got in, and she took off. "Aren't we waiting for the cops?"

"No."

"You okay?"

"No."

She nodded, took a corner, then another, picking her way toward the highway. "Where to now, boss?"

"Home," I said. "I need a shower."

15

Mason and Jeremy were alone together in a jail cell. The chief had put him in a private one, on the premises, and there were strict orders to keep it that way. The son of a homicide detective shouldn't be in a cell with others. It was common sense, not kindness.

He was furious with Chief Cantone. With the system. With everything.

"I need to know. About Dad. You get that, right?"

Mason brought his focus back to Jeremy. "I know you do. But this isn't the time."

"I fought with him, before he did it. Shot himself. For a long time, I thought it was because of me."

Mason looked Jeremy right in the eye and said, "It had nothing to do with you. He had…he was messed up, Jere. Mentally. He was doing things that left him racked with guilt, but he didn't feel like he could control himself. He couldn't live with it."

Jeremy's brows lowered. "What kinds of things?"

Mason looked at his kid, honestly, his son. He loved

Jeremy as much as he could ever love his own son. He said, "Jere, the details will do you more harm than good."

Jeremy lowered his head, closed his eyes and said, "It's that bad." It wasn't a question. Then he sighed heavily.

"It wasn't him. I will never believe it was him. I think Rachel can explain that better than I can, but…he killed himself so he wouldn't do any more harm. It was the only way he could see to make sure. It was a selfless act, really."

Jeremy sat very still, eyes focused on the space between him and the wall.

"I *will* tell you the rest, if you want to know. I'd just prefer we work through this crisis first."

"You don't think I can handle it." His voice was toneless, dull, and deeper than Mason's own.

"Like you keep telling me, you're an adult now. You know what you can handle better than I do. But if writing an essay about your mother sent you into a drinking binge, then…" He didn't finish the sentence. He didn't need to. "We'll get you bailed out after the arraignment tomorrow."

Celia Moon had come and gone already, promising Jeremy would only have to spend one night behind bars. "We'll get you home. We'll get you on solid ground, and then we'll tell you everything. But in the meantime, Jere, it's real important you don't bring this up with anyone else. Especially here."

"Why?" he asked.

"Because Rachel and your mother and I are the only three people in the world who know the truth. And I'd just as soon keep it that way."

The kid lowered his head. He muttered, "You should go," and his voice was thick.

Mason's heart clenched up, and he put a hand on Jeremy's shoulder from behind. "Jere–"

"It's okay. It's okay, I just need to get my head together. Get some sleep."

"Okay. All right, Jere." He got up and went to the cell door. "We're gonna talk it out. I promise. Soon as you get home, if you want. Or when all this is over, if you think that would be better. It's your call."

He didn't reply, didn't turn around.

Mason left the cell and went back through the hallway to the secure doors. But as he stood there, waiting for a guard to buzz him out, a chill ran down his spine. All of the sudden, he had a horrible feeling that Jeremy might already know the truth about his old man.

He got his phone back at the desk, along with a lot of sympathetic looks from the detectives and staff. Rosie was waiting for him, clasped his hand, and hugged with the other arm. "Cantone feels like shit for this, partner."

"She should," he said, then more softly as they walked into the hallway together. "What's the new evidence? What brought this on?"

Rosie glanced behind them, then leaned close. "Campus security footage. He said in his sworn statement he never left his dorm room after the encounter with the professor on Thursday. But he did. He took his car out of the parking lot, was gone for an hour. Parked in a different spot when he got back."

"Someone else moved the professor's car that night, probably with him in it, then put it back after. Is that on camera, too?"

Rosie shook his head. "I thought of that, too. But no. Broken camera in that area. Probably not a coincidence, if you ask me."

"Is that all they've got?"

"All I know of. If I hear anything more, I'll let you know."

"Thank you for that."

"He's your kid. Listen, Mace, is he okay?"

"He's still drying out. That's between us."

"Not really. He admitted he'd been drinking in his statement. Cantone transferred me to guard duty for as long as he's here. I'm not going home until he does. I'll make sure he's okay."

"Thanks, Rosie."

"The body they found, earlier–does that have anything to do with all this?"

"Maybe. She belonged to the same support group as those women I sent you the plate numbers for. You ever get the rest of those run down?"

"Yeah, yeah, so much going on I forgot to send it. I'll text you the file."

Mason's phone pinged. He glanced down and saw ten messages from Rachel on his screen. "I've gotta go." He didn't say why, and Rosie didn't ask. They both knew Mason was off to find the real killer and clear his kid. He headed out, and it felt like he was leaving most of his insides behind.

MASON GOT home around ten thirty. I was glad. Being alone in the house was creeping me out. I'd got used to having the Brown men around. Sure, I had Myrtle and Hugo, but it wasn't exactly the same. The dogs were great company, but they'd let anyone slit my throat for a Scooby snack.

That was a morbid thought.

Sure was, Inner Bitch.

He threw his keys on the stand by the door, heeled off

his shoes, came through the foyer into the living room where the lights were down low. I was curled on the sofa in sweats and cushy socks, with a laptop and a cup of hot cocoa.

"How did you know about Gloria Orr?" he asked. No hello, or how are you holding up, or so much as a kiss. My alarm bells started jangling.

"She was the missing member from the support group. No one's heard from her in three days. I told you that. And my stuff said her name in my head. So I found her address on the net and went to see her. Found her dead."

"Looks like an overdose," he said.

"Not according to Gloria."

He closed his eyes slow. I could see the strain on his face. He didn't have lines around his mouth, he had dimples. This was not the Mason I was used to seeing.

"I asked 'who killed you,' and she said, 'not just me.' That was all I got. Other than the medallion–"

"Matched the one in the professor's car, and in the photo of Ivy Newman," he said. "I saw that, too." He wasn't right. I felt it.

"I made you cocoa. Well, I dumped the packet into the mug. Water's still hot."

He nodded, but didn't move to go to the kitchen to get it. He looked dead on his feet. I got up, set my mug on the coffee table and went over to him. "Hey, are you okay?"

He pressed his lips, looked away a little, tried to talk and then had to swallow before he could get a word out. "I think Jeremy knows, Rache. I think somehow, he already knows."

"Knows what?" I knew the answer before I finished the question. "You mean about Eric?"

He nodded. "I said we'd tell him everything as soon as he's back home. But I think he already knows."

The breath left my lungs like it was evacuating the place. "This was probably inevitable."

"Probably." He sank onto the sofa, pulled my laptop around to face him. I hadn't bothered closing it. "What's all this?"

"Medallion research. The image is Nemesis, Goddess of Vengeance. Also known as Rhamnousia, which I gather also translates to Goddess of Vengeance."

He glanced quickly my way, then back to the images I'd pulled up. In some of them, the goddess was winged. In some she carried a set of scales. But in all of them, she wielded a double-edged sword and was apparently very pissed off.

I wandered to the kitchen, poured hot water into his mug, and carried it back, stirring as I went.

"This links Gloria Orr to the murders."

"Links all of them to the murders," I said. "Potentially, anyway." I handed him the mug and sat down beside him, leaning over him to click through the photos I'd taken. "I think almost all the group members wear one. Look, see? Several of them are wearing chains around their necks. Ivy's is the only one with the medallion visible. The rest are tucked into their blouses."

His brows bent and he leaned closer to the screen.

"I've been mulling this all afternoon. This is a support group for victims of childhood sexual assault, all of them wearing a symbol of retribution."

"They're vigilantes," he said.

"Maybe not all of them. Otherwise, why would Gloria be dead?"

"She couldn't handle the guilt."

"No. I said suicide and she screamed in my ear, 'No fucking way'."

He looked at me, waited, like he thought I'd say more. Then he said, "Is that everything?"

I frowned.

"Did you take anything from the crime scene? Or leave anything behind?"

"No."

"Did anyone see you there?"

"I don't think so. No one but Amy, at least."

"Have you talked to Ivy about this?"

"Ivy? Why the hell would I talk to Ivy about this?"

He stared at me for a long moment, not answering, and I rose slowly from the sofa. "Mason, why the third degree?"

"I'm just asking, Rache. I'm Just asking."

"And I'm just answering. No. I have not talked to Ivy about this."

He nodded slowly, then said, "If they all have the same pendant, then we just need to figure out which one is missing to know who killed the professor."

"And who killed all the others," I said.

"Not *all* the others. Ivy killed Dwayne," he said. "You know it and I know it." He took out his phone and started tapping its screen.

Inner Bitch said, *Doesn't matter what you know. It's what you can prove.*

And we don't have a shred of evidence against Ivy, I thought back. *NFP is inadmissible.*

We arrived in the courtroom promptly, and sat right behind Jeremy and Celia Moon. The District Attorney presenting the case was not a Rachel de Luca fan. He had expressed the opinion online that my books were bullshit, to which I had replied something along the lines of, "you wouldn't know a good book if I smacked you upside the head with one, which I'd be happy to prove, should we ever meet."

I shouldn't have done that, especially considering that I used to think the same thing about my books.

We all rose as the judge walked in. Jeremy looked back at us, and it was a knife in my heart to see the fear in his eyes. He was scared shitless.

"Be seated." The judge was a large black man who looked like a body builder, had close cropped salt and pepper hair, and square framed red glasses. I loved that particular style choice.

"I've seen the evidence and I'm ready to set bail, unless either side has anything to add. Counsel?"

Celia Moon rose from her chair. "Your honor, we have several witnesses who say the professor provoked Mr. Brown deliberately. We want to reiterate that my client is profusely sorry for losing his temper, but also that punching someone who richly deserves it does not indicate a capacity for murder."

"Oh, come on! His DNA was found in the car, your honor!" The prosecutor didn't even get up on his feet.

They have DNA? Holy fuck.

"Transferred from the professor himself when he got in immediately after a physical altercation with my client," Moon stated.

"And what about the other victims?" the prosecutor snapped. Still not getting up, acting like he hadn't just dropped a bombshell.

"Other victims?" Judge Reynolds lowered his glasses halfway down his nose.

"The police department has a string of unsolved homicides with similarities to the professor's abduction."

Celia was shaking her head the whole time the DA spoke. "Absolutely false, your honor. Those bodies were dumped in locations where they would be easily found. The professor is still missing, and we have no reason to believe he's been killed."

"Four of the five victims were tortured before they were killed," the DA said. "Maybe the professor hasn't yet suffered enough to die."

A soft cry, and then a woman got up and hurried out of the courtroom. The professor's wife. Man, this DA was a heartless bastard. A loud murmur rose from the people in the courtroom.

The judge pounded his gavel and everyone settled down. Then he nodded at the DA to continue.

"Your Honor, the defendant's mother is in a locked psych unit for a string of grisly murders."

Celia said, "That's meaningless, inadmissible, and a transparent attempt to influence this court! Your Honor, there has never been a serial killer whose offspring was also a serial killer–"

"That we know of," the DA said over her.

"–and we're not even sure that's what we *have* in this case." Celia Moon never even paused in her rant. "This young man intends to enter the police academy after college. He's the nephew and ward of a decorated detective and a spiritual self-help author."

The DA snorted.

I tried to set his hair on fire with my eyes.

"He has a clean record," Celia went on. "He's an outstanding young man."

The judge pursed his lips and nodded slowly. Then he looked at the DA and said, "Any bad blood between you and this family, Taylor?"

"Not unless you count him publicly trashing my work all over the net," I said, on my feet and out of order.

The judge gave me a look. "When I want to hear from you, Ms. de Luca, I will tell you so. Sit down."

"Sorry, Your Honor." I sat.

"Your Honor, may I speak?"

I was surprised to hear Chief Vanessa Cantone's dulcet tones from the back of the courtroom, and turned to see her standing up, facing the judge.

"Chief Cantone, if you feel you have something significant to add, by all means."

She said, "I know Jeremy Brown quite well, the entire family, as a matter of fact. These are good people. I do not believe for a minute that this young man is capable of true violence. A punch in the nose when provoked, sure, but who among us hasn't done that?" She looked around. The DA reluctantly raised his hand. Celia rolled her eyes. "Further, I can reiterate that we have not determined the other recent murders are the work of the same killer, and have even less basis for suspecting the professor's disappearance is connected to them."

The judge nodded slowly, then looked right at Jeremy. "You have anything to say, Mr. Brown?"

"I'm innocent, Your Honor. But if I hadn't been drinking, I wouldn't be in this situation right now. For that, I'm more sorry than I can say. I'm sorry for what this is doing to my family, especially my little brother. But not for myself. This is all my own fault. I'm done with alcohol, and I mean it. I deserve to go through hell for being such an idiot. But I did not abduct or harm Professor Ashton." He looked the judge right in the eye when he said it.

The judge saw his soul, I think. "I'm going to release you on house arrest. You'll wear an ankle monitor, submit to random, unannounced drug and alcohol testing, and stay within one hundred yards of your uncle's home at all times. Be on your best behavior, son. You mess up, you live in a cell until trial."

"Yes, sir. Understood. Thank you, Your Honor."

"Your Honor," the prosecutor said. "I object strenuously to this–"

"Shut up, Taylor. I've made my decision. Trial date is set for…three weeks from today. You'll receive official notification." He banged his gavel. "Get out. Bailiff, call the next case."

Two officers came in, spoke briefly to Jere and Celia, too low for me to hear, then took Jeremy out a side door.

"Wait…where–?"

Celia held up a hand. "They need to put the ankle monitor on. It'll be a minute. Come with me, you can drive him home."

We walked out the main entrance of the courtroom into a hall with domes and hardwood and art deco lights. Chief V came out behind us, rocking her short skirt and blazer combo like nobody's business.

"Mason, a minute?"

He turned to her. He was still furious, turned back and walked away without a word.

I hung back. "Thank you for helping out in there, Chief," I said.

"I did what I could."

"You lied. We all know the murders are connected."

"Not officially."

"Still, I appreciate it."

"I know you do. I hope Mason does, too."

"He does. And if it's any comfort, he's a little pissed at me, too, right now."

"What did *you* do?"

I shrugged.

"Are you…" She glanced around us before continuing, then lowered her voice, "…*getting* anything on all this?"

"I'm getting close," I said.

"You two are investigating this off the books, aren't you?"

"What do you think?"

"Don't fuck up the case, Rachel, and don't let Mason fuck up his career. Be careful."

"I know. We know."

"Okay. Good." She looked at her watch. "I have to go."

It had to do with this mess, I felt it to my toes. "Where?" I asked.

She looked at me. "I do have other cases besides this one, you know."

"Yeah, but where you're going has to do with this one."

She held my eyes. "It creeps me out when you do that."

"I don't fucking care. And you might as well tell me, because I'll just follow you if you don't."

She sighed, rolled her eyes. "We found a body yesterday."

"Gloria Orr, I know."

"Of course you know. Why wouldn't you know?"

"So?"

"She rents a storage unit out in the sticks. We found a receipt in her papers. We're meeting the owner there to get a look inside."

"I want to come, too."

"No shit, and Mason too, I bet, but I can't let you."

"Yes, you can."

"You want me fired? You want some hard ass in here who hates you both? No. Go home. Take care of Jeremy. I'll fill you in as much as I can, and Mason's faithful partner will tell him everything that I can't." My eyes must've widened, because she said, "What? You think I don't know Rosie's keeping him apprised? I tried shutting that down, but the other cops keep Rosie apprised. They love Mason."

"He's a lovable guy."

"Go home." She walked away, down the hall toward the exit.

I ran the other way, the way Mason and Celia had gone. Just when I worried I wouldn't find them, they came out a door with Jeremy between them. Thank God.

I ran up to them, hugged Jeremy's neck, and he hugged me back. Mason looked dour.

"Celia," I said. "I need a minute with my guys."

Celia nodded "I'll meet you out front."

As soon as she was out of earshot, I said, "Gloria Orr had a storage unit. Cantone's on her way there. I need to be there when they bust it open."

"I'll go," Mason said.

"Yeah, and get fired, or worse," I said.

"Who's Gloria Orr?" Jeremy asked.

"Mace will fill you in on the way home." I looked my man in the eyes. "I might be able to get something the cops can't. Please, let me do this."

I told him with my eyes, with my heart, that I needed his trust. I told him this was an important moment. And I think he heard me.

He took out his keys, handed them over. "Take the car. I'll find us a ride."

"Thank you. I love you. Both of you. See you at home."

I took the keys and ran down the hall to the exits, hoping I could still catch sight of Vanessa's car so I could follow her. As I went, I heard Jeremy ask, "So? Who's Gloria Orr?"

16

Mason thanked Celia for the ride and he and Jeremy headed for the house. He stopped at the door. "All right, here's the deal-I have to go out in a little bit. Don't go anywhere."

"I'm not gonna go anywhere," Jeremy replied, like he should've known that. But Mason's faith in the kid's common sense was a little bit shaky at the moment, so he reiterated his point. "That monitor has been activated by now."

"I'm aware of that. The little green light was a pretty big clue." He turned his ankle and hiked up the leg of his jeans to illustrate his point.

"Your brother will be back in two hours. I'll be back by then, too." He looked at Jeremy, shook his head. "I don't know if I can just leave you on your own after all you've been through today."

"Or maybe you just don't trust me," Jeremy said.

"I do trust you. I don't expect you to do anything deliberately. I am a little bit afraid you'll stumble headfirst into more trouble, though. Maybe for perfectly legitimate reasons but still..."

Jeremy sighed. Then he said, "I guess I had that coming." Then he tapped his phone to life and turned its face toward Mason's, showing him some texts. "Misty's on her way over. See? I'm not going anywhere."

Two hours alone with his girlfriend. Okay, he wasn't going anywhere. Mason felt better. Then he clapped Jere by his nape, and pressed their foreheads together. "I love you. You know that, right?"

"Psssh." He turned his head away. "I know it. I love you, too. You going off to solve the crime and save my ass?"

"Gonna do my best." He let go of Jeremy's neck, opened the door and they went inside. Jeremy headed upstairs, probably to make sure he was minty fresh for Misty.

He brewed a cup of coffee, went into the living room and opened Rachel's laptop. He knew her password. She knew his. They didn't have any reason to keep them from each other. He logged in and found the photo file, automatically backed up from her phone. She'd named it "Victim Vigilantes."

He smiled a little and wondered if she was thinking of novelizing the case once it was solved. She'd always talked about writing a thriller.

He copied the whole file to himself, then forwarded it to Chief Cantone's personal cell number, and waited.

He didn't have to wait long.

"What the hell is this?"

"List of suspects we should round up for questioning," he said.

"Right. And it came to you by magic, being that you're supposed to be staying out of this case."

"By magic. Yeah. Gloria Orr and these other women were members of the same support group. They all have the same pendant as the one we found in Ashton's car. It's a vengeance goddess, by the way. The license plates will ID them. Run the tags."

"I can do that. It's flimsy on cause, though."

"I don't want you to do anything but pick them up for questioning. And coordinate it so they don't have time to contact each other, get their stories straight or whatever."

"That makes sense."

"And tell me when it's go-time."

"Why?"

"Because I want to pick up one of them myself."

"But you're on leave."

"So take me off leave."

He heard her exhale nasally, could picture the slight flare of her nostrils because he'd seen it on many occasions when he'd pushed her patience to the brink. "Any one in particular?" she asked at length.

"Yes."

"What aren't you telling me, Mason?"

"Nothing I can prove," he said. "Nothing there's a shred of evidence for. Yet. If there was, you'd have it. My kid's on the line here."

"I know. I know. How is he holding up?"

"He'll be better when we find out who did all this and clear him. So? Will you text me when it's go-time?"

"Yeah. And it'll be soon."

"Anything in that storage unit?"

"We're opening it right now. I'm sure your busybody better half will fill you in."

"She's hard to shake, isn't she?"

"Like a fucking tick. Gotta go. Don't do anything stupid."

I WATCHED from my car in a parking lot behind a McDonald's. I had a pretty decent view of the storage place, which was next door with nothing but a couple of raised beds indicating the border between the two. I'd parked strategically, a Dumpster mostly blocking the car from view of anyone over there. They were too occupied to notice me, anyway. Although Chief V knew I was nearby. She'd looked right over here a second ago. Not much got past her. It was good she'd accompanied the team to the site. Her hands-on approach was popular with the public, but that wasn't her motive. She liked the action. She missed being a cop. I don't know if she knew I was aware of that.

I munched my fries, because, what? I'm gonna be this close to a McD's and *not* get food?

Not on my watch, Inner Bitch promised.

So, I munched my fries and watched as Chief Cantone pocketed her phone. A guy with a big chomping tool cut the padlock off the unit. I chewed faster, leaning over the steering wheel. The sectioned metal door rolled upward. It was dark inside. I got out, taking my fries with me, moving closer, no longer caring whether anyone saw me. I had to see what was in there.

Someone found a light switch, turned it on. I walked faster. I was wearing pumps, because I'd dressed nice for court, so the tap-tap-tap of them over the pavement was loud as hell. But everyone was staring at the unit's interior, and when I got close enough to see, so was I.

My first impression was of blood. Splashes, spatters, streaks on the walls. A dark puddle on the floor. And a flash of pain that shot through my entire being before I slammed the door on it, not even knowing how. I was moving closer, on auto-pilot. My feet were driving, my head still trying to process what I was seeing, while my stuff was telling me that Professor Ashton was no longer alive. I dragged my gaze off the blood, widened my focus. There was a table in the middle of the unit with built-in leather restraints. There was a meat hook hanging from above.

I had moved right up beside the chief, when I blurted, "What the actual fuck?"

Cantone turned to send me a look that was irritated, but not surprised. "Nobody goes inside," she said. "Get forensics out here. First thing I want is that blood analyzed. Find out if it's the professor's."

"I'm pretty sure it is," I said. "But Gloria Orr didn't do this. She still had her pendant."

"You can't be here," she said, instead of asking what I was talking about.

"It's okay, I'm not staying long."

"You can't be here, Rachel."

"I understand. You're absolutely right." I craned my neck to see more of the unit. The left wall had knives and a hatchet attached to a pegboard meant to hold tools. Well, they were tools. Bloodstained tools. Tools of murder. There were other items, too. "Is that a cattle prod?"

"*Rachel–*"

"I'm going." The other wall was just a wall. "He must've been here the whole time," I said. "Until they killed him."

"We don't know anyone killed him."

"You're gonna want to find out how fresh that blood is," I said. "So you can tell if he was moved before or after Gloria Orr was murdered."

"Gloria Orr overdosed."

"Not voluntarily."

Ivy, said a voice in my head. It sounded a lot like Gloria Orr.

Chief V looked at me, then looked harder, frowning. "You should tell me what you know."

"I just did tell you what I know. And now I have to leave." I headed back to the car, and tossed my fries into a wastebasket on the way.

I CALLED OUR LANDLINE. Jeremy picked up, and I smiled, glad to hear his voice. "How are you doing, kid?"

"Glad to be home, that's for sure. I didn't need the ankle bracelet to keep me from leaving. Misty's here."

"Good." I looked at my watch. "Remind Mason to make Josh an after-school snack. He'll be home soon."

"Mason's not here, and Josh can make his own snacks. He's thirteen, Aunt Rache."

"What do you mean, Mason's not there?"

"He said he had to go. Something about the case."

And he didn't text us? Inner Bitch asked, sounding about as offended as I felt. *I thought we were working this together.*

IVY, said the voice in my head.

"Anything wrong, Aunt Rache?"

I had been quiet for a few beats too long. "No, no, I'll text him and find out what's up. No worries, kid. We're on this. Love you. Bye."

I couldn't tell him the professor had been tortured and murdered in a storage unit. Not until I could also tell him the evidence cleared him of the crime.

I texted Mason. "Where R U?" Then waited.

There was no reply, not all the way to Dilmun. And I didn't know whether to be pissed off or worried. The voice in my head chose worry. My love for my kid leaned the other way. I pulled through the open gate and along the driveway to Reginald D'Voe's gothic monstrosity.

I got out and went to the front door, my maternal ferocity wrapped around me like a she-bear's bristled fur. I was here, so I was going to make good use of the opportunity to make Ivy Newman tell me what she knew about all this. *All* of it.

Ivy opened the door before I even knocked and stood there looking at me with those big wounded eyes of hers.

I wasn't going to soften under their dampness, though. I clung to my fury. "I don't know if you heard yet, but Gloria Orr–"

"She's dead. I know." She tipped her head to one side. "But how do you know?"

"I live with a cop, remember?"

"I mean, how do you know I even know her?"

"Let me in and I'll tell you."

She frowned and said, "Are you angry at me for some reason?"

"Let me in and I'll tell you," I repeated. I wasn't up for bullshit and I wasn't here to comfort her on the loss of her friend. I was here to get some answers and clear my kid.

She opened the door wider, waved an arm sarcastically. "By all means, come in. Nothing could top this day more perfectly than a visit from a pissed-off, crime-solving psychic."

"I am *not* fucking psychic." I went inside, though, past her.

She swung the door closed behind me. "According to Reggie, you are." She turned and walked further into the house, past the comfortable living room off to the left, and straight through the foyer to the kitchen off the far side. "And Reggie doesn't lie."

"He's mistaken then. Doesn't matter. My kid's in trouble, Ivy. He's in trouble for something he didn't do."

"Sit. You want anything? Coffee? Tea?"

"I want answers." I didn't sit. I stood behind the chair, though, at the small table for two near the tall windows, arms crossed over my chest. That was automatic, that pose. Like I was trying to keep something out, when what I needed to do was let something in. I forced my arms to my sides, tried to open myself to her.

She poured herself a cup of coffee, poured me one, too, set them both on the table. "Cream?" she asked, opening the fridge.

"Who killed Gloria?"

I felt a cold shock ripple through her, despite that the fridge door blocked her from my view.

She closed the door slowly, a pretty porcelain cream pitcher in one hand, and turned to look at me. "Someone killed her? Mel didn't tell me that on the phone."

"Mel?"

"Yes. My therapist."

"The one who leads the support group?"

Her eyes went round. I reached out, caught the pitcher just as her hand went limp. I'd moved before she'd even dropped the thing. She was unimpressed.

"How do you know about my support group? I go all the way to Endwell to protect my privacy."

I turned, put the cream pitcher on the table. "I followed you. I know the names and addresses of all the members." I didn't yet, but I would as soon as Rosie ran those plates for Mason. "I know you all wear a pendant with the image of Nemesis, goddess of vengeance–"

"Justice." She said it so fast I knew she'd blurted it without forethought.

"You wearing yours now?"

Blinking rapidly, she tugged the chain from underneath her blouse. "Why wouldn't Mel tell me Gloria was murdered?"

"Because as far as anyone is yet admitting, it was a run-of-the-mill overdose."

"Overdose of what?"

"Toxicology will tell for sure, but it looks like heroin."

"God." It was a whisper, maybe even a prayer. She was still standing. Her knees were jelly, though, I could tell by the way she wobbled.

A little bit of my tough bitch attitude cracked. "You need to sit down."

"Yeah. Let's uh…take this to the living room."

I picked up both mugs and followed her into the living room. She moved like someone who was almost too tired to put one foot in front of the other. But it felt like an emotional exhaustion more than a physical one.

There were coasters, so I used them, set our mugs on the coffee table, and took a small chair. She sat in the big one that I sensed was Reggie's. It felt like he was hugging her when she sat in his big chair. I got all that as she sank into it. I also got that Reggie was upstairs, asleep.

"I don't believe Gloria was a drug user," she said.

"She only had one track mark."

She wanted to ask how I knew that, then decided she didn't want to know. "And you're sure it wasn't...self-inflicted?"

"I'm sure. She had a storage unit. It was set up like a torture chamber. Table with restraints. Saws and knives and tasers hanging from hooks on the wall. Blood all over the floor."

She burst into tears, and *burst* is the word, like water

balloon meets porcupine. She cried noisily. I sipped my coffee, looked at my mug, and tried to feel her.

Not Gloria, not Gloria, it couldn't have been Gloria.

"The working theory will be that she killed all of them," I said. "But that theory probably won't hold up to the physical evidence in the locker. You'd better believe I'm not letting my kid go down for this."

"Your kid?"

"Yeah. He was the top suspect, before they found Gloria's locker. So I need you to tell me everything you know, Ivy, and I need you to tell me now."

I heard a vehicle. A familiar one. A car door slammed.

"God, what now?" Ivy muttered, but footsteps pounded up the porch stairs, and the knock was only for show. Mason opened the door and walked right in.

He looked at me. Clearly he'd seen my car outside, so he already knew I was there. But his eyes wouldn't hold mine. He shifted his focus straight to Ivy.

"I need you to come to the police station with me, Ms. Newman. You are a material witness in a murder investigation, and if you don't come voluntarily, I'll–"

I shot across the floor and grabbed his arm. "Mason, what the hell are you doing? What's going on?"

"We're bringing all the members of the support group in for questioning," he said. "Picking them up at the same time to prevent them from collaborating on a storyline. What the hell are *you* doing? You come to warn her?"

"How could I warn her when I had no idea you were planning this?"

"You were with the chief when I texted her."

"I did not know you texted her," I denied. "You used *my* research."

"I did. We had Rosie running the plates, anyway, to clear Jeremy."

"That's *exactly* my goal here."

"You could've fooled me."

"I'll come," Ivy said loudly. She probably would confess, if we kept up the stupid arguing in front of her. Talk about torture. We sounded like a pair of idiots who didn't appreciate what we had in each other.

Ivy got to her feet and let her head fall forward. "I'll come with you, Detective."

"You will do no such thing!" The bellow came from the top of the stairs, and it was followed by the footstep-cane-thump cadence of Reginald D'Voe descending. He wore his signature smoking jacket; long black satin with red swirls and a wide red lapel.

Ivy ran to the foot of the stairs to grip his arm and help him. "It's okay, Reggie, I need to do this–"

"What you need to do, dear girl, is sit down and be quiet. And I mean that with every cell in my body. Not another word." He shoved her off him, toward the sofa.

She stumbled three steps, clearly stunned and wounded, looking at him like she'd never seen him before.

"Detective Brown, I'll text my attorney to meet us at the police department. I presume you're willing to transport me there?" He tapped his phone as he spoke.

Mason looked at me, and for a second it was like before. Us communicating without a word. Him asking *WTF?* and me replying *Damned if I know*. Then he shifted back to the dying actor again. "Mr. D'Voe, I need to question Ivy. You're not a material witness–"

"Not any sort of witness, my good man. I am the Riverside Strangler."

"Reggie, no!" Ivy cried.

"Not. One. Word." He sent her a firm glare, then returned his gaze to his phone, and hit a few more keys before pocketing it and facing Mason again. "I did it. I killed them all. I insist you take me in and accept my confession. I'll give you all the details you need, providing certain conditions are met. Ivy, of course, knows nothing about any of this. Moreover, she's under psychiatric care and on medications that would render anything she has to say regarding this matter, entirely unreliable and likely inadmissible, as well."

"Sir, I get what you're trying to do, but–"

"I know details only the killer would know, Detective. I know about the pendant you found in the professor's car. It was mine. I had a copy made, as a show of emotional support to show solidarity with Ivy and her fellow survivors. I can even tell you where to find the newest body, if you like."

I grabbed Mason's arm, and he looked at me, and I shook my head side to side very slightly. The actor was spewing lies. Possibly even reciting lines. There's no way Reggie D'Voe tortured anyone, much less had access to Gloria Orr's storage locker. He didn't even *know* Gloria.

"I knew all the girls in the support group," Reggie said. And I sent him a stunned look. Dammit, he was reading me. He was reading all of us. "We hosted several gatherings here. Teas and dinners and the like. Gloria mentioned the storage unit and I knew it would be the perfect spot to use. I stole her key from her bag. I'm not prone to tell you more until you comply. If you refuse to take me in, I'll have my lawyer pick me up here instead of meeting me there. Either way, this is happening."

"I can't let you do this, Reggie," Ivy said. "Please, don't–"

"If you ever loved me, Ivy, respect my wishes in this now. My *dying* wishes."

"But Uncle Reggie–"

He hit the floor with the stick so hard it sounded like a gunshot, and Ivy jumped out of her skin. So did I. "I don't have all day, Detective Brown." Reggie walked to the door, opened it, and headed down the steps to the car.

"Meet us there, Ms. Newman," Mason said. "I still have questions for you."

"You will stay right here, Ivy, until and unless you are presented with a warrant," Reggie called, not even looking back. "You will speak to no one until Attorney Helmsford has advised you. Understood?"

"Yes, Uncle Reggie."

"No one," he said again, and he did look back then.

She had tears streaming. "Everyone will know you're alive," she whispered.

"Indeed. It will be quite the media circus." He shrugged. "It'll be nice to be on the front pages again, one last time."

Mason followed the old man out to his car. He didn't look back at me, didn't say shit. Doors opened, doors closed, and the car pulled away. I turned to Ivy.

"We both know Reggie didn't kill anyone."

She pursed her lips, met my eyes through her own very wet ones, and said, "I'm afraid I can't talk to you anymore right now, Rachel. Please go."

"I'm not going anywhere until we–"

"I said get out!" She lurched at me like a maniac, fire in her eyes, and she pushed me right through the door, then slammed it. Locks snapped into place. I stood there gaping, stunned right to my core.

I didn't know she had it in her.

Had I been reading her wrong this whole time? Was that even possible?

I CALLED the kids to check in, yes while driving, but I used the handsfree crap that really doesn't help at all. I mean, come on, admit it. You still have to look away to make it work. I stand by my claim that some laws are moronic, and I break those laws at will, despite that my love interest is a cop.

I hoped that situation wasn't about to change, because damn he was mad at me.

Jere picked up his cell. "Hey, Rache. What's up?"

No "aunt" just "Rache." Probably because Misty was there to impress. It shouldn't bug me, but it did. "Good news and bad news, kid."

"Good news first," he said. "I'm putting you on speaker. Josh and Misty are right here."

"Okay, the good news. Someone has confessed to the crime you're accused of. Or is about to. Mason's driving him in now."

Misty whooped out loud, and I think she hugged Jeremy. The phone got all muffled for a second. Josh said, "YES!" and I could imagine him pumping his fist in the air. Hugo snuffle-barked, picking up on the excitement. I didn't hear Myrtle, but it took a lot to get her excited these days.

"Myrt with you guys?" I asked.

"Yeah, she's right here," Josh called. "She's sittin' on my foot right now."

Then Jere said, "What's the bad news?"

"He didn't do it."

"The guy who's confessing?"

"Right. Totally didn't do it. He only confessed to protect someone your uncle was about to drag off in manacles, who also didn't do it. Mostly. I think."

"Shit."

"Put a dollar in the swear jar. And don't worry. This is all pointing us closer to the truth. We're going to get to the bottom of this, Jere, and very soon. But in the meantime, I imagine you'll be off the cops' radar. Maybe you should give your lawyer the heads-up so she can get the ball rolling on your behalf."

"I will. Are you coming home?" he asked. It broke my heart that he sounded so deflated.

"Yeah. I was going to go to the PD, but…I miss you guys. And I desperately need some bulldog love."

"Good. I was just gonna grill some burgers outside. Want me to throw one on for you?"

"Yeah, thanks Jere." That was a switch. Normally he'd have asked me to bring home food. He was growing up, or trying to. And if a hard childhood could make or break a man, I was betting on it making this one. He was good through and through.

SOMETIME AFTER ELEVEN, Mason came through the front door, heeled off his shoes, scuffed straight through to the kitchen and opened the refrigerator without turning on a single light. I could see the dark circles under his eyes in the glow that spilled from the fridge.

I was sitting at the bar in the dark waiting for him and sipping Diet Coke spiked with the vodka I'd stashed in my office, where it wouldn't tempt Jeremy.

"There's a burger for you. Bun, lightly toasted. Veggies already chopped. All in separate containers. I know how you hate when things get soggy."

He stiffened when I started talking, waited until I was

finished to close the fridge and turn around. "You didn't have to wait up."

"Of course I had to wait up. We're on the fritz and I want to know why. Did you really think I ran out there to warn Ivy Newman you were coming for her?"

"Why the hell else would you have been out there? *Again*? Without even telling me?"

"Um, first off, I love you, but you do not own me. I don't have to tell you everywhere I go and everything I do and you have no right to demand that. Furthermore, you went out without telling me where, and then when I texted you, you ghosted me."

"I don't have to tell you everywhere I go and everything I do," he said, heavy on the sarcasm.

"I went to Ivy's to find out what she knew about the murder of Gloria Orr and clear Jeremy. And also because I'm pretty sure the aforementioned Gloria told me to. Fuck, Mason, that you'd even come up with any scenario other than that is bullshit."

"You've been protecting her."

"Not at Jeremy's expense. And not at yours."

He slid onto a stool across from me. I pushed the second drink I'd made across the counter to him.

"You knew I was on my way."

"I was saving time. Knew I'd want at least two. Possibly four or five."

He looked at the glass, then pushed it away.

I pulled his glass over next to mine. "I was hiding behind a dumpster at the McD's next door while you were texting with the chief. I saw her on the phone right before they opened the unit. But how was I supposed to know you were going to try to drag Ivy in for questioning?"

"How do you know anything you're not supposed to?"

"Not by going through my lover's computer when he's not home, that's for goddamn sure."

"There shouldn't be booze in the house when Jere's home."

"It's hidden in my office, which is off limits, and also locked since he's been home. Any other critique you'd like to share?"

He lowered his head, looked away.

I looked at my two drinks, took a deep breath, blew it out slow.

He's right, Inner Bitch said.

I know he is.

"So you gonna tell me what went on with Reggie D'Voe at the station, then? Is his confession worth a shit?"

He shrugged. "He told us where to find the professor's body and we found it there. So yeah."

I was stunned. And then I wasn't. "He has it. What I have. And then some. That's how he knew. He was reading us right there at the house. He knew what I'd seen in the storage locker. He knew that it belonged to Gloria Orr. He knew everything."

"What, you want to clear *him* now, too? Do you *want* Jeremy to go down for this?"

"Whoa, what the hell, Uncle Mace?"

We both jumped like school kids caught smoking in the restroom. Jeremy came into the kitchen, snapping on the light, damn near blinding me. Not to mention revealing my possibly red eyes. And not from the vodka. Speaking of....

I took both glasses to the sink and poured them out, rinsed the glasses, and then my mouth.

Jeremy was standing there in the doorway, looking from one of us to the other like he'd never seen either of us before. "Are you two *fighting* because of my screw-up?"

"No."

"Of course not."

We spoke over each other. I looked Mason's way, and he looked back and we sort of agreed silently to get along in front of the kid.

God, what are we becoming?

Jeremy came in, sat on the third of four stools, on my side, so he could show his uncle what an asshole he was being to me, and also to make me super self-conscious about the possibility of vodka on my breath. Yeah, okay. I was going to dump the rest. This was going to be a dry household from now on. If we couldn't live without booze, how could we expect Jeremy, who was addicted to it, to live without booze?

I nodded to myself, feeling good about the decision.

And then he dropped the bomb.

"Was my father a serial killer?" And he looked at his uncle. "Is that why he shot himself?"

Mason looked like he'd been punched right between the eyes. He didn't move, just looked at the kid, blinking.

"Where did you get an idea like that?" he said at length.

"Mom told me. But Mom's crazy, so I thought I'd ask you."

"Look, Jeremy, I just don't think–"

"Rachel?" Jere asked, cutting him off and turning to me. "You know about this, too, don't you?"

I nodded. "Me, and nobody else, kid."

"Rachel–"

"For fuck sake, Mace, he's a grown-ass man."

Mason closed his eyes.

"Tell me, Uncle Mason."

After a long, anguished pause, Mason said, "Your dad texted me that night, from my place. The apartment. He sounded off, so I rushed home. He pulled the trigger just as I opened the door." His voice broke. He looked at the water ring on the counter where his glass had been sitting, and I bet he was wishing he hadn't refused it. "He left a note."

"What did it say?" Jere asked, in a voice rubbed in sandpaper.

"He confessed to a string of deaths I was investigating."

"Murders. Not deaths. Murders," Jeremy said.

Mason nodded. "I destroyed the note. Found the evidence and destroyed that, too. It was my lowest day as a cop."

"And your finest day as an uncle," I said. "As a *parent*. Jeremy, your dad felt as if there was some other force inside him committing the crimes, one he was powerless to fight. He took his life because he thought it was the only way he could stop it."

But Jere was looking at his uncle like he'd never seen him before. "You destroyed evidence? How could you do that, and still serve?"

I stood up. "Hold on, kid. Listen to me–"

"This is between me and Mason, Rache."

"The fuck it is. My brother was one of the victims."

That got his attention. He looked at me, horrified. "My dad killed your brother?"

"Yeah. And I helped your uncle cover it up, once I knew the whole story. Jeremy, your father was dead. He couldn't hurt anyone else. We found the bodies, so the relatives had closure. The truth coming out would have devastated your family. Your mother was pregnant at the time. And think about your grandmother, what it would've done to her. Think about Josh, for God's sake."

I reached across the bar and covered Mason's hand with mine. "It was the right thing to do. Not the *legal* thing, but the right thing. For the right reasons."

"Mom knew," he said softly. "That's what drove her nuts."

"She probably had underlying issues," I said. "But yeah, it was probably a contributing factor."

"So, the guy we all busted at the lake, the guy who went to prison for the crimes?"

I looked at Mason. He nodded at me to go on. "Well, this is where it gets weird, kid. Your dad donated his organs. That guy got your dad's heart, and kept on killing. I got his corneal tissue, and my NFP. Which I think your dad probably had, too. He just couldn't handle it."

Mason seemed to have pulled himself together. He looked at my hand over his on the counter, and I moved it away. Then he faced Jeremy. "He was sick."

"Mom, too," Jere said. "No wonder I'm so messed up."

"You're not messed up. You're a normal, healthy young man who's susceptible to alcohol addiction. Murder isn't genetic."

"How the hell do you know?"

"Jere," I said, "It wouldn't matter if it *was* genetic. A gene like that could only express under the right conditions. Stress, anger, negativity. You're the opposite of all that. You have a good life with people who love and support you. You're a good person."

"So was my dad."

Mason opened his mouth, closed it again.

"What?" Jeremy asked. "What were you gonna say?"

"Just that...Eric killed things even when he was a kid. Josh's age."

Jeremy lowered his head, swearing in a whisper.

"Younger even," Mason went on. "If this thing was in you, the way it was in him, you'd know it by now."

"Jeremy, it could have cost Mason his entire career. He

could've done time for the decision he made. He did it to protect you and your brother, and your grandmother."

Jere took a deep breath, then he said, "I know. I know you did, Uncle Mace. I guess I'd have done the same thing."

All the breath rushed out of Mason. Jeremy closed his eyes, and then they were off their stools and hugging each other and I was suddenly leaking saltwater all over my face.

17

LEGENDARY ACTOR REGINALD D'VOE FAKED OWN DEATH, screamed the headline. And the sub-headline added, Confesses he's the Riverside Strangler.

Some version of that story was on every front page and 24-hour news network in the country. It was irresistibly glamorous. The man who'd played monsters and crazed murderers on the silver screen for fifty years, was claiming responsibility for a string of grisly murders, some of which had included torture. Even juicier, he'd been the public's favorite suspect in the death of his fiancée, Hollywood darling Jez Parker, decades ago, a crime that was still unsolved.

The arraignment was a circus, as Reggie, surrounded by bodyguards and lawyers, was brought into the courtroom. He'd spent the night in a cell, but if we thought Jeremy had received special treatment, it was nothing compared to what Reggie must be getting. No handcuffs, and he got to wear his own clothes. And yet he looked terrible. There was a gray caste to his skin, and his eyes were tired.

Mason, Jeremy and I sat in the back of the room, trying to

be inconspicuous. Celia Moon had shown up with an officer of the court to remove his ankle monitor last night. The courtroom was packed with press, none of whom were paying any attention to us.

Reggie admitted his crimes, the DA stated he had evidence to support the confession, and Reggie's lawyer asked for his release on his own recognizance until sentencing, arguing that Reggie was a dying man. His doctor had submitted a statement saying Reggie didn't have the strength to harm a puppy right then, much less a human being.

The judge granted the defense's request. Didn't even require electronic monitoring, because it was obvious Reggie was no danger to anyone. What *should* have been obvious was that he never had been. Certainly not as recently as a few days ago.

We managed to sidle out just before the judge banged his gavel and the circus resumed.

"I wonder why Ivy wasn't here?" I asked as we walked out of the courtroom, down the steps, onto the sidewalk. We'd parked a block away, so we'd be able to get out again in the crush.

Already throngs were pouring out of the courthouse behind us. We headed down the steps to the sidewalk.

"Look," Mason said, "I know you two have some kind of…weird bond–"

"Don't be like that." Things were still tense between us and I hated it.

"I want you to stay away from her." He leaned closer. "We both know Reggie didn't kill anyone. But maybe she did."

"Maybe she did." There was a commotion behind us, and I looked over my shoulder, then clutched Mason's arm. "Something's happening."

He stopped, too.

Reggie was standing at the top of the courthouse stairs, holding up his hands for quiet. There were a dozen microphones shoved in his face. His lawyer was close to him, one hand on his back for support.

"Mr. D'Voe, why did you do it? Why did you kill all those men?"

"Mr. D'Voe, why did you fake your own death?"

"Mr. D'Voe, what's all this really about?"

The same question was shouted by several reporters.

He looked at his lawyer, said something. The lawyer shook his head angrily. Reggie just smiled. "I have a brief statement. I won't be taking questions," he said. "First, I want to apologize for pretending to be dead when I wasn't. The truth is, I was diagnosed with cancer. Terminal. The end won't be pretty, and I wanted to do that part in private. So, I faked it. Attended my own funeral in disguise. Got quite a charge out of that, as a matter of fact.

"Facing my own demise led me to reassess my life, the work I had done, and I felt...well, frankly, I felt like it wasn't enough. And then, through means I will take to my grave, I heard about a man who was abusing a child." He stood there in silence for a moment, then shrugged. "So, I killed him. And it seemed such a good idea, that I learned of others doing the same, and I killed them, too."

"Are you alleging all your victims were pedophiles, Mr. D'Voe?"

"I'm not alleging it. I'm stating it flat out. They were. And now, they are not. I have not one regret. That's all I have to say. Please, part the waters and let me get to my car." He moved through the crush, and down the stairs. Two young men in suits walked ahead, splitting the crowd for him, creating a wide channel. His lawyer held his arm as they descended through the mob toward a waiting limo.

"But Mr. D'Voe, some of the dead men were tortured," a reporter shouted above the others.

Reggie paused, hand on the car's open rear door. "Do you think their victims were not?" And then his eyes rolled, and he sank toward the ground.

The two men and a couple of cops held back the crowd, while the lawyer managed to wrestle Reggie into the car. Then it sped off.

"Holy shit, he collapsed. Mason–"

"I know. We'll go to the hospital."

"You go," I told him. "I have to–"

"Don't tell me. You have to go to Ivy."

"Something's wrong. She would've been here. I *have* to go. If you don't trust me, Mason, there's nothing I can do about that, but *I* trust me. That's the thing. *I* trust this stuff I have. I trust my inner knowing. I trust my instincts, and they're telling me to go to Ivy right now. I don't know when you lost faith in me. In us. I hope to hell you can get it back. But either way, I'm going."

I jumped into the Crosstrek, went to slam the door, but he got in the way. He leaned in and kissed me on the mouth. "I love you, goddammit. Be careful." Then he closed the door.

IT SHOULD'VE BEEN a pleasant drive, all those trees, their colors in infancy, getting ready to pop into full blown vivid adulthood, their limbs arching over the roads leading to Dilmun. Cayuga lake's dark waters rippled under the sun. Layer upon layer of mountains unfolded in every direction. But I drove too fast to enjoy it. And for me to speed past such breathtaking vistas without visually devouring them was a rare thing. But there was this feeling deep in the pit of my stomach that got worse with every mile. A sense of urgency nipped at my heels like a pissed-off chihuahua.

The wrought iron gate was closed, so I parked on the road and squeezed in through the opening along one side, then brushed off my clothes as I walked quickly along the curving driveway. The D'Voe mansion seemed as if it was in mourning. I wondered what made it seem that way, but it wasn't something I could see with my eyes. It was something I could only feel. The tall windows with their ornate gothic trim felt like the empty eyes of a being without a soul. The white paint seemed dull beneath a haze of gray loneliness.

I trotted up the wide stone steps that would bear Jack-o-lanterns on either side of them most Octobers. I'd seen photos. Probably not this year, though. At the door, I rang the bell. Its deep, funereal chimes didn't seem as entertaining anymore. They seemed morbid.

Impatient, I followed by ringing it again, and then knocking on the door but there was no sound from inside, so I tried the knob.

Unlocked.

When I opened the door, its hinges groaned in pain, and I stepped inside. "Ivy? Ivy, are you here?" The place felt empty. I closed the door behind me and walked farther in, wondering why I felt like I should tiptoe and whisper. There was no logical reason. But I did it anyway.

The foyer was empty, as was the big sitting room with the fireplace. Reggie's picture above the mantle seemed to look right into my eyes. It felt almost like he was validating my feeling that something was wrong, and urging me to get on with it.

I didn't bother searching further. My intuition or whatever

told me to go upstairs, so I did. I walked past the room full of mannequins. Its door was wide open, and even in daylight, it creeped me out. *Somebody's in there*, whispered through my mind. "Don't be stupid," I whispered back.

Ivy was lying in Reggie's bed, pillows clutched in her arms. The only part of her that moved was her back, with the involuntary sobs that racked her.

I moved in slowly, right up to the bed, and then, I don't know why, I was compelled to lie down beside her, and wrap my arms around her, and hold her while she cried. She didn't even acknowledge my presence for a minute. And then she did, her hands clutching my arm to her chest.

"It's not fair. It's just not fair. It's not fair."

"I know, Ivy. I know."

"Reggie would never hurt anyone."

"I know he wouldn't." Her words were slurred, I realized, and sat up, looking around for a bottle or a glass or anything. "Have you been drinking?" I asked.

"No, of course not."

"Did you take something?"

She nodded, her chest spasming. "My doctor gave me something for the stress."

"Did you maybe take too much?" I asked. I got up onto my feet. "Where's the bottle?"

"What?" She rolled onto her back, blinking at me. Her pupils were pinpricks.

"Where are the pills she gave you? How many did you take?"

"I don't know." She sniffled.

I got out of the bed and went to her night stand, but there was no pill bottle, only a small brown envelope. It had nothing written on it, and it was empty.

"I never meant for this to happen," Ivy said. "I'm not a

bad person. I just wanted to save Juan the way Reggie saved me. That's all."

"I know that."

"Reggie told me to stay home. I can't stand not knowing. What happened? Is he still in jail?"

"No. No, he's not in jail."

She blinked away tears. Their salt had burned paths into her cheeks and reddened her eyes. "Is he okay?"

"He–"

"Did something happen? Omygod omygod." She scrambled her phone off the nightstand, tapped rapidly, then clapped a hand over her mouth as the video of Reggie's collapse played on a tiny screen.

She lunged out of the bed and into the attached bathroom, leaned over the tub, not the toilet, and was violently sick.

I went in behind her, held her hair, rubbed the spot between her shoulder blades. "It's okay, it's going to be okay. He's being cared for. I promise. I can get an update from the hospital right now if you want."

Ivy got weakly to her feet, scuffed to the sink, turned on the taps and used her cupped hands to rinse her mouth. Then she brushed her teeth, and rinsed it again. "I don't think I can drive. Can you take me to the hospital?"

"Of course I can." And maybe get her checked out, too. Whatever she'd taken, she'd taken too much. But I hoped she had expelled a lot of it.

She returned to the bedroom, swayed, almost fell. I wrapped her arm in mine to help her back to her bed. She sat down.

My phone chirped. Mason. I read it silently, then aloud, "Reggie's stable and resting comfortably. They gave him fluids, and they want to keep him at least overnight. He's sleeping right now."

She nodded and whispered, "Thank goodness."

"Maybe give yourself a few minutes. I'll help you find clothes, if you want."

Looking down at herself, she seemed to only just then realize she was still in a pink satin robe. I texted a thank you to Mason, told him I was with Ivy and everything was good and not to worry. And then just as I tapped send, she said, "You wouldn't think it would be so hard. Killing a pedophile."

My eyes widened. That was all but a confession. And if she was going to confess, I couldn't keep it from Mason and fuck things up between us even more. I quickly texted "Facetime. Be silent." Then I switched apps, tapped his image, and casually set my phone on the nightstand.

"Is that what you've been doing, Ivy? Killing pedophiles?"

She was quiet for a long moment. Then she said, "I know what Reggie's doing." And then she lay down, turned onto her side, and drew her knees up. "Everyone knows how much he loves kids. The big Halloween party he throws every year for the local children is his Christmas. It's his favorite thing to do."

"He told the press his love for children is why he killed all those men they found by the Susquehanna," I said, slow and careful. "He said they'd all been hurting kids, and he wanted to keep them from hurting any more."

"It's easy to believe. That's why he confessed. But it wasn't him."

"I know." I had balanced the phone against a lamp on the nightstand. I didn't know for sure if it was recording her image, but it was definitely getting her voice. "Who was it, then? Who really did kill them? Was it you?"

"He saved me from one of those kinds of men, you know. When I was just a little girl. He protected me from then on."

Just like I've been trying to do, I thought. Something about her must bring that out in people.

"But I'm not weak."

"I know you're not weak. I know."

"Yes, you know," she said. "You've known from the beginning, haven't you?"

I nodded, hoping she'd get specific.

"But I didn't kill those other men they found by the river. And torture, that's…not…I couldn't. I don't want to *hurt* anyone. I just want to save children from pigs like the one who stole my life."

"I get that. I mean, I can't say I understand. I don't think anyone can understand who hasn't been through that. I'm a full-grown adult and when some perv grabs my ass in an elevator, I want him to get the electric chair."

She wasn't really hearing me. I was just filling the space in between her lines, so she wouldn't fall asleep on me. She'd used the word "other." "I didn't kill those *other* men they found...." I didn't know if it was enough to count as a confession. I didn't want her to have done it. But I wanted Jeremy cleared, and I didn't think Reggie's confession would hold up under close scrutiny.

"Reggie didn't torture those men, either," Ivy said at length. "He only confessed because your husband suspected me."

"He's not my–"

"Reggie could never hurt anyone, though. No matter what."

"Then who?" I asked.

"I don't know. If I knew I would tell you. I don't want Reggie to die in prison, Rachel. All he wants is to end his life in peace, here at home in his own bed. And that can't happen until we find who really did it."

She was sounding a little clearer, I thought. But it didn't look as if she was going to confess. I was half frustrated and half relieved. "I should call your sister. Why isn't she here?"

"She and Vince went whale watching. I didn't want to ruin their trip."

"They don't even know what's going on?" I was sure one of Chief O'Mally's officers would've clued him in that Reggie D'Voe was alive and well and living with his sister-in-law.

"I think Gloria knew who it was, though," Ivy said. "I think that's why she died. She must've figured it out."

"Or it was her, and she couldn't stand the guilt," I said.

"No. No, Gloria...no. But I don't know who. One of the others, I suppose."

"One of the others in your support group?" I asked. "Is that what you mean?"

"It's not like we talked about it. I didn't know anyone else was…thinking along those lines. Much less…acting." She shivered, and closed her arms more tightly around herself. I pulled a blanket off the foot of the bed and draped it over her.

She pulled her necklace from underneath her robe and eyed it absently. The pendant with the vengeance goddess.

Justice, Inner Bitch reminded me.

"I was doing better. The private sessions with Dr. Guthrie were helping so much."

"Dr...Guthrie?"

"Mmm."

"She's the support group leader? And you had private sessions?"

She nodded.

"Did you talk about Juan and his father?"

"Of course we did. It was killing me that I couldn't do anything to fix it."

She knuckled her eyes and sat up in the bed. I glanced at the phone. I had the screen turned away from us, so she couldn't see that it was streaming. There was a glass of water on the nightstand, and I got it for her. She drank deeply. I thought she looked a little better.

"Dr. Guthrie said it was a gift to humanity that Dwayne Clark was dead. That's when she gave me the necklace. A badge of honor, she said. Everyone gets one, when they make great progress."

I went ice cold, and flashed back to Gary, his tormented eyes, his nearly incomprehensible ranting. *I can't do it her way. I'm not strong enough.*

"Ivy, after your private sessions with Dr. Guthrie, what made you decide the only way to help Juan was to–?"

"There was no other way."

"Yeah, I get that, but whose idea was it? Was it her idea, Ivy?"

"Dr. Guthrie's? *No*! Of course not." She lowered her head, closed her eyes. And then her eyebrows crinkled a little.

She was remembering.

I reached out to take her hand and closed my eyes, too.

I want you to relax, the doctor said.

The shift in my perception was so sudden and so vivid I almost got whiplash. I was not in Ivy's room anymore. I was in a smaller room, lying on a white leather fainting couch with a silk throw over its back. Dr. Guthrie was sitting in a chair, kitty corner, above my head, so I couldn't see much of her without craning my neck.

Ivy's neck, that is. Because I was riding along inside her mind, inside her memory.

"Relax and listen to the clock," Dr. Guthrie said. She had

a deep voice, a little bit raspy with age, but strong and confidence-inspiring. She was speaking very slowly, very calmly. "Hear it, ticking? Isn't that the most soothing sound you've ever heard?"

"It is," Ivy said. She said it aloud in real-time, and thought it aloud in the world within.

"Breathe nice and deep. In." There was a long pause. "And out."

Ivy started breathing to that cadence, as Guthrie repeated it in a voice like gritty molasses, over and over. "Now from this very calm place, this place where your emotions are still and quiet, where panic and fear don't exist, where there's only the gentle, steady ticking of the clock, and your slow, perfect breaths. In…and out. From this place, without emotion, you know that Juan needs your help."

"Juan needs my help."

"No one else can help him."

"No one else can help him," Ivy and I repeated in unison. Her voice was softer and higher than mine. Sort of wispy and afraid. Mine was deeper and fuller.

"The system won't help him. The system has failed him. His own mother has failed him. You're all he has left."

"I'm all he has left."

"His father's going to rape him this weekend, unless his father dies."

I popped back into the here and now so fast I felt the impact of the landing. Ivy sat up straight in bed at the same moment, and her eyes were very wide and locked onto mine. "It was Dr. Guthrie's idea!"

I wondered if every member of that support group who sported a medallion had killed a child molester.

"Well, now, I didn't expect to see you up and around,

much less with company, Ivy." A dignified, slender, platinum-haired woman stepped into the room, pointing a gun at us.

"Dr. Guthrie," Ivy whispered.

She pulled the trigger, and I flinched as a lightning bolt of shock shot up my spine

18

I spent long seconds trying to locate where the bullet had penetrated my body. Then I realized she'd shot my phone. Its pieces had exploded outward in all directions. She must've seen that I'd been streaming.

"Now I'm going to have to kill him, too. You realize that, right?"

"Him, who?" I asked, standing still, afraid to move and make her squeeze that trigger again.

"Whoever was on the other end of that phone," she said. "Your husband, the cop, I presume?"

"We're not married. How do you know he's a cop?"

"I've been keeping an eye on the both of you since the first body was found. I read about you, your off-the-record crime solving skills, your uncanny insights. Some say you might be psychic."

"I am *not* fucking psychic," I said. But I didn't expect that to keep working much longer, if the word was out.

"I had a patient who was a fan. Talked about your crackpot books in session all the time. It was easy to convince him to follow you around and report back."

"Gary," I said. "Seems like you're pretty good at convincing your patients to do your dirty work, aren't you, Doc?"

"Therapy, meds, and post hypnotic suggestion work on some. Not on everyone."

I nodded, thinking she was a monster. But I held myself back from saying that out loud. I just needed to stay alive until Mason could get here. I just needed to stretch this out as far as I could to give him time.

"Listen, before you shoot me, I'd really like to know why." I lowered my hands, which I'd been holding up since she'd burst in. Moving by millimeters, I sat down on the edge of the bed. I was trying to read her, but I was too scared to take my eyes off her. Visual stimulation was too distracting, and way louder than my more subtle senses.

"You're stalling, giving him time to get here. It won't matter."

"You think the local cops aren't already on their way? The Dilmun police chief is Ivy's brother-in-law. You gonna kill them all?"

She blinked at me like a robot processing my words.

"It happened to you, didn't it?" I asked, and I softened my tone. "Someone hurt you when you were a little girl."

"I'm not a victim."

"You're certainly not. But *she* was. The little girl you used to be. She was."

She averted her eyes. I forced myself to close mine, so I could feel her. "You thought helping other women heal from the same kind of abuse might help you figure out how to heal yourself."

I tapped into her mind, just briefly. Foul breath in her face, the feeling of being split in two. I couldn't take it, so I opened my eyes again.

"There *is* no healing from what happened to me. To any of us," she whispered.

"YOU TOLD ME THERE WAS!" Gary Conklin burst into the room behind her, and she swung around, her gun leading the way.

I jumped to my feet and shot past her holding out my hands. "Don't shoot him. Don't shoot him. First do no harm, right? Don't shoot Gary. Don't do that. Stay still, Gary. Just stay still."

"No! She said the only way to make it stop hurting was to kill my old man, and I did it! I did it, but it's still there! Everything he did to me is still there. She lies. You lie, Dr. Guthrie, you lie, you lie!" He lunged toward the doc, and like an idiot I got between them and put my hands firmly on his shoulders. "Gary, she's got a gun."

He stopped, seemed to realize that for the first time. He blinked into my eyes, and reminded me of my brother again. He said, "I won't let her hurt you, Rachel," he moved me gently aside. "She told me you might be in danger. To follow you and tell her everything you did, everywhere you went, to keep you safe, but she lies. I shouldn't have listened. I won't let her hurt you, though."

"She doesn't want to hurt me," I said. "She doesn't want to hurt innocent people the way a bad man hurt her when she was just a little girl. But she's broken. She can't tell you how to make your pain go away, because she hasn't figured out how to make her own pain go away."

"What are you doing?" Guthrie demanded. "Are you playing amateur analyst with *me*?"

She was facing me now. I saw Ivy looking at my shattered phone, probably just then realizing what I'd been up to. Her head was clearing. I wondered if throwing up had saved her life.

"It's all gone wrong, hasn't it, Melissa?" I used her first name, hoping it would help. "You wanted to make things better and wound up becoming the very thing you hate."

"I have not become like them!" she shouted.

"No?"

Shut up, Rache! You're gonna get us shot!

Maybe so, IB, but she's gonna hear the truth before I go out. I was good and pissed.

"I think you've become exactly like them. You hurt innocent people who don't deserve it. People like Gary. People like Gloria."

She flinched. I saw it. "Gloria figured it out. She would've talked."

"So you killed her. To protect yourself. And you tried to kill Ivy tonight, too, didn't you? Because you knew she wasn't going to let Reggie take the fall for this. She'd have told whatever she knew and the police would figure it out from there. Another innocent. Another one of your victims. You're just like the men you killed."

"Stop saying that!" She stood there, still pointing her gun at Gary and me, her entire body shaking with rage or fear or both.

I heard cars skidding into the driveway, doors slamming.

"Go to the window," she said, waving her gun at me. "Now."

I gave Gary an "easy" signal with my hands, and did what she said. She had nothing to lose, and I was still hoping to get out of this alive. I got to the window, and she came right up behind me, smashed the pane with her gun then pressed it to my head. "I have hostages," she shouted. "Stay outside or I'll kill them all."

There were two Dilmun Police SUVs down there. Chief O'Mally must've got the word and returned from whale watching early. He and both his officers were crouched behind open car doors, weapons drawn. Mason must've called them. They were closer than he was.

"We won't come in," O'Mally shouted. "Don't hurt them."

She dragged me away from the window and around near the foot of the bed with one arm locked around my neck. Ivy was sitting in the bed with her knees drawn to her chest. Gary was standing near the nightstand on the side away from the window.

"Killing them didn't help, though, did it, Melissa?" I asked.

"It wasn't enough."

"You planned it all. How to make the garrote. Where to bury the bodies. So it would look like a single killer and throw the police off the trail."

She didn't respond, but my theory was coming together now. "Why the burlap?"

"So they'd go on a wild goose chase, thinking the Craig's List Ripper had come back. They didn't take the bait."

No, but I almost had. Not that I was going to admit that.

Keep her talking, Inner Bitch advised. *She stops talking, she's gonna shoot you. So just keep her talking.*

I thought you wanted me to shut up.

"The world is a better place without those men," Dr. Guthrie said.

I didn't feel like I was going to die today. I kind of thought I would feel it if I was. I said, "You said it wasn't enough, killing them. So you had to punish them, torture them. Was *that* enough, Melissa?"

"I burned my father alive," Gary said. "It wasn't enough to make me better. And now my mom's hurting as much as I am. You did that."

Guthrie glanced his way, gave a crooked half smile. "No, it wasn't enough for me either. I couldn't torture them enough before they died. And I guess I know now that it's never going to be enough. Eternal hellfire wouldn't be enough."

"Then why?"

"To end the pain!" she screamed. She pressed the heal of her hand to the side of her head, like it hurt right there.

"But it didn't work," I said. "So why keep doing it? Why kill Gloria and Ivy just so you could keep doing it, if it wasn't working?"

"Because I thought I could build something. My vision was so much bigger. Maybe I couldn't end my pain, but I could *use* it." She shook her head. "But now...it's over now. It'll never happen now."

"I'd like to hear more about that," I said. "Your vision. What was it?"

Her jittery gaze had been jumping between the three of us, the window, and bedroom door, but it came to mine when I said that.

I shrugged, and said, "What the fuck else have you got to do? You're not going anywhere."

The bedside landline rang. We all jumped, and Ivy reached for the phone.

"Leave it!" Guthrie barked.

"It's the cops calling," I said. "They want to negotiate with you."

It rang again. She pulled the trigger and the phone exploded. Ivy screamed.

A bullhorn-enhanced voice said, "What the hell is happening!"

Guthrie snapped an arm around my neck and dragged me to the window again. "I shot the phone. Leave me the hell alone!"

"Are the hostages all right?" Chief O'Mally asked.

"All three of us are fine," I shouted before the insane doctor had the chance to reply, thus telling him it was not just Ivy and me in here. I didn't see Mason yet. I was longing to see him with my whole being, but I didn't see him yet. It wouldn't be long. It hadn't *been* long. Minutes were like hours in this room.

"I swear to God if you say another word in the next ten minutes, I'll kill one of them."

Then she released me, ducking away from the window. I stayed on that side of the bed, so I could see out the window without standing right in front of it.

"What was your vision?" Ivy asked. "I want to know, too."

There was a rocking chair near Melissa Guthrie. She sat down in it, and rested her gun hand across her thighs. Its barrel was pointed toward Ivy and me, for the moment. Gary was still on the opposite side of the bed. Guthrie's hand remained on the grip, her finger on the trigger.

"I wanted you all to know about each other," she said to Ivy. "I wanted us to be a team, to organize, maybe even expand. Form other groups, all over the entire country, dedicated to protecting children."

I was stunned. "Dedicated to killing child abusers."

"Pedophiles, yes. There's no treatment, you know. No cure. You can castrate them, they'll still be compelled to sexually assault children. As long as they're alive, they are a threat to children. There's no life sentence for their crimes. So there has to be a death penalty. And they're mostly all men, so we can't expect our male-dominated government to make better laws. We have to take action ourselves." Raising her free hand, palm up, she said, "It's them or the children, Rachel. Can't you see that? It's them or the children. It's not wrong to kill them. How can it possibly be wrong? It's a service to the world."

I didn't even disagree with her all that much.

What would your books say? Inner Bitch asked.

That if you kill one, ten more will pop up to take their place. That it's only by changing from within that we can change the world around us. But I'm not fucking telling her *that.*

Vanessa Cantone's car skidded to a dusty stop in front of the house. I could hear sirens too, so there was more backup coming. State, I figured.

Then Mason's black Monte Carlo left rubber and he got out, gun drawn, eyes on the house.

I'm okay, baby. I'm all right. Don't freak out.

To Melissa Guthrie I said, "I think it's a crime against nature to take a life. But I think it's a crime against nature to hurt a child, too, so–"

"It doesn't matter. I can't get relief. No matter how many of them I kill. No matter how much I hurt them. I killed all those bastards and it still hurts. It still hurts so bad." Her voice broke on that line. Then she said, "I just need this to be done."

She raised the gun, pointed it right at me.

"No!" Gary made a sudden move, hurling a lamp at her, and she swung his way and fired before it hit her.

Ivy screamed. Gary dropped the lamp with a crash, staggered backwards, hit the wall, one hand on his belly where blood was gushing. Ivy scrambled out of the bed onto the floor with him. She dragged a blanket behind her, and wadded it up and pressed it to his bloody shirt.

I spun to Guthrie, who still had hold of her damn gun. She lifted it, I held my hands flat in front of me, like they could stop a bullet. "What did you do? What did you fucking do?" I shouted. I wanted to go to Gary, but when I moved, she shook the gun at me to stay still. "You keep telling yourself you're not like them, but you are. You just proved it. Gary's an innocent child in every way that matters. Just like you were."

"Shut up shut up shut UP!" She cried. "I didn't mean to. I didn't mean to."

"You meant to. You meant to kill Gloria. And if Ivy hadn't puked, she'd be dead, too."

And if Reggie hadn't collapsed, Ivy wouldn't have seen that news clip and vomited, Inner Bitch pointed out. *Funny how things work out.*

"End this now, Melissa Guthrie. Put the fucking gun down and end this now."

Her breaths were coming short and rapid, her eyes darting. She was freaking out. "Bring me Ivy's phone," she ordered. "Do it!"

I took the phone from the nightstand, brushed a few bits of my late phone from its face.

"Unlock it."

I looked at Ivy, still kneeling beside Gary, weeping, trying to help him, holding a blood-soaked blanket to his belly. "Ivy?"

"I d-don't know what to do for him," she stammered.

"Tell her your pass code," Guthrie snapped.

"Ten thirty-one."

Halloween, I thought. Reggie's favorite holiday.

Then Guthrie said, "Lay him down. Elevate his feet. Put a blanket over him," and then to me, "Key it in."

I did. It was an old phone, four-digit passcode, not six. "Open the camera app to video. Point it at me. Hurry up, they're coming in."

My hands were shaking, but I managed to do it.

"Is it running?"

"Yeah. Yeah, it's recording."

Guthrie said, "I am the Riverside Strangler. The men I killed were pedophiles and even those I tortured deserved far worse than they got. I hurt innocents, too, directly and indirectly; Gloria Orr, Ivy Newman, Reginald D'Voe, Jeremy Brown." She looked over at the two on the floor and tears brimmed. "Gary Conklin. No one else was involved in any of this. It was all me." Then she said, "Turn it off."

I tapped the stop button. Guthrie looked at Ivy. Ivy looked back. She was weeping, holding the blanket so hard her arm was trembling. Gary was limp, but conscious, his head tipped over onto his shoulder.

Guthrie said, "My vision could still work with the right person guiding it. You're the best of all of us, Ivy. I'm sorry I hurt you."

Then, in a split second, she pressed the gun barrel up under her chin and pulled the trigger. I lunged toward her and then I kind of skidded and fell on my knees as a spray of blood, brain and bone exploded from the back of her head. The chair rocked backward so hard it went over as the gun thudded to the floor. There was shouting from below, thundering feet, doors crashing open.

I scrambled upright and around the bed to kneel beside Gary. He lay against the wall, head limp, eyes open. His breaths were coming short and quick. I heard footsteps pounding up the stairs. Ivy was still beside him, still holding pressure, but her eyes were wide and staring at the flipped rocker, or the body, or the spatter on the wall behind it. Something in that general vicinity.

"Gary." I pressed my hand to his cheek, tears pouring down my face. It was like Tommy all over again. "Gary, everything's okay. You don't need to be scared. I promise you, everything is really okay."

He frowned a little, but then his entire face relaxed. The pain left his eyes and his brows rose in gentle arcs. He whispered, "It really is. Wow." He covered my hand with his. I felt a rush of unfathomable relief, and the sensation that I was made of light. And then that sense whooshed away, and his hand fell to his lap, and his eyes closed, and he was gone.

The bedroom door burst open and Mason charged in with the most horrified expression. He spotted me still on the floor, and then he was on his knees and catching me up in his arms all at the same time. He pulled me up and away from Gary.

Vince O'Mally was right behind him, going to Ivy who was also on the floor. He checked Gary's pulse, shook his head sadly, and pulled a clean corner of the blanket up to cover his face. Then he helped Ivy to her feet. As soon as he touched her, she burst into tears, and then he hugged her to his chest. "It's okay, little sis. Holly's on her way. We headed back as soon as we heard. God, Ivy, why didn't you tell us Reggie was alive this whole time?"

"What difference does it make?" she asked softly. "What difference does anything make?"

Vanessa came in behind them. I saw her over Mason's shoulder. She kind of blocked the flow of inward traffic there in the doorway, the only one thinking about proper procedure.

"It wasn't Reggie," Ivy said, not just to Vince, but to everyone in the room. She said it loudly and firmly as she pulled free of her brother-in-law, and climbed over the bed to take her phone from the floor where I'd dropped it. "It was Dr. Guthrie. She confessed to the murders. She said she killed all of them." She looked right at me when she said it. Because she knew that I knew she had killed Dwayne Clark. But I couldn't prove it.

She handed the phone to Chief O'Mally. He tapped it, and I heard Guthrie's voice again. "I am the Riverside Strangler.

The men I killed were pedophiles and even those I tortured deserved far worse than they got. I hurt innocents, too, directly and indirectly; Gloria Orr, Ivy Newman, Reginald D'Voe, Jeremy Brown. Gary Conklin. No one else was involved in any of this. It was all me. Turn it off."

"We need to get everyone out of here so we can process the room," Chief Cantone said. "If no one's injured–"

"I'm fine," Ivy said. She sounded remarkably okay.

I said, "Guthrie gave her some kind of sedative. Never said what. She vomited and I think it might've saved her life. But she should get checked out."

Mason's arm remained locked around my shoulders as we made our way out of the bedroom into the hallway.

"Will Reggie be released now?" Ivy asked, coming out behind us, Chief O'Mally at her side. "He thought you suspected me, so he confessed to protect me."

The chief squeezed her shoulder. "Ivy, he collapsed after the arraignment."

"I know," she said. "I need to see him. I need that so much."

"I'll take you."

Tears welled up, but she didn't break down. She said, "I'd like to get cleaned up first. Is that all right, Vince?"

He nodded. "I'll make it all right. We'll have to bag the clothes you're wearing and–"

"Ivy!" Holly came pounding up the stairs, crashing past Vanessa and almost knocking her over to get to her sister. She wrapped Ivy in her arms, sobbing. "Are you okay? Oh my God, are you okay?"

"I'm okay." Ivy endured a powerful hug, then unwrapped herself, and walked into the hallway and toward her bedroom. Holly sent her husband a questioning look, and he shrugged, then nodded at her to go with her sister.

"Let's go outside," Mason said, his arms still around me. "There's too much going on in here."

Not to mention two dead people, neither of whom were talking to me, thank God. But I knew Gary was okay. I'd felt him let it all go. I'd felt the pain just fall away. I wondered if Melissa Guthrie had the same experience.

"This was dangerous, and I shouldn't have come here alone," I said, before Mason could say it for me.

He held me a little tighter to his side. "You must really be traumatized. You'd never admit that in your right mind."

I leaned my head on his shoulder as we walked down the stairs together, through the foyer and out the front door. Police were swarming, and there was an ambulance waiting. But we went straight to Mason's car. He opened the passenger door and put me inside. Then he went around it and got behind the wheel.

His text pinged. He pulled out his phone. "Vanessa says to take you home. They know where to find you to get your statement. It can wait. She thinks we need some down time."

"Damn straight we do."

He turned toward me, put his hands on my shoulders, looked me square in the eyes. "I love you. You know that."

"I was beginning to wonder." I made a face. "That's a lie. I never doubted it. You might piss me the hell off, but you'd never stop loving me."

He smiled a little, maybe relieved, maybe amused. "I don't like secrets between us, Rache."

I took a deep nasal breath, brought my hands up and put them on his shoulders. "I love you, too. You know that."

He smiled a little. "Yes, I do. And like you, I never really doubted it."

"Once," I said, "not all that long ago, you had to make a choice, Mason. You had to choose between the legal thing to do and the right thing to do. Between following the law, and protecting your family. And you chose right, and it's haunted you ever since. It damn near tore your heart out having to admit to Jeremy that you burned your brother's suicide note and concealed evidence. And it'll do the same when you have to admit it to Josh someday. Not just that their father was a murderer, but that you, the man they respect most in the world, lied about it."

"All that's very true," he said. "I couldn't have got through it without you."

"So how could I, the woman who loves you beyond reason, ever tell you something that would put you into that same position all over again? How could I ask you to make that choice again?"

He looked at me for a long time, his eyes searching mine.

"If you knew what I knew about Ivy, if you knew the truly evil things Dwayne Clark was doing to that little boy, and the horror she was feeling over it, and the nightmare she went through as a child–if you knew those things the way I do, you wouldn't have wanted her prosecuted any more than I did. And then you'd have been faced with that choice again. I just wanted to find a way through this mess without you having to do that."

"And now.…?" he asked.

"There's not a scrap of physical evidence against Ivy. There's nothing but my stuff, and my stuff is inadmissible. But I would die for you, Mason Brown. I would die for those boys. And if you ever doubt that again, I will kick your noble, upright ass."

He sighed. "Nothing Ivy said when you were streaming the video to me was a confession," he said. "There's no physical evidence against her. There are no eye witnesses. And we have a full confession from Guthrie."

"But I think—"

"Like you said, your stuff is inadmissible." He pushed my hair behind one ear, gazed into my eyes, his absolute love for me right there to see. "Everything's okay. We're okay. I'll try to never doubt you again."

"I'll try to never keep things from you again."

He kissed me slow. Then he started the car. It rumbled like a motorhead's dream, vibrating beneath us. He backed it around, and picked his way among the official vehicles flashing all around and eventually through the now broken gate, and onto the road.

EPILOGUE

The campfire was warm and dancing against the night sky, sending sparks so high they vanished among the stars. We'd set our chairs all around it. I was lounging in the double Adirondack chair with my man beside me and my dog lying on my feet. Jeremy and Misty sat on a blanket on the ground, arm in arm, looking all sweet and sappy. Josh had Hugo on his lap. Sandra and Jim sat in side-by-side lawn chairs, their hands joined between them. Angela and Christy were toasting marshmallows on long sticks and giggling together. Mason's mother had become as much a grandmother to my nieces as she was to Jeremy and Josh. I thought my mom approved of that from the other side. Amy was in a folding chair, watching the way the sparks from the fire rose into the night sky.

Reggie D'Voe was back home with his beloved Ivy, living out his final days just the way he wanted to. I'd visited twice. I kind of loved the man and he loved me back. We talked about our "gift" in ways neither of us had ever talked about it with anyone else.

Ivy seemed good. Stronger, somehow, now that it was all

over. I chose not to think about Dr. Guthrie's final words to her, the ones she'd spoken after the camera was off. But I'd told Mason about them. I'd decided from now on, I was telling him *every*thing.

Mason sat up a little straighter and said, "So I have this thing I've been waiting to do."

Everyone looked at him, including me. He was so handsome, I thought. Especially so tonight, with the lake behind him all dark and majestic, and the fire in front of him, painting his face in light and shadows.

And then to my utter astonishment, he dropped down onto one knee in front of my chair.

"Holy fu–"

"We both know we're gonna be together forever, Rache. And we're already husband and wife in every way that matters." And then he took a ring out of his pocket, and held it up like an offering. "What do you say we make it official?"

The stones danced and winked at me in the firelight.

"I say it's about fu–" I looked at the smiling, beaming faces around me. My sister had prayer hands pressed to her mouth. Misty was tearing up. Amy and Christie high-fived.

Jeremy had his arm around Josh, and they were both smiling so hard I thought their cheeks might split.

I cleared my throat, and returned my attention to the man in front of me. "It's about time you got around to asking."

He grinned. "Is that a yes?"

"Well of course it's a yes!" I thrust out my left hand, and he slid the ring onto it while our audience cheered. We got upright, and kissed like the end of a rom-com.

Sandra sprang from her chair. "You're getting married!" She ran around the fire pit to hug me. Christy yanked her stick out of the fire so her mother wouldn't trip over it, the marshmallow fell off, and Myrtle lunged and caught it as efficiently as a frog catching a fly. Lack of eyesight didn't hamper her at all.

"This is wonderful!" Mason's mom said, handing her own, perfectly toasted marshmallow to Christy. She got up and came over to hug me, too, and then her son. "Honestly, I thought you were going to wait forever."

Jeremy and Josh locked eyes, grinned at each other, and Josh winked.

"What's that about?" I asked, accepting hugs from Misty and Christy in turn while Amy was still pumping her fist and repeating,"Yes!"

Myrt was on her feet, senses on full alert in case more marshmallows magically fell from the sky in celebration of whatever great thing was going on. Hugo danced around her, thinking she must want to play.

"We saw the ring *weeks* ago," Josh said.

Jeremy nodded. "We got so sick of waiting for Uncle Mace to get his nerve up, we discussed giving it to you ourselves."

Jere looked good. Clean and sober and happy. Hitting AA meetings three nights a week. He was still attending classes, but he'd decided to commute from home, at least for this first semester. And our house was officially dry, for good.

"Will you do a big wedding?" Misty asked. "A fall wedding would be amazing, wouldn't it?"

"Not unless you mean *next* fall," Angela said.

"My favorite weather guy says the foliage will peak in a couple of weeks," I said. "Wouldn't it be nice to get married outside, surrounded by all that color?"

"A couple of weeks!" My sister and future mother-in-law exclaimed in such perfect unison and perfect horror I'd have thought they'd practiced.

Mason stood up, took my hands in his, and said, "A

couple of weeks, it is. Outside, among family and our closest friends, at the peak of fall color."

My heart was swelling in my chest like that scene from *How the Grinch Stole Christmas.*

"We need to go dress shopping tomorrow!" Sandra said.

"We need to book a caterer!" Angela pulled out her phone and started tapping.

I didn't hear any of them. I was too busy being swept into Mason's big strong arms, kissing him like there was no tomorrow, happier than ever before. And come on, I was pretty damn happy before, so that's really saying something.

THE END

There will be more Brown and de Luca to come!

Continue reading for an excerpt from Ivy's story,
Gingerbread Man.

New York Times Bestselling Author
MAGGIE SHAYNE

"Intricately woven...
Haunting."
~Publisher's Weekly

GINGERBREAD MAN

GINGERBREAD MAN

"ARE MY CHILDREN still alive?" Sara Prague asked the question in a quiet, steady voice that he heard very clearly despite the noise around her. Cops coming and going, keyboards clicking, phones ringing. She looked haggard. Hard. She hadn't always, Vince figured. The worry lines bracketing her eyes, her mouth, the dry skin, the chapped lips, the sense that she really didn't give a damn what she looked like—those things had been strangers to her that first day. The day her kids hadn't come home from school. Now those lines, that hardness, had made themselves at home. It looked as if they planned to stay awhile. This shouldn't have happened to Sara Prague, a PTA mom whose world revolved around her kids. It shouldn't have happened to her husband. Mike, full-time plumber and part-time Little League coach. It shouldn't happen to anyone. Ever.

Vince walked around his desk and eased Sara Prague into a cracked vinyl chair, ignoring the chaos around them. He poured her some stale coffee from the pot on the nearby stand, just as he had every day for the past three weeks. She came in here like clockwork—something the Center for

Missing and Exploited Children had probably told her to do. He thought she would keep doing it, too. For years, if necessary.

It wouldn't be necessary, though.

She took the foam cup and sipped automatically. It was all part of their daily ritual. "You haven't answered my question. Detective. Are Bobby and Kara still alive?"

"Mrs. Prague, we're doing everything we possibly can." He walked back around his gray metal desk, pulled out his chair, sat down. It gave him a chance to school his face. It gave him a chance not to look at hers. She was just... bleak. Looking into the woman's eyes was like looking into a black hole. Nothing left. "Every lead is being meticulously followed. We're pursuing every avenue of—"

"I don't want the party line you give to the press, Detective O'Mally. I want the truth."

Things crossed his mind. Things every cop knew—like the fact that, in most cases, kids abducted by strangers are either found in the first twenty-four hours or not found at all. Not alive, at any rate. He shook the thought away. It was irrelevant. This was *his* case. The outcome would be different this time. He wouldn't fail.

He forced himself to look her in the eye and managed not to shiver at the dead gray chill of her gaze. "I do think they're alive," he told her. "And I'll keep thinking it until and unless I have a reason to think otherwise." He painted his face with a hopeful expression, reached across the desk, and squeezed her cool, limp hand. "Try to hold on to hope, Mrs. Prague."

"I have to. Detective. I don't have anything else left." Pulling her hand away, she set her coffee cup on his desk, adding a new ring to a file folder already covered with them. She reached inside her purse.

Vince bit back a groan. God, here came more pictures. He

couldn't take much more of this daily torture. Then again, he didn't imagine it even began to compare to hers.

"I brought this for you." She pulled it out—a silver frame that folded in half, like a book. With her free hand she pushed aside some papers—the ring-marked file folder, the wrapper from his mc-breakfast—making a single bare spot on his desk. Then she set the frame there so that it faced him. One side held a photo of five-year-old Kara. Dimples. Freckles. Carrot-colored pigtails and sky-blue eyes. She held a scrawny tiger kitten in her lap. The other side of the frame held a photo of seven-year-old Bobby, posing in his Little League uniform, bat at the ready.

Keeping a professional distance had never been what Vince O'Mally did best. Hell, it was the one thing he wished he *could* do by the book. But he wasn't a by-the-book kind of a cop. His methods were more instinct than science. His gut had gotten him further than any procedural manual or training course ever would. He trusted it. But sometimes it got him too close.

And this was one of those times.

This woman—coming in here every day, with her photos and her red, puffy, lifeless eyes—was dragging him into her anguish. He barely slept nights anymore. Every spare second, on duty or off, he was working this case. It gripped him in a way nothing ever had.

Sara Prague was a needy woman. Not a weak woman, but needy. He didn't do well with needy women. He tended to want to save them. Always a mistake.

"Mrs. Prague ..." he began.

"I notice the other photos I've brought aren't on your desk anymore. What do you do with them after I leave?"

He got up and paced away from her, pushing a hand through his hair. "I keep them. Just... in a drawer. It's too distracting to have them on the desk like that." Turning, he faced her again. "I understand what you're trying to do, but I need to focus on the case. On chasing down leads and analyzing evidence. Not on how ..." His gaze strayed to the photo against his will, and his throat closed up. "Not on how goddamn bad I'd like to come to a game next spring, and see Bobby hit a homer."

Sara Prague nodded, her huge haunted eyes never leaving his. "I suppose it seems cruel of me to keep bringing photos. Please understand, I need to know you won't forget that these arc my children, Detective O'Mally.'" Her hand moved to the largest pile of paperwork on his desk, settling atop it. "They aren't in these files. They aren't a case number or a statistic or an investigation. They're Bobby and Kara Prague." She moved her hand to the photo, forcing his gaze to it again. To Kara's baby teeth. To Bobby's unevenly trimmed bangs. "They're *my children.*"

He tried to look away from her, from the need, the plea in her eyes. But he couldn't. She didn't speak, but he heard her anyway. Her eyes said it all. *Tell me it's going to be all right. Tell me you 're going to find my babies safe and sound, and put them back in my arms where they belong.*

He knew better. He knew damn well better.

Tears welled in her eyes. Something deep inside him quaked. He said, "It's going to be all right, Mrs. Prague. I'll find your kids. I promise you."

He saw a hint of light come into her eyes, dull, dim, flickering, but fighting its way through the fog of despair. He'd given her hope. It would help her get through the day. Maybe even a couple more beyond that. But at what cost?

Vince O'Mally didn't make promises he couldn't keep. How the hell was he going to keep this one? The photograph dragged his gaze back to it, like a supercharged magnet pulling shards of metal.

She reached across the desk, squeezed his hand. "Thank you for that." Then she got up and left him standing there staring at the photo. He heard the door swing closed when she left, and he still couldn't look away. Even when his vision blurred, he kept staring at those little faces staring back at him.

Then a big hand swung into his line of vision, and swiped the frame off his desk in one brisk motion.

"That woman isn't gonna let up until she drives you right over the edge, is she? Dammit, Vince, you're letting her get to you. I can see it."

Vince sank into his chair, cleared his throat and tried to shake off the grimness that squatted on his shoulders like a lead demon. "Hell, no, I'm not letting her get to me," he told his partner. "I know better." It was a lie and he knew it.

"I used to think so." Jerry tossed the frame onto his own desk, leaving it folded closed. "But look at you, pal. You haven't been right since they handed us this case, and you're getting steadily worse."

"That's bullshit"

"Is it?" Jerry shoved a stack of file folders aside, and perched on the edge of Vince's desk. He wore a white shirt that could've been whiter, and a striped tie that he'd tugged loose. His belly hung two inches over his shiny black belt, and he had less hair on his head every day. "So, what else are you working on, Vince?"

Vince shook his head, ignoring his partner.

"You're not working on anything else, are you? Nothing but this."

"Get off my back, Jerry."

"I heard you just now."

That brought Vince's gaze up. Jerry looked worried— a little scared, even. "Why the hell would you make a promise like that? You know better."

"It helped. The woman is barely standing these days."

"Yeah? And what do you suppose it's gonna do to you if you can't keep it?"

Vince's fist clenched. "We'll never know, because that's not gonna happen."

"Vince—"

"I'm gonna find those kids, Jare."

Jerry sighed, studying his friend's face for a long moment. But when he spoke again, his tone was closer to normal than it had been before. "Still following up on registered sex offenders?"

"Only the pedophiles. And, hell, I've only made it through the first five hundred or so. You know how many convicted perverts we got living like normal people in this city?"

"No, but I'm sure you're gonna tell me."

Vince just looked at him. "I meant what I said. I'm gonna find them."

"Because you're Detective Vincent frigging O'Mally. Decorated supercop who always gets his man. You know, my friend, this case might be easier on you if you'd ever once failed at anything in your entire life."

"You don't know what the hell you're talking about."

"I know this. You're not infallible, Vince. And if this one goes bad, it's not gonna be because you fucked up."

"It's *not* going to go bad," Vince said, meeting his partner's eyes. "And I *don't* fuck up."

The telephone on his desk rang. Jerry grabbed it up before Vince could, probably just to piss him off a little and distract him from the case.

"Detective Donovan," Jerry intoned automatically. Then

he listened, and his gaze shot to Vince's, and his face went pale. "Shit. Okay, yeah. We're on it."

Jerry put the phone down. "Maybe you'll want to sit this one out, buddy."

Vince got to his feet, grabbed his coat, and tried to fight the dread building in his belly.

***

"THERE'S NOT GOING to be anything in here." Vince stood just outside the door of a dilapidated house on Syracuse's east side and said words he didn't really believe. Jerry was on the other side of the door. Their guns were raised, their backs to the outer wall. The light wasn't good. Overcast skies tinted everything in sepia. A stiff autumn wind rode herd on dried-out leaves, so they crackled over the sidewalk like rattling bones. "We checked this place out already."

"The caller said there was a bad smell," Jerry said, keeping his voice low. "I don't smell anything, do you Vince?"

Vince didn't really sniff the air. He couldn't make himself do it. He said, "No, I don't smell a damned thing. Probably the same neighbor who reported seeing that beat-up van near here the day the kids were taken. Probably just likes calling the cops. Makes her feel important."

"We checked it out that day," Jerry said. "We didn't miss anything."

Vince looked at his partner. "We didn't miss anything."

Jerry nodded, and Vince turned and pushed the front door open, backed away, then entered cautiously. The place was falling down. Not a piece of glass remained in a single window, but plenty littered the splintered floors underneath thick layers of dust and plaster.

There was a closed door on the far side of the room, its once-white paint peeling off it in great strips. Boards lay here and there, and the floor creaked under their feet Vince took another careful step. A floorboard broke and his foot went right through. He swore under his breath and yanked his foot free. Then he looked in the hole his foot had made, frowning. A child's storybook lay under the floor, its cardboard cover warped and bent, colors faded. It looked as if it had been lying there for years. Still, Vince carefully picked it up with two gloved fingers to take a closer look. A thick coat of dust covered the title. *The Gingerbread Man.* Odd place for a children's book. There were gaps in the floor all over the place. It must have fallen through one of them, who knew how long ago? Opening the cover carefully he saw a library card pocket. The words "Dilmun Public Library, Dilmun, NY" were stamped there, along with a series of dates. He yanked an evidence bag from his coat pocket—he always carried a handful of them—and dropped the book into it telling himself it was probably unnecessary, because this place had nothing to do with Bobby and Kara Prague. Nothing. He wasn't going to find a damn thing here.

His instincts were disagreeing vehemently with his mind on that, but he refused to hear them. Still, he jotted a note about the book on his notepad.

Stuffing the bagged book and the notepad into his coat pocket, he looked at the closed door, took a single step toward it. Then the pungent scent hit him and his entire soul recoiled.

"Ah, shit," Jerry said, turning his nose into his collar. "Vince, the smell... it's coming from in there." Jerry nodded toward that same closed door at the far end of the place.

Damn, he didn't want to do this. Everything in Vince was screaming at him not to go over there. Not to open that door. Just to turn around and leave. He stepped forward even as his partner reached for the broken door with a trembling hand.

Vince put his own hand on Jerry's shoulder, stopping him. "Why don't you check the other rooms, partner?"

Jerry frowned at him.

"It's my case, Jerry."

"It's *our* case."

Vince lowered his hand. "You've got kids."

"And I've got a partner. We'll go together."

Finally, Vince nodded. Swallowing hard, Jerry pushed the door open. The odor sprung from the pitch darkness and hit them both like a physical blow. Jerry turned his back on it, a knee-jerk reaction. A second later Vince heard his partner's staggering footsteps as he headed back through the house and out the front door, then he heard him retching someplace beyond it. Hell, it looked like Vince would be doing this alone after all.

Stiffening his spine, Vince pulled the lapel of his coat up over his nose and mouth, pulled out his flashlight, and flicked it on.

The beam pierced the darkness, the floating dust specs, the invisible veil between blessed blindness and hell. The pale light spilled onto the bodies of Kara and Bobby Prague, and Vince turned away, but not before the image had burned itself into his brain. He lurched out of the room, and a second later he was outside, on his knees beside his partner. He wasn't puking. Just kneeling there, ice cold, his entire body rigid, eyes wide and unable to erase what they had seen. Unable to silence the voice in his mind telling him he had failed. He'd promised to find those kids—but not like this. *Goddamn,* not like this. He kept seeing Sara Prague's eyes, the hope he had put in them.

"Vince? Vince, what the hell was it... ? Jerry wiped his mouth with a handkerchief, getting to his feet to lean over him. "Was it the Prague kids? Was it them?" When he didn't answer, Jerry swore and turned to go back inside.

Vince got up, grabbed his partner, jerked him around. "Don't go in there."

"The hell I won't." Jerry pulled free.

Vince punched him. Just like that, he clocked his partner in the jaw, knocked him flat on his back. Jerry lay there, blinking up at him in shocked silence.

"No man with kids has any business seeing what's in that room," he muttered. Then he stepped over Jerry to reach into the car for the radio mike, and, keying it, requested a coroner and a forensics team.

Three days later, Vince and Jerry sat in Chief Rogers' office. Jerry and the chief seemed to be taking turns shooting worried looks Vince's way, but he did his best to ignore them.

The chief didn't waste a lot of time before coming to the point. "You two are off the Prague case."

Vince surged to his feet "What do mean? Jesus, chief, we don't even have the autopsy report yet!"

The chief held up both hands and kept talking. "The FBI has it. They've taken over. They have three other cases with what they say are striking similarities in Pennsylvania, Massachusetts, and Jersey. They've got a task force in place to deal with it, and they don't want any locals stepping on their toes."

"That's bullshit," Vince snapped. "I've been working this case for almost a month, dammit. I have to get this guy."

"You're off the case, O'Mally."

"*I have to get this guy.*"

The chief glanced sideways at Jerry, then focused on Vince again. "Sit down."

Vince sat, but stiffly. He braced himself on the edge of the chair, his hands balled into fists on his knees.

"When's the last time you shaved, O'Mally? Huh?" The

chief eyed him, looking more concerned than stern. "How long since you've eaten a full meal, or had a few hours' sleep? Have you walked by a mirror lately?"

Vince averted his eyes. "I've been busy."

"You're running on empty. You can't possibly be thinking clearly. Now, I know that crime scene got to you. It got to all of us. The forensics team that went in there is undergoing group counseling, and they admit they're having trouble. And these guys have seen damn near everything."

"I'm fine," Vince insisted.

"No. I don't think so. Do you think he's fine, Jerry?"

Jerry shook his head. "No sir, I don't think he's fine at all."

"Jerry, for crying out—"

"I'm sorry partner, but you've been messed up since you came out of that room. I don't know what the hell to do about it. You insisted on talking to Sara Prague yourself—breaking the news, when I begged you to let someone else do it. When you came out of her house that day you looked... dead, Vince. You looked dead. You're drowning in this case, man, and I don't know how to pull you out."

Vince tipped his head back, rolled his eyes at the ceiling.

I'm gonna give you a choice, O'Mally," the chief said slowly. "Take a thirty-day leave, get out of here, get away from this thing, and see if you can shake it off."

"No way. I'm seeing this thing through to the end, Feds or no Feds. What's behind door number two, Chief?"

"An hour a day with Dr. Feltzer."

"The shrink from hell?" The chief nodded. "For how long?" Vince asked.

"Until she says you're passably sane."

"Hell, she didn't think I was passably sane the day they hired me."

"Your decision. Either way, you're off this case. I want everything you have on my desk in ten minutes. That goes for you, too, Jerry."

"So you can turn it all over to the Feds?" Vince asked, disgusted by the thought.

"Those are my orders. After that, I want you to go home. Take the rest of the day off, and let me know what you decide—the leave or the shrink."

"But—"

"I'm done talking," the chief said. "You can go now."

"But, Chief, I—"

"Go. Now." He lifted an arm, pointed at the door.

Vince stormed out of the chief's office and headed for his desk. Jerry was right on his heels, but he ignored his partner as he pulled file folder after file folder off the sloping stacks on his desk and dropped them into the little wastebasket beside it. Papers flew like confetti. He could feel everyone in the place looking at him as if he'd lost it. He ignored them all, opened drawers, rummaging through them, gathering up every scribbled note and every paperclip that had any connection to the Prague case. Slamming one drawer closed he yanked open another, and then another, until at last, he opened the drawer with the pile of framed photos inside.

He stopped, frozen, and stared down at the freckled faces. His shoulders quaked, but he caught himself, held himself in a hard, merciless grip.

"Those ... probably ought to be sent back to the mother," Jerry said, his voice hoarse.

"Yeah."

"I'll take care of it for you."

Vince nodded, then reached in and picked up the most recent photo. He handed it to Jerry. "All but this one, okay?"

"Vince?"

"I want the Feds to have this one. Tell 'em to look at it every day. Tell 'em this is what that bastard killed, not that pile of paperwork. This."

Jerry nodded and took the framed photo. "So ... you gonna take the time off, or the treatment?"

"I don't know yet." He picked up the wastebasket, handed that to Jerry as well. "Give this to the chief for me." Reaching for the computer on his desk, he peeled off a half dozen yellow sticky notes, wadded them up and tossed them into the trash can as well. Lastly, Vince ejected a flash drive and dropped it into his shirt pocket.

"What's that, Vince?"

"What's what?"

Jerry scowled. "What did you do? Did you keep a copy of your files on this case?"

"Shit, pal, when did you ever see me organized enough to think of something like that?"

"Vince. You gotta let this one go."

Vince met his partner's eyes for one long moment, then looked away. "I'm going home. I'll see you later."

Jerry sighed as Vince left the office.

Halfway back to his apartment, three miles from the police station, Vince glanced down and noticed his coat lying on the passenger seat. It had been warm for this late in the fall. He hadn't worn the coat since ...

The kids. The house. The book. His senses prickled. He'd turned the book in, and then forgot he had. But there had been something...

Slamming on his brakes, he jerked the wheel and brought the Jeep Wrangler to a jerky stop on the shoulder. He grabbed his coat, searched the pockets and found his dog-eared notepad. Flipping it open, he read what he had written there: *The Gingerbread Man.* Dilmun Public Library, Dilmun, NY.

ABOUT THE AUTHOR

New York Times bestselling author Maggie Shayne has published more than 50 novels and 23 novellas. She has written for 7 publishers and 2 soap operas, has racked up 15 Rita Award nominations and actually, finally, won the damn thing in 2005.

Maggie lives in a beautiful, century old, happily haunted farmhouse named "Serenity" in the wildest wilds of Cortland County, NY, with her soul-mate, Lance. They share a pair of English Mastiffs, Dozer & Daisy, and a little English Bulldog, Niblet, and the wise guardian and guru of them all, the feline Glory, who keeps the dogs firmly in their places. Maggie's a Wiccan high priestess (legal clergy even) and an avid follower of the Law of Attraction.

Find Maggie at http://maggieshayne.com

- facebook.com/maggieshayneauthor
- twitter.com#!/maggieshayne
- instagram.com/maggieshayne
- bookbub.com/authors/maggie-shayne

ALSO BY MAGGIE SHAYNE

Sleep with the Lights On

Wake to Darkness

Dream of Danger

Innocent Prey

Deadly Obsession

Cry Wolf

Girl Blue

Printed in Great Britain
by Amazon